AT THE END OF HIS ROPE

Above the sentry box stood an enormous horse chestnut tree, just now a solid mass of bright green leaves and tall candles of white bloom. Max was under it, staring into the greenery. On his face was an expression of total disbelief.

"Max, what's the matter?" Sarah panted. "What's up there?"

"Don't look."

"Why not?" Sarah was already looking, of course. "I can't see anything, the foliage is so dense. Wait, what's—darling, are those feet?"

All he said was, "Did you get hold of Bill?"

"I met Abigail. She's sending him along. Max, answer me."

"All right, they're feet," he admitted. "Rufus's feet."

"What's he doing up there?"

"Hanging."

S0-AYW-724

Silver Ghost

ALSO BY CHARLOTTE MACLEOD

Vane Pursuit*
The Recycled Citizen*
The Corpse In Oozak's Pond*
Grab Bag
The Plain Old Man
The Curse of the Giant Hogweed
The Convivial Codfish
Something the Cat Dragged In
The Bilbao Looking Glass
Wrack and Rune
The Palace Guard
The Withdrawing Room
The Luck Runs Out
The Family Vault
Rest You Merry

*Published by
THE MYSTERIOUS PRESS

ATTENTION: SCHOOLS AND CORPORATIONS

MYSTERIOUS PRESS books, distributed by Warner Books are available at quantity discounts with bulk purchase for educational, business, or sales promotional use. For information, please write to: SPECIAL SALES DEPARTMENT, MYSTERIOUS PRESS, 1271 AVENUE OF THE AMERICAS, NEW YORK, N.Y. 10020.

ARE THERE MYSTERIOUS PRESS BOOKS
YOU WANT BUT CANNOT FIND IN YOUR LOCAL STORES?

You can get any MYSTERIOUS PRESS title in print. Simply send title and retail price, plus $3.50 for the first book on any order and 50¢ for each additional book on that order. New York State and California residents add applicable sales tax. Enclose check or money order to: MYSTERIOUS PRESS, 129 WEST 56th St., NEW YORK, N.Y. 10019.

CHARLOTTE MACLEOD
The Silver Ghost
A SARAH KELLING MYSTERY

THE MYSTERIOUS PRESS

New York • London • Tokyo • Sweden

If you purchase this book without a cover you should be aware that this book may have been stolen property and reported as "unsold and destroyed" to the publisher. In such case neither the author nor the publisher has received any payment for this "stripped book."

The Kellings, the Bittersohns, and all their relatives, friends, and undesirable acquaintances are just as fictitious in this adventure as they have been all along. Even the Billingsgates' bees behave in decidedly atypical fashion. Any resemblance between the persons and incidents in the book and actual people or events would have to be coincidental. Some resemblance between the Billingsgates' bees and real bees is unavoidable since, no matter how aberrant their behavior, bees will be bees in fiction as in fact.

MYSTERIOUS PRESS EDITION

Copyright © 1988 by Charlotte MacLeod
All rights reserved.

Cover illustration by Mark Hess

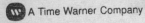 Mysterious Press books are published in association with
Warner Books, Inc.
1271 Avenue of the Americ
New York, N.Y. 10020

A Time Warner Company

Printed in the United States of America

Originally published in hardcover by The Mysterious Press.
First Mysterious Press Paperback Printing: August, 1989

10 9 8 7 6 5

For Julia
and All The Daniels

1

Professor Ufford favored the loveliest woman at the revel with a condescending smile. "I suppose you subscribe to the popular fallacy that Henry the Eighth introduced morris dancing to England."

Sarah Kelling Bittersohn shook her head, not only in denial but also to make sure the underpinnings of her hennin hadn't come loose. "Why should I? Wasn't it John of Gaunt?"

"Er—probably." The professor switched off his smile and turned on a supercilious sneer. "The theory that the dance may have been inspired by the Morisco, or Spanish fandango, is of course absurd. My most recently published book offers conclusive arguments for a Flemish origin. Do I gather that you've been reading *Terpsichore Totters*?"

"Because I happen to know about John of Gaunt?" Now quite sure of her hennin, Sarah tilted back her head to give Professor Ufford the kind of smile her Aunt Emma had been seen to give a guest who slopped red wine on her white damask tablecloth. "Doesn't everyone?"

That was nasty. Sarah herself happened to be informed on the subject only because her Cousin Lionel had backed her into a corner at Aunt Appie's Easter luncheon and talked about morris dancing until she could think of a nonviolent way to stop him, which was no small task with Lionel.

Anyway, she'd managed to stop Professor Ufford. He

1

touched the wide, circular brim of his black straw hat and wandered off, perhaps to find another pretty lady who hadn't yet heard about John of Gaunt.

Sarah could have told Ufford where he'd got the idea for his costume, too. That hat, with its crown shaped into a truncated cone wrong end up, had appeared in van Eyck's portrait of Giovanni Arnolfini and his wife. She couldn't think why the professor had chosen a style that suited him so ill. It hadn't suited Arnolfini all that well, either.

There was some excuse for Arnolfini, since the costume had no doubt been all the rage back in 1432. But why had the professor gone to so much trouble and expense to get himself up like a pregnant giraffe? His long neck and longer, bonier head stuck up in an almost grotesque continuum above the bulky calf-length cloak. Far too much of his stringy shins stuck out below. The green stretch tights he'd pulled over them were a forceful argument for a middle-aged man's keeping his trousers on.

Perhaps Sarah simply hadn't yet adjusted to the mediaeval mystique. This was the first year she and her husband, Max, had attended the Billingsgates' annual Renaissance Revel. Bill and Abigail were close friends of her Uncle Jeremy Kelling. Normally Jem would have been here instead of the Bittersohns. This year, however, Jem was yachting with a different set of cronies. Sarah and Max were here on business, though nobody was supposed to know.

The Billingsgates' problem was an unusual one for them to become involved with. Stolen paintings, jewelry, and objets d'art were their specialty. This was the first time they'd ever been asked to track down a missing 1927 New Phantom Rolls Royce.

The crux of the matter was that the Phantom shouldn't have vanished at all, considering the lengths to which Bill had gone to keep his precious antique safe. Only somebody closely connected with the family, it seemed, could have got the car away. That was why Nehemiah Billingsgate, to give him his proper name as almost nobody ever did, had put in a frantic last-minute call to Jem's niece and nephew-in-law instead of to the police.

The Renaissance Revel had provided a perfect excuse to get the Bittersohns on the scene and introduce them to the family's inner circle, along with a good many circumferentials. As soon as they got a chance, they'd have to get together with their host and employer to sort out who was who. For now, Sarah and Max had set themselves to mingle.

Max was taking the assignment as something of a joke, so far. He'd insisted on entering this nest of affluent WASPs as the Merchant of Venice's business rival. His own academic robe, which he'd bought when he got his PhD and now wore when he had to speak in front of learned gatherings, as he was increasingly asked to do, made an acceptable costume for Shylock. He'd added his father's black yarmulke and suggested carrying a salami to symbolize the contested pound of flesh. Sarah had drawn the line at the salami.

"I am not going to the Billingsgates' with a man who smells like a delicatessen. It's unprofessional. Besides, Abigail might think you were afraid she wouldn't give you enough to eat."

The contrast between a typical Kelling party spread and the amount of food considered minimal at even the smallest Bittersohn family affair had been a source of wonderment between them ever since they'd met. Max often had to stop for a hamburger upon leaving the former, and Sarah usually went on a two-day diet after the latter. Even Max's mother, though, couldn't have thought anybody likely to starve at the Billingsgates'.

Their house was one of those architectural **vag**aries that used to be indulged in sometimes during the golden age of cheap labor and no income tax by romantic millionaires with Miniver Cheevyesque yearnings. Max and Sarah had arrived to find red and yellow pennons flapping from the turrets and a red-and-white striped pavilion set up outside the portcullis. Under this vast canopy were long trestle tables already laden with cates and dainties to keep body and soul together until such time as the revelers might get down to serious feeding.

Along with the food there were punches and possets, but mostly there was mead. Mead was a big thing at the Billingsgates'. They brewed it in their cellar from honey gathered by Abigail's thousands upon thousands of bees. Most of the potent product was sold to entrepreneurs who ran mediaeval feasts on a commercial basis, but Abigail and Bill kept their choicest bottlings for themselves and their friends.

Today, the bees had all been lured off to distant fields. Abigail was trying to convince her guests that they could go where they chose without running the risk of getting stung. Some were strolling along the nearer garden paths, but few were bothering to risk the apian panzer divisions in the back acres. Here by the pavilion, the grass was like plush and the entertainment was lively enough.

A space had been cordoned off with ropes for dancing. Nearby, another miniature pavilion had been set up for the musicians. Lorista, daughter-in-law of the Billingsgates' good friends the Dorks and sister to Sarah's aforementioned Cousin Lionel's wife, Vare, was in her glory here. She'd left her dulcimer at home, to Sarah's relief, but brought her recorder. Instead of playing the instrument she was conducting with it while an assortment of kindred spirits tooted their crumhorns, twanged their lutes, or thumped their tabors.

All were in Renaissance garb, loosely speaking. Lorista herself was the most renascent of the lot, as might have been expected from a woman who hadn't even been able to sing "Eentsy-Meentsy Spider" to her infant daughter without first getting herself up in seven petticoats and thick white stockings cross-gartered to the knees. The aim of the consort's amalgamated discords was to provide an accompaniment to a group of men in green hose, scarlet doublets with dagged and slittered edges, and bright yellow liripipe hoods. Each had a string of bells tied garterlike below each knee. At the moment, each was carrying two beribboned white batons which he clicked against other men's sticks. The men's movements were precise and spirited. John of

Gaunt would have been pleased. As Sarah paused to watch, Max dodged a passing farthingale and came over to join her.

"Is that Lionel? I didn't know he danced."

"He told me he did, but I hadn't realized he was so good," Sarah replied. "Who are the others, do you know?"

"The one beside Lionel must be Dork the Younger," Max said. "He looks just like his father, poor guy. The tall one in the middle's the Billingsgates' son-in-law."

"Lucky Melisande. He is good-looking, I must say. You don't suppose his name is Pelleas?"

"Who knows? His last name's Purbody. He told me to call him Tick when I came out here yesterday. There must be a few Whets and Tolbathys in the bunch, they always hang together. Too bad Jem's on the high seas. Or half seas over, more likely. He'd know who's which."

"And he'd tell them all what we're here for, once he'd got his nose in the mead," Sarah added.

She didn't have to worry about being overheard. The jangling and clacking combined with the twanging and tooting and thumping to produce a fairly high noise level. Whoever the dancers might be, they were taking their fun with the same dogged concentration as the musicians.

"They do flutter a lot," she went on. "What do you bet Lorista designed the costumes?"

"Stands to reason," Max agreed. "By the way, did you get a chance to call Miriam?" His sister was baby-sitting the youngest Kelling, since their housekeeper had the day off.

"Yes, dear. She says Davy finished his bottle, ate every bite of his carrots, and hasn't cried once since we left. He doesn't miss us a bit." Sarah tried not to sound disappointed, but didn't quite manage.

"Ah, he's just putting on a brave front," Max consoled her. "Come on, I'll buy you a sack posset."

"Ugh, no thanks. I'd adore a cup of tea but I suppose it's out of period. Shouldn't we mingle some more?"

"I suppose so. I'll mingle right and you mingle left. That means you get to mingle with your Aunt Appie."

"Max, you beast! Where is she? I can't see over all those padded headdresses."

"She's under that big tree, talking with some woman wearing a Queen Mary hat."

"Good heavens, I'll bet that's Aunt Bodie. I didn't know she was coming. Are you sure my hennin's on straight?"

"Looks perfect to me. You're far and away the best-dressed woman here."

Max spoke with only a modicum of prejudice. Considering that Sarah and her sister-in-law had whipped together her costume only the night before, after she'd learned they were expected to show up in mediaeval dress, Sarah did look totally delightful. She'd constructed her tall conical head-dress from a sheet of heavy watercolor paper that she'd painted in a millefleurs design. A piece of green mosquito netting borrowed from Cousin Brooks, the family naturalist, floated from the tip and could be whisked into use should Abigail's bees decide after all to join in the festivities.

Her gown was, in confidence, a pink satin nightie she'd bought for her honeymoon and never been given a chance to wear. Over it she wore a sumptuous pale green houppelande made from a pair of brocaded draperies Miriam had picked up at a yard sale ages ago. The sleeves reached almost to the ground and were a heavy responsibility, as was the short train wagging after her, but the effect was so enchanting that everybody who caught sight of her turned around to look again. As she swept across the close-clipped lawn, Apollonia Kelling hailed her with rapture.

"Sarah, how too utterly utter! Isn't she too ravishing for words, Bodie?"

"I can't imagine your ever finding anything too anything for words, Appie."

Boadicea Kelling wasn't being consciously rude, merely stating the facts as she saw them. "I daresay you could use that redingote affair for a negligee afterward, Sarah, if you shortened the sleeves and took up the hem. You don't plan to waste so much expensive material, of course."

"Why not?" Sarah answered brazenly, glancing back to

make sure her train was disposed to best advantage. "One never knows when one might need a houppelande. Besides, my daughter might like to dress up in it someday."

"But you don't have a daughter," Boadicea Kelling reminded her. "David Josiah is a boy."

"Yes, thank you, I had noticed that. But Max and I are thinking we might try again sometime, now that we've got the knack. How are you, Aunt Bodie?"

"Well as always, thank you. My blood pressure stays at 130 over 80, I still do my brisk four-mile walk each day, and my weight hasn't varied by more than a pound and a half during the past thirty-six years."

"Ah, but it will have by the time we get up from the banquet," crowed Appie.

Boadicea shook her Queen Mary toque. Sarah knew the hat well. When she was a little girl, it had been a rich purple color. Gradually the velvet had changed to a strange bronzy taupe, now it was almost cream. Boadicea had become too much a Kelling to fuss over trifles like that.

"I realize the custom is for guests to gorge themselves to the limit, but I have no intention of doing so. The leftover food won't go to waste, I've already verified that point with Abigail. She and Bill are having their respective Sunday School classes over tomorrow, to eat up the perishables and stage their own modest version of a Renaissance revel. This will be an educational experience for the young people. They are expected to improvise their own costumes. Otherwise, you could have left yours for one of them to wear, Sarah."

"No, I couldn't. I didn't bring anything else to put on."

Her aunt refrained from commenting on Sarah's lack of foresight. Her niece would know better another time, now that she'd been made aware of her shortcoming. Boadicea never nagged, she merely pointed out the proper course of action and assumed thenceforth it would be followed. She had read Norman Vincent Peale's book *The Power of Positive Thinking* as a young woman and never forgotten its message. She was thus able to find a positive word for Lorista and her consort, even though Lorista had now begun singing a ballad about the ratcatcher's wife and the fiddle-de-dee.

"Such diligence is commendable. I assume the musicians are donating their services. Bill assures me they're going to stop soon. He's scheduled a program of uninterrupted Renaissance music to be played over his local radio station during the banquet."

"Dear me, can one do that?" cried Apollonia. "I must get hold of WCRB about our church bazaar. Bach and Purcell, don't you think?"

"Nonsense, Appie." Boadicea spoke crisply because one really had to be crisp with Apollonia Kelling. "Bill can choose his own program for the reason that he owns the station. His object is to allow the listening audience to share our enjoyment of the auditory portion of the revel, thereby furthering the spirit of universal brotherhood to which he and Abigail are so laudably dedicated."

"But the audience won't know we're reveling and they won't get any mead." Appie investigated her own pewter flagon and discovered it to be empty. "I believe I'll wander off and see if I can find a serving wench, or do I mean potboy? Shall I get some for you, Bodie?"

"Thank you, no. I'm fine for the moment. We must concede, Sarah," Boadicea added as the other aunt took herself off wenchward, "that Appie's point is well taken. Some of the experiments Bill performs with those radio stations of his seem to presuppose a higher level of rapport with his public than may in fact exist. With regard to the mead, however, delivering their fair share to the listeners would be difficult to achieve and quite possibly a violation of the alcoholic beverage distribution laws. It's as well Bill abstained from making the attempt. I do hope Appie doesn't break her neck tripping over that skirt."

2

Most of the revelers had obliged their hosts by showing up in mediaeval or Renaissance costumes. Sarah wasn't enough of a scholar to sort out which was which and didn't suppose it mattered. Even experts could be ambiguous as to exactly when the Middle Ages left off and the rebirth of culture began. A few seemed to be of the opinion that the Renaissance was still going on. This left plenty of latitude for choice and the guests had used it all.

Some would have simply rented appropriate garb for the day. Others, like Professor Ufford, must have had authentic costumes made to order at no small expense. Spectacular outfits such as his had probably been gracing the Billingsgates' revels already for some years and would no doubt appear again and again, so the expense would be amortized over a long period. Then there were those who'd chosen to improvise, of whom Apollonia Kelling was definitely one.

Sarah realized that her aunt's costume must be based on the evening gown Appie used to wear on opening nights at the Huntington Avenue Opera House. Sarah only knew about these openings from hearsay, the opera house having been torn down shortly before she herself was born, but she had seen clippings in Uncle Jem's scrapbook. This was the gown that had strained the society editors' ingenuity to the point of cracking. One year Mrs. Samuel Kelling would be reported as having appeared in kingfisher blue, the next year in teal blue, the following year cobalt blue, then on to cerulean blue, azure blue, bluebonnet blue, forget-me-not blue, and finally back to kingfisher.*

By now the gown was a decidedly faded blue, but Appie had cheered it up with a screaming orange overblouse, probably borrowed from her daughter-in-law, and a good many strings of beads relatives had brought her from time to time as souvenirs of places they'd visited. Chains of polished quahog shells from Maine joggled together with seed pods from Papua and fake scarabs from Cairo, perhaps symbolizing the far-flung explorations carried out during the Renaissance.

For a headdress, Appie had simply pinned the open end of a white linen pillowcase around her head like a coif and let the rest of the case flop down her back. It was rather flapping than flopping just now, as a brisk wind had sprung up. On Appie's tall, gaunt figure the effect was that of laundry blowing around a clothes pole. Boadicea gazed after her cousin, interested but not censorious.

"Appie is enjoying herself. I myself saw no reason to bother about a costume. The dress I have on is middle-aged enough as it is, and so am I. Have you seen Drusilla Gaheris around anywhere, Sarah?"

"I'm afraid I shouldn't know her if I did."

"Not unless you were introduced today. There was that possibility. Drusilla is almost certainly here, since she's Abigail's house guest. I do realize, however, that you and Mr. Bittersohn—"

"Do call him Max."

"Very well, if you wish me to," Boadicea conceded. "That you and Max, as I was about to say, had not been acquainted with the Billingsgates and their circle before that unfortunate business with Wouter Tolbathy.** I grant you Wouter was

---

*Cleveland Amory in *The Proper Bostonians* described a similar adjective effort's having been expended over a period of years on the white gown of a Boston lady. If either wearer ever noticed, she was probably mildly amused.
**The Convivial Codfish

always an odd duck, but so many inventors are, don't you think? Too bad he was never able to adapt his undoubted genius to any useful purpose. Ah, here comes Drusilla now, with Hester Tolbathy."

"Oh, good," said Sarah. "I do like Hester so much."

"It's quite likely you'll enjoy Drusilla, too."

Sarah thought it possible. Mrs. Gaheris looked sensible enough, anyway, in a drab-colored costume with a lighter coif. Sarah thought at first Aunt Bodie's friend had come as a nun, then she remembered the habits worn by religious orders until recent years were in fact survivals of middle-class sixteenth-century housewives' daily garb.

Hester, on the other hand, had flung herself headlong into the festival spirit. Her gown was of purple satin over a wide-spreading farthingale, with a gold embroidered stomacher and a stiffened lace collar that must have been hell to wear. Her abundant white hair was dressed high with artificial roses and a chain of real amethysts. Rings flashed on thumbs and finger joints as she held out both hands to Sarah.

"The little mother! How lovely you look, Sarah dear. Did you bring your baby with you?"

"No, Davy's not quite ready for grown-up parties yet. He's back at Ireson's Landing with his aunt and his grandma."

"Being gloriously spoiled, no doubt. But he's thriving?"

"He was fine the last I heard."

"Which was?"

"About fifteen minutes ago," Sarah confessed. "Max teases me about being overanxious, but if I don't keep checking, he reminds me."

"That wears off after the first one," Hester assured her. "And you really like living year-round at Ireson's Landing? You don't miss Boston at all?"

"Not a bit. We love our new house and it's marvelous being so close to the ocean and to Max's family. He grew up on the North Shore, you know, and I've spent so many summers there that we felt at home from the very first day. Anyway, we do still have the Beacon Hill house. My cousin Brooks and his wife live there, but we keep a couple of rooms upstairs for ourselves to use whenever we decide to stay in town."

"That sounds like an ideal arrangement. Bodie, how good to see you. Did you drive all the way from Wenham by yourself? Drusilla Gaheris, do you know Bodie's niece, Sarah Bittersohn? She was Walter Kelling's daughter."

"Then you must be Lionel's cousin," said Mrs. Gaheris. "How do you do, Sarah? Lionel married my niece, Varine."

"Oh, Vare, of course. She mentioned an aunt who lived abroad."

"Yes, my husband was with the State Department. He died in Switzerland this past year and I decided I didn't want to stay over there by myself. I must say it's lovely to be among my own connections again, and to be meeting so many new ones. I missed both Vare's and Lorista's weddings, along with far too many other family functions, though I'd known both Lionel and Dorkie as little boys. They're quite good, don't you think?"

The morris dancers were still leaping and kicking, still in perfect unison, still with no sign of flagging. With their ribbons and bells, they made a merry sight to watch, even though their faces were grim enough. Like true Yankees, they were determined to have a good time if it killed them all. Even the wheezings and creakings of Lorista's consort didn't sound too bad in the open air. Village bands of the sixteenth and seventeenth centuries probably wouldn't have been any better, Sarah told herself.

Soon, though, Lorista raised her recorder high and brought it down with a savage slash, narrowly missing the *cor anglais*. Music and dancers came smartly to a halt. Onlookers clapped. Potboys bustled up with fistfuls of flagons. Lionel stuck his batons into the belt of his doublet and walked over to where the four women were standing.

"Well, Aunt Bodie, Aunt Drusilla. Good to see you, Mrs. Tolbathy. Where's Max, Sarah?"

"Around somewhere."

"Ungh. Seen Mother?"

"Appie was with us a little while ago," said Boadicea. "I

believe she may have gone into the pavilion. Allow me to compliment you on your dancing, Lionel. The morris dance is of ancient origin, is it not?"

"That depends on what you call ancient," was his gracious reply.

"I call myself ancient," said Hester Tolbathy, "and my feet are going to start aching in about one minute if I don't find a place to sit down."

"What about that bench under the tree?" Sarah suggested.

"It looks as if the birds have been there first," Mrs. Gaheris objected. "Isn't there someplace cleaner, and softer?"

"We could go into the pavilion," said Hester.

"Or up to the car shed," said Boadicea. "I must confess that when the reveling gets a bit too much for me, I always slip off and sit in one of Bill's Rolls Royces."

Drusilla Gaheris raised her eyebrows as far as her starched coif would allow. "I know Abigail and Bill each drive a Rolls. Don't tell me there are more?"

"Nine in all, I believe."

"No, ten," Hester Tolbathy corrected. "Bill gave Abigail a 1927 Silver Cloud for Christmas this past year. They're all antiques, Drusilla. Heaven only knows what they're worth by now."

"Oh, but we mustn't give Drusilla the idea Bill simply went out and squandered a lot of money on them," cried Boadicea. "How it started, Drusilla, was that Bill's grandfather bought one of the early models in 1908, I believe it was. Then of course the cars kept getting better, so he bought another in 1916. Then Bill's father was given one for his graduation from Harvard in 1924 and his sister Eglantine got hers as a wedding present."

"And then the Depression came along and people were selling off their Rollses for whatever they could get," Hester went on, "so the Billingsgates picked up a couple more for Bill and his brother Ralph to drive when they got old enough. Naturally one doesn't trundle a Rolls off to the junk yard and I suppose it seemed rather vulgar to turn them in, so they simply accumulated. After a while, the Rollses became something of a family joke. Bill's parents gave him and Abigail a 1945 Sedanca de ville to go honeymooning in, and so it went. It's got so that whenever Bill sees an old Rolls going at a bargain, he just buys the car and stuffs it in with the rest of them."

"What a fascinating hobby," said Mrs. Gaheris. "Do they all work?"

"Oh yes," Hester assured her. "I'm sure you'll be dragged off to a rally as soon as we've recovered from the revel. We go in a bunch: Tom and I and the Dorks and the Whets and our various offspring and their wives. Or husbands, as the case may be. And Bill and Abigail, needless to say. I expect you'll get to drive the New Phantom."

"Me? I'd be scared to touch it."

"When were you ever scared of anything? Remember how we used to pile into that Chevy roadster of yours with the rumble seat and go whooping around like a pack of Zelda Fitzgeralds? Ah, those were the days and aren't you glad we don't have to live them over? Come on, Drusilla, let's go see the cars."

But they couldn't. Sarah wondered whether or not she should be the one to break the news that the car shed had been declared out of bounds for the day. She didn't particularly mind sending Aunt Bodie on a wild goose chase, but it did seem a shame for Hester Tolbathy to drag her farthingale all the way up there for nothing.

Luckily, the matter was taken out of her hands. Two of the musicians, now carrying brass trumpets fully a yard long and wearing tabards emblazoned with what was presumably the Billingsgate coat of arms, a bee *volant* on a field *semé*, marched to the front of the pavilion and began creating a terrible din. The banquet was announced.

And a banquet in sooth it was. Renaissance revelers had evidently been hearty feeders, when they got the chance, and the Billingsgates weren't about to dishonor the tradition. Even Max was impressed.

"My God, this looks like a Newton bar mitzvah. What is all that stuff, anyway?"

There'd been some fudging of recipes to suit modern tastes, and a few pardonable subterfuges. The peacock pies, for instance, were only turkey under borrowed plumage and the swans but geese. The baron of beef, the larded capons, and the sallets of herbs were authentic as could be. So, no doubt, was the huge silver bowl full of something gruelish that sat square in the middle of the laden trestle. Even Sarah couldn't guess what it might be.

"Frumenty," said Marcia Whet, who happened to be standing beside them. "Just whole wheat boiled in milk and spices, actually. Abigail always sets it out because she feels it's the thing to do, but she doesn't really expect us to eat any. Take half a spoonful for manners and leave it on your plate, that's what I always do."

As she spoke, Marcia gave herself a generous helping without seeming to notice she was doing so. Max decided to pass up the frumenty, then shrugged and helped both himself and Sarah to a dollop.

"*Ess, ess, mein Kind*. It's probably good for you."

"It must have some redeeming feature. Enjoy your dinner, dear. I'm going to mingle some more."

Sarah took her plate over to one of the long tables and sat down. There was no printed menu; she supposed not all the lords or ladies of the period would have been able to read one. At least everybody got his own knife and fork, although it appeared the forks were anachronistic. The gentry hadn't started introducing them to their tables until sometime in the seventeenth century, and even then many considered them a silly affectation.

She knew all this because Professor Ufford told her so. She'd picked a seat next to old Tom Tolbathy, whom she liked very much, assuming she'd be able to have a comfortable chat with him about who was who and why. Tom would have been only too glad to oblige, but Ufford had zeroed in on the empty seat at her right. Since then, neither of them had been able to get a word in edgewise. Her neighbors across the table, Buck Tolbathy and Young Dork, were no help. They were deep in a low-voiced conversation about the finer points of morris dancing, and eating frumenty almost as if they liked it.

Well, it probably didn't matter that she wasn't accomplishing anything here. Marcia Whet and Hester Tolbathy had Max cosily tucked between them at the next table; no doubt he was gleaning plenty from them. Sarah tried to tune out the professor's drone and concentrate on her dinner and the charming Renaissance music being piped in from Station XBIL. Pretty soon she'd find an excuse to change her seat.

That wouldn't be hard to do, plenty of people were table-hopping. Though any number of potboys and serving wenches were rushing about with trays and plates, and Melisande Purbody's five Afghan hounds were foraging among the rushes that covered the floor of the pavilion, service was mostly do-it-yourself. Somebody would get up, wearing his napkin around his neck and carrying his cutlery as well as his plate, collect another helping of peacock pie and frumenty from the buffet, then plop himself down beside some other reveler he hadn't yet got to revel with.

Even after the surfeit stage ought to have been reached, Sarah couldn't notice much thinning around the boards. The pavilion was more inviting now than the lawn. As so often happens on a May day in Massachusetts, a stiffish east wind had sprung up. The sky that had been so azure or perhaps cerulean an hour before had become overcast with the darkish gray clouds that foretold a shower.

Sarah herself was comfortable enough in her silken gown and heavy brocade houppelande, but Abigail was sending a couple of the serving wenches who also happened to be her granddaughters into the house for extra wraps to protect the more thinly garbed. Apollonia Kelling, sitting over beyond Young Dork, was accepting a shawl with loud cries of gratitude.

"Just what the old bones needed. Bodie ought to have one, too. Her rheumatics always kick up if she gets a chill."

"I'll take it to her," Sarah heard one of the young Purbodys offer. "Where is she?"

"Let's see. There—no, that's Henry the Eighth. Or is it the seventh? Anyway, not Bodie."

Appie started prowling up and down between tables, turning the Kelling nose this way and that like a particularly undecided weathercock. "I can't seem to see her. How odd. Sarah, have you seen Bodie?"

There'd be no rest for her until she responded. Sarah murmured "excuse me" to Tom Tolbathy, who was working his way through an extra helping of frumenty with a somewhat bemused expression on his face. "I'm coming, Aunt Appie."

Sarah scanned the tables in her turn, but Boadicea Kelling's well-ordered countenance appeared nowhere. "Sorry, Aunt Appie. Aunt Bodie did mention that she wasn't going to eat much at the banquet, as you may remember. I expect she's doing her four miles around the clover fields, or something of that sort. Here, give me the shawl and finish your dinner. I'll go find her."

She was passing the buffet table, noticing to her surprise that the frumenty bowl had been scraped clean as a whistle, when she spied Professor Ufford. He was heading her way, and the smile on his face was not professorial. Sarah flipped her train into reverse and made a beeline for Max.

"Darling, I'm sorry to break up so attractive a threesome, but could you come and help me find Aunt Bodie? She's somewhere out in the grounds and Aunt Appie's afraid she'll get cold without a wrap."

"Sure. See you later, ladies."

Max climbed over the bench and took his wife's arm, leaving Hester and Marcia to exchange comments, no doubt, about what a charmer he was; and Professor Ufford to seek what consolation he could find among the Afghan hounds.

3

"**W**hat's so urgent about finding your aunt?" Max wanted to know when they'd got clear of the pavilion.

"Nothing, really, I don't suppose," Sarah answered. "It's just that Aunt Bodie was talking before we went in to dinner about going to sit in the Rolls Royces. She's a bit of an antique car buff herself. As far as I know, she's still driving a beige and gray Daimler her mother bought in 1946."

"So?"

"So I'm hoping she hasn't got into trouble with whoever's guarding the Billingsgates' cars, that's all. Aunt Bodie can be pretty sniffy when somebody tries to keep her from doing whatever she's set her mind on. Where's the car shed?"

"This way, if I'm not mistaken."

They picked their steps down a picturesque but rather damp path through a bosky dell that lay to the right of the terrace, and over a quaint stone bridge that spanned what had probably been laid out to represent the castle fishpond.

"It's too Horace Walpole for words, don't you think?" Sarah observed. "Where's the fern'd grot, I wonder?"

"I wot not of the grot," Max replied, "but the car shed's just over the hill."

"It would be."

Sarah's pink slippers hadn't been designed for climbing hills. She was glad of Max's helping hand as they navigated another rise of closely mown greensward on the other side of

18

the bridge. "How do they get the cars out to the road, for goodness' sake?"

"You'll see. Remember how we drove into that big graveled circle down behind the house?"

"Where you parked the car, yes. Then we walked through that long hallway and out over the drawbridge."

"That's right. Abigail told me Bill's grandfather didn't want carriages and automobiles driving up to the front of the house because he thought they'd spoil the effect of the portcullis. It's a stupid arrangement, but anyway there's another drive that leads from the circle up to the car shed, which is behind that stone wall up ahead of us."

The wall was of undressed granite chunks, about seven feet high surmounted by a spiked iron fence. As they got closer, Sarah could see a beautifully raked gravel drive. It snaked up from among some tall hemlocks that masked the house from view, and ran at last between iron gates that were set into the wall. These were heavily padlocked; beside them stood a dapper little wooden sentry box with a peaked red roof. Inside, Sarah could see only a wide gravel turnaround and a large, utilitarian, one-story building of unromantic concrete blocks roughed up to look like stone but not succeeding. Like the gates, the building appeared to be locked up tight.

"I don't see any sign of Aunt Bodie," she said.

"I don't see the watchman, either." Max was not happy. "He ought to have challenged us by now."

"Might he have gone to get something to eat?"

"He's not supposed to. He got a lunch break at noon and a coffee break at three o'clock. He's not due for another till six. One of the potboys is supposed to come by every hour on the hour to see if he needs a quick relief, and stay till he gets back. Bill left strict orders that the gate's not to be left unguarded for a single minute. Besides, Rufus—that's his name—is part of the entertainment. He's in mediaeval peasant costume and carries a *Totschläger*."

"What's that, some kind of war club?"

"A flail, actually; a hollow handle with a ball of iron

attached to the tip by a short chain. They were designed for bashing holes in an opponent's armor and came in a great many variations, jocosely referred to en masse as holy water sprinklers. Those mediaeval knights were a barrel of laughs. They had one that had a big ball studded with long iron spikes. It was called a *Morgenstern*, which of course means morning star. *Totschläger* just means dead-whacker or something of the sort, so Bill's great-grandfather probably got the name wrong. Not that it matters. This whole revel's about as authentically Renaissance as a Cranach painted on Masonite, as you must have realized by now."

"Rufus isn't supposed to flail anybody, then."

"Oh, no, the weapon's just there to provide positive reinforcement in case guests insist too much on being admitted to the car shed. Bill doesn't want anybody in there because they all know his collection and would notice the New Phantom was missing."

"Couldn't he say the Phantom was off at a rally or something?"

"Bill tell a lie? You've got to be kidding." Max took hold of the padlock and rattled it against the gate. Nothing happened.

"Sarah, I don't like this a bit. Would you mind going back to the pavilion by yourself and finding Bill? You'd better stick to the drive, it's shorter. Don't push the panic button, just get Bill aside. Tell him we found the gate unguarded and thought he'd better know."

"Yes, of course."

Sarah gathered up her train and started toward the house, sticking to the grassy verge and studying the gravel as she went along. Inside the fence, the gravel had been raked smooth as an ironing board. If Rufus had gone inside to the car shed, he must have walked on the narrow strip of grass that edged the turnaround. Outside the gate, there had been some scuffing of the gravel where the sentry might have paced or guests ambled over to chuckle at Rufus with his *Totschläger*.

Aunt Bodie must have been among the most recent

visitors, assuming she had in fact come here with the expectation of sitting in one of the cars. Sarah would be surprised if it turned out she hadn't. Boadicea Kelling wasn't one to indulge in idle chat. Had she bulldozed Rufus into letting her enter the car shed in defiance of Mr. Billingsgate's orders, then dragged him off to confess his dereliction? Sarah wouldn't put it past her.

Or had she irritated Rufus into chasing after her with his *Totschläger*? Sarah found something oddly agreeable in the thought of Aunt Bodie's being put to rout by a mediaeval peasant, even a make-believe one.

But it wouldn't do. Aunt Bodie wouldn't flee to the bee fields, she'd do a brisk about-face and march back to the pavilion. She'd deliver a concise report of the regrettable incident to whichever Billingsgate she happened to meet first, then she'd append a polite but firm request that this nonsense be stopped and she be admitted forthwith to the car shed.

She must have gone for her four-mile walk, after all. It was to be hoped she'd continue walking until whatever was wrong at the car shed could be ironed out. Sarah walked faster, found the door to the long hallway, and had the luck to encounter Mrs. Billingsgate coming back into the house for more shawls.

"Oh Abigail, I'm so glad it's you. Could you possibly do Max and me a big favor?"

"Of course, Sarah, what is it? Not the baby, I hope?"

"No, nothing like that. It's just that we need Bill up at the car shed. You can drop the message more easily than I without making people wonder, so would you?"

"Certainly, but what's the rush? Is something wrong there?"

"We don't know. We just went to check. The gate's still padlocked and the car shed shut up, but your guard's nowhere to be seen."

"That's odd. Bill gave Rufus strict orders to stay put till he's relieved."

"Yes, he told Max. That's why we're concerned. Max is standing sentry duty for the moment."

"You slip back and tell Max I'll scoot Bill along as soon as I can wiggle him loose. Oh dear, and I promised Ethelyn Frome I'd bring her something to put on. What a nuisance."

"Here, take this." Sarah realized somewhat to her surprise that she was still carrying the shawl Apollonia Kelling had given her to deliver. "I was supposed to take it to Aunt Bodie, but I didn't find her. I'd expected she'd be up by the car shed, berating the guard for not letting her in."

"I'm surprised she wasn't," said Abigail. "Bodie was always like that. We were in boarding school together, you know, along with Drusilla. But this is hardly the time for schoolgirl reminiscences. I'll get Bill."

She took the shawl and sped off, a buxom little figure looking much like the Wife of Bath. Her bright blue, full-skirted gown was short enough to show close-gartered scarlet hose and handmade shoes of soft brown leather. Her kerchief was of heavy white linen, probably one of those vast old-fashioned dinner napkins sized to encompass nine-course Edwardian paunches, Sarah thought. Abigail had drawn a wimple of white lawn around her face and topped it with a black felt hat hardly as wide as a buckler or targe but big enough to keep the sun off her nose. That was most likely why she wore it; she was already rosy-hued enough.

Sarah felt a moment's anxiety about her hostess's blood pressure but didn't stop to worry. It was hardly three minutes since she'd left Max, but she didn't like the thought of his being all by himself in that strangely silent place. It was not easy to hurry uphill with those many yards of brocade swirling around her, but she was almost running by the time she got back to the gate.

Above the sentry box stood an enormous horse chestnut tree, just now a solid mass of bright green leaves and tall candles of white bloom. Max was under it, staring into the greenery. On his face was an expression of total disbelief.

"Max, what's the matter?" Sarah panted. "What's up there?"

"Don't look."

"Why not?" Sarah was already looking, of course. "I can't see anything, the foliage is so dense. Wait, what's—darling, are those feet?"

All he said was, "Did you get hold of Bill?"

"I met Abigail. She's sending him along. Max, answer me."

"All right, they're feet," he admitted. "Rufus's feet."

"What's he doing up there?"

"Hanging. You can't see it because you're not tall enough, but there's a rope tied around that branch over your head, running up the trunk."

"And he's on the other end of it," Sarah finished.

Max shrugged. "Where else?"

"Then shouldn't we cut him down?"

"Not on your life. There's nothing we can do for him, I've already climbed up to see. And messed things around in the process, no doubt, though I tried to be careful. My guess is that he was dead, or at least unconscious, before he was hauled up."

"Max, how awful!" Sarah moaned. "Why do you say that?"

"Because the foliage around him isn't disturbed. A person being hanged doesn't usually die right away. That's why hanging as a form of execution used to be such a popular form of public entertainment back in the so-called good old days. Sometimes the poor bastard would put up a lively struggle for several minutes."

"Yes, I've read about such things." She wished she hadn't. "The hangman would have to tug at their feet to quiet them down. Those are heavy boots, aren't they?"

"That's right, and Rufus was no ninety-seven-pound weakling, either. He'd have kicked and squirmed and clutched at the branches trying to save himself. His hands show no stains or abrasions, his clothes aren't torn or dirty, and those boots look to have been freshly cleaned and oiled."

"But why kill him first if you're going to hang him anyway?"

"Mainly because dragging him that high into the tree would have been a hell of a job if he struggled. The ground would have been littered with debris off the tree and there'd be breakage all the way up," Max explained.

"Yes, of course. I should have thought. Then the object of the hanging was simply to get the body up where it wouldn't be seen. Don't you think that shows some degree of premeditation? How did you happen to look in the tree, anyway?"

Max shrugged. "It's an old dodge. The theory is that people searching for something seldom think to look over their heads."

"So naturally you did. Boost me, will you, dear? I'd like to see how that rope is tied."

"My pleasure."

Max took Sarah by the waist and swung her up to his shoulder. She slid an arm around his neck to steady herself and examined the lethal strand.

The rope appeared to be quite new and couldn't have been better chosen for its purpose. Its dead brown color blended so well with the tree bark that only an observer as keen as Max would have noticed it from the ground. It was thin but strong-looking and made Sarah think of Cousin Lionel.

"Max, I'll bet this is a mountain climber's rope. Cousin Lionel has one he takes on those survival hikes. And the knot's a clove hitch."

"Meaning what?"

"That's a kind of sailor's knot used to tie up a boat. The harder the boat pulls at the mooring, the more secure the knot becomes," Sarah informed him.

"From which we deduce that whoever hanged the guard climbs mountains and ties boats," he replied.

"In short, Cousin Lionel. Darling, I can't say I find that particularly amusing. Put me down now, I think I hear Bill coming."

"Sorehead."

Max gave her a quick kiss just below the hennin and set

her down in time to be looking professional when his current employer came hurrying up from the house.

"What's the matter, Max? Abigail says you've lost Rufus."

"I'm afraid we've found him, Bill. You're not going to like this."

"Good Lord, you don't mean he's badly hurt?"

"I wish I did," Max answered.

Nehemiah Billingsgate stared, then shook his head. "I don't believe you. Where is he?"

"Up there."

"In the tree? Max, this is absurd. I see nothing but leaves."

"Try for boot soles."

Either because Nehemiah Billingsgate was a religious man or because the garb was loose and comfortable for an elderly, somewhat overweight man who'd known he was going to be on his feet most of the day, he'd got himself up as the friar of orders gray. When he spotted the hanging boots, Bill's face turned grayer than his habit.

"Dear merciful God," he whispered, "whatever possessed Rufe to do a thing like this?"

"I think we're going to find he didn't," said Max. "I climbed up and took a look. There's a noose around his neck, but I don't believe he put it there."

"How could that be? What would be the sense?"

"Of killing him? I don't know yet. As for hanging him up the tree I assume it was to conceal the fact that he was dead and give the killer a chance to get away. Rufe was part of the show. That means your guests have been strolling up here to take a look at him off and on ever since the revel started, right?"

"Yes. A number of people have commented on how amusing he looked." Bill almost didn't manage the "amusing."

"So during the banquet would be the least risky time to kill him because everybody was in the pavilion then together. But there was still the off chance that somebody would come along, so the killer had to work fast. Leaving the body by the sentry box would attract attention too soon, but dragging it away to hide would take too much time. Hitching his body to a rope and hauling him up into the tree wouldn't take more than a few seconds."

"Assuming one had the rope ready in advance." Bill wasn't so thunderstruck as to overlook the obvious.

"Yes," Max agreed. "I'm afraid that's a foregone conclusion."

Bill shook his head, with the fake tonsure that everyone had been finding as amusing as they had Rufus and his *Totschläger*. "Whoever would have thought to look for him there? We might have left him hanging until—the crows found him, I suppose. Max, this is appalling! Will you help me get the poor fellow down?"

"We mustn't, Bill. The police will have to see him as he is."

"The police?" Nehemiah Billingsgate bowed his head and swallowed hard. "Oh yes. Stupid of me. And we were all having such a marvelous time. Except Rufe. You don't think he suffered, Max?"

"There's no sign that he did. I'd say he never knew what hit him."

"Poor old Rufe! Well, the Lord giveth and the Lord taketh away. Rufe always said he wanted to die before he got old and useless. Then you want me to telephone the police?"

"First, if you don't mind, we ought to check out the cars," said Sarah. "Can you open the gate, Bill?"

"No problem. I have my keys right here. I've gone a bit paranoid about security since the New Phantom disappeared. Which I expect is why Rufe got killed. If only I hadn't been so mean-spirited about setting a guard!"

"Bill, you did what anybody with a grain of sense would have done," said Max. "Rufus had keys, too, I suppose?"

"No, as a matter of fact, he didn't. His are back at the house, locked up in the library safe. There was no reason for Rufe to be carrying them, you see. He wasn't required to go inside the gate, merely to let visitors know the car shed was out of bounds. He thought if anybody got too insistent, he could merely explain that he had no keys with him, then nobody could accuse him of being uncivil. Furthermore, my wife forgot to put any pockets in his costume, so he'd have had no place to keep them anyway," Bill added with a rueful smile. "Dear God, if Rufe was killed for the keys he didn't have—well, let's use mine."

Bill's keys were part of his costume, a great ring of them hanging from a cord around his waist. "Abigail insists that if I'd ever gone into holy orders, I'd have wound up as a sacristan, so we decided I might as well play the role," he explained as he fitted a black iron key about six inches long into the massive padlock. "I expect most of our guests thought these were plastic, if they noticed them at all. Sarah?" He opened the gate and motioned her through.

"I've been noticing how beautifully the gravel's raked," Sarah remarked as they walked across to the car shed.

The unsteadiness was back in Billingsgate's voice. "Rufe spent hours out here yesterday helping Bob tidy the place up for the revel. We do have a special tractor with a wide rake on it for the gravel, but with our cars going in and out so often, the drive's generally a good deal less orderly than you see it today. We'll go in this little side door, if you don't mind. Ah, I believe this is the key."

"I'll go first this time." Max stepped inside and took a careful look around. The car shed was the size of a skating rink, with concrete walls and floor and a steel-girdered ceiling. There was nothing in it but Rolls Royces. "Quite a place you've got here, Bill."

Sarah's reaction was more personal. "What marvelous old cars!"

"We think so," Bill confessed. "Some mean more to us than others, of course, because of the family connections. The New Phantom belonged to my brother Ralph, who died thirty-five years ago. That's why I was so particularly upset to lose—dear God in heaven, the Silver Ghost!"

4

"**W**here?" demanded Sarah. Bill was so pale, she thought he must have seen an apparition.

"I don't know where," he babbled. "It's gone. It was parked right here betweeen the Barker Saloon Cabriolet and the Drop Head foursome Coupe. It's not the famous Silver Ghost AX201 of 1907, needless to say, but one of the subsequent models and the gem of our collection. Except for the dear old Roi des Belges, I have to admit. Great-grandfather bought her in 1906. But the Roi's a bit cranky to drive if you're not used to her. The Ghost's a dream. Max, I— I don't know what to say."

"You're saying another of your Rolls Royces has been stolen, Bill," Max Bittersohn pointed out reasonably enough. "When did you last see your Silver Ghost?"

"Half-past twelve or thereabouts. Rufe had just finished his lunch and I was getting him settled in his sentry box because people would be starting to arrive. I'd brought his costume with me and we'd come in here so he could change."

Bill led them into a small room at the back where several chauffeurs' uniforms of different vintages hung, along with some motoring dusters and veils, a brown tweed jacket with leather patches at the elbows, and a pair of wrinkled chino pants washed almost white. Bill nodded at these last with a twisted smile.

"Rufe's Old Retainer suit. That's what Melly calls it. She and Rufe always had great fun teasing each other. He'd known her since she was knee-high to a hubcap, of course."

"He was with you a long time, then." Sarah could sense what Bill must be feeling. She'd had losses, too.

"All his life," sighed Bill, "and his father before him. Rufe was terribly feudal in his ideas. He wouldn't have dreamed of leaving the castle, as he always called it, and we'd certainly never have wanted him to. We'll hold the funeral service right here in our own private chapel, and lay him to rest in the family plot. Rufe would like that, dear soul. Anyway, it may help to make the rest of us feel less miserable at losing him. Sarah, Max, I do beg your pardon. When I mentioned my wretched little problem, I had no intention of dragging you into something like this."

"Don't apologize, Bill," Sarah told him. "At least we know now why Rufus was killed. Once we get a line on how the Silver Ghost was taken, I expect we'll be able to wind things up quickly."

"But the Ghost can't have been stolen, don't you see? The only way it could have been taken out was through the gate and down the drive. But the gate was locked and the drive was undisturbed. You said so yourself. It makes no sense."

"It will," said Max. "Rufe's death didn't make sense a couple of minutes ago."

"That's true. I'm sorry. I'm overwrought, I suppose." The older man made a brave effort to pull himself together. "You say Rufe was killed to keep him from stopping the theft of the Ghost, and hung in the tree to gain time for the thief to get away. That much I'm willing to grant. I myself would never have thought of looking in the tree. I'd have wasted time searching the grounds, the castle, his own rooms."

"Where are they? In the castle?" Max asked him.

"No, in the gatekeeper's lodge. Silly name, but that's what it's always been called. You may have noticed a small house to your right as you entered the main drive from the road. We do have gates down there, though we almost never shut them. I think my great-grandfather's fancy was to keep a rosy-cheeked old lady in the lodge who'd pop out and bob a curtsey as the gentry drove up, but I'm sure it never happened. Anyway, Rufe was born in the lodge. Lately he's been sharing the place with our cook and her husband, who's the Bob I mentioned. Bob gardens for us and some other people around town."

"Where is he now?" Sarah asked.

"Off to one of his other customers, Eric Hohnser, who lives about a mile up the road."

"On Sunday?"

"Yes, Hohnser made rather a thing of Bob's working today because he'd missed one day last week when it rained. Bob didn't mind. He was afraid that if he stuck around for the revel, we'd put him into velvet pantaloons like Rufe. Which we would have, I expect. What fools we mortals be. I'm babbling."

Bill took a few deep breaths. "Anyway, if the Ghost was driven away, then the drive must have been raked by hand afterward. But if the thief was in such a desperate rush that he couldn't even spend a minute or two to knock Rufe out and drag him in here instead of—you do see what I'm getting at?"

"We see it, Bill, but we can't get around the fact that Rufus is dead and the car's gone. Perhaps he wasn't killed to save time but because he recognized the thief."

"Then you're suggesting one of our guests did it. But that's unthinkable. They're all our friends."

"Or friends of friends," Max suggested. "Or business acquaintances, or neighbors you didn't want to slight even if you don't know them all that well?"

"All right, Max, you've made your point. I realize this is no time to piddle around with the amenities. I suppose this is when we call the police."

There was a telephone in the car shed. Most unhappily, Nehemiah Billingsgate used it.

"They said they'd be right along. Wretch that I am, I wish we could have waited until the guests leave."

"Why don't you walk down to the front gate and intercept

them?" Sarah suggested. "At least you can keep them away from the front of the house. Max, you don't mind staying with the—evidence, do you? I think I'd better keep looking for Aunt Bodie."

"What the hell for?"

"To head her off, dear. If she happens along while the police are here, she'll start giving helpful advice and land the whole party in jail. Don't worry, I'll stay within screaming distance."

She went out the gate and struck off across the crest of the hill. There were tall hedges of lilac to skirt before she could get a good view of the bee fields, but they didn't worry her much. It was most unlikely whoever had killed Rufus and stolen the Silver Ghost was lurking around to accost straying women. Max didn't think so, or he'd have put up more than a routine husbandly protest about her wandering off on her own.

Most of the revelers must be dancing by now; she could hear what sounded like a minuet, muffled and sweetened by the distance between her and the pavilion. Sarah had rather looked forward to trying the ancient dances herself. What a burning shame the party into which the Billingsgates had put so much time and love had ended like this. Remembering those two feet dangling high in the horse chestnut tree, Sarah shuddered in spite of her houppelande.

"How adorable you look."

The voice came out of the lilacs. Sarah drew breath for a good, loud mediaeval scream. Then the speaker emerged and she snarled instead.

"Professor Ufford! Why aren't you dancing?"

"Because I promised myself a beautiful partner and wasn't able to find her."

"Then your standards must be incredibly high." He was no Adonis himself, the old goat.

"Indeed they are, Mrs. Bittersohn. That's why I came looking for you. Do say you'll give me the honor of your company for the galliard and the *volta*."

"Sorry, but I've never even heard of either one. You'll do far better to ask Lorista Dork. I'm sure she knows them all."

"Ah, Lorista." The kind of smile that accompanied those two short words could have made Ufford a fortune in the movies back when sophisticated rotters were in vogue. "Come now, don't be shy of me. You and I have so much in common."

"I can't imagine what you think it is, Professor Ufford."

"Enchanting Sarah, do call me Vercingetorix."

"Whatever for? Excuse me, I must get back to my husband."

He appeared ready to commit some more audacious familiarity, but the one really useful thing Sarah had learned from Aunt Bodie was the art of quelling an encroacher with a look. Her look wasn't quite up to Boadicea Kelling's look, but it packed enough wallop to wipe the leer off Ufford's unlovely visage. She sketched him the ghost of a curtsey and sailed back to the car shed with her houppelande billowing out behind her like a spinnaker in reverse.

Max must have locked the gate. He was sitting outside in the sentry box with his eyes shut. Asleep, she thought fondly. He'd acquired the useful knack of snatching quick naps under the most unlikely circumstances.

"Wake up and rescue me, sluggard!" she ordered.

"Huh? What's the matter?"

"Vercingetorix is after me."

"Come to papa, I'll protect you."

Max spent a few protective moments to the satisfaction of both before he got around to inquiring, "Vercingetorix who?"

"Ufford. That old prune in the Arnolfini getup. He says we have a lot in common."

"The insufferable cad!"

"He asked me to dance the *volta* with him."

"I'll punch his ugly face in."

"By all means do, if you feel the urge," Sarah agreed. "What's a *volta*, anyway?"

"A lot of hopping and leaping, then the guy grabs the girl

by the upper thighs or the corset cover, whichever turns him on, and waves her around his head. Which way did the bastard go?"

"Darling, don't be mediaeval. He's old enough to be your father. But nowhere near good-looking enough," Sarah qualified. "Aunt Bodie was nowhere in sight."

"Why the hell wasn't she?" her husband demanded. "Where were you?"

"Heading for the clover fields. I thought she might have gone to get stung for her arthritis."

"Sarah!"

She gazed at him in cool wonderment. "You do get upset over the oddest things, dear. Don't you know bee stings are supposed to be beneficial in certain cases? It would be quite like Aunt Bodie to try, if she could find a suitable bee."

"How'd she know which bee was suitable?"

"She'd know," Sarah replied confidently. "I gather the police aren't here yet?"

"No, Bill's still waiting. Why the hell do these people do it?" Max wondered. "He's already lost one Rolls Royce, so he throws a big wingding for all the people who common sense ought to have told him are his prime suspects."

"I know, dear. So does Bill, or he'd have called the police instead of us in the first place. But what else could they have done? Short of a death in the family, they couldn't have called the revel off at the last minute. Abigail's the one I feel for, having to go on playing the perfect hostess when she must be having fits about what's happened to Rufus."

"She'll know soon enough," Max said grimly. "Bill says things will be winding down soon. People generally begin drifting off once they've trodden a measure or two."

"But will the police let them go?"

"Probably. That's why it might not be a bad idea for you to nip back down there and find out whatever you can while they're still around. If your aunt shows up, I'll give her a look. And if Ufford comes along, I'll rip him to shreds and stamp on the pieces."

"What a splendid idea," said Sarah. "I think I'll go back by the drive, just in case. I do hate being jumped out at."

But nobody jumped. Sarah didn't meet a soul until she was through the long corridor and back out on the front terrace. Then she headed straight for Abigail.

"Did you find Rufe?"

Sarah had expected the question, and managed to answer without flinching. "Yes, we found him. Don't worry, Abigail. Max and Bill are back there with him."

She turned away before Abigail could ask any more. Cousin Lionel was her next target, she'd decided. Those sharp gooseberry eyes of his didn't miss much, and getting him into one of those prolonged bickerings that often passed for conversation among the Kelling clan was no trick at all. Sarah had only to offer flat statements and wait for him to contradict her. He'd be right more often than not and he wouldn't gloss over the rough spots. Cousin Lionel had no scruples against speaking ill of his neighbor.

"I hadn't realized Young Dork and Tick Purbody work for the Billingsgates' radio stations," was her opening gambit.

"That's because they don't," Lionel was only too happy to reply. "Young Dork works for his father; and Tick Purbody, in my candid opinion, works for Tick Purbody. That's not to say Tick won't want to hire Young Dork as soon as he manages to snatch the reins from his father-in-law. Those two have been thick as thieves all their lives."

"But you say Young Dork is in his own family's firm."

"Who knows for how long?" Lionel could sneer almost as well as Professor Ufford. "At the rate small businesses are being gobbled up by the conglomerates, it's only a matter of time before he's among the unemployed, like me."

Sarah wasn't about to waste any tears on Lionel. Helping his mother cash her dividend checks and wheedling her out of the proceeds kept him well enough occupied.

"But if the Dorks get gobbled up, why shouldn't the Billingsgates?" she argued. "They're not exactly the National Broadcasting Company, are they?"

"No, but Tick's a damn sight smarter than Young Dork.

Once he takes hold, you're going to see some big changes, believe me."

"Why do you say that? Has Tick talked to you about his plans?"

"That's a stupid question. Of course he hasn't."

She'd hit a nerve. Naturally none of his friends ever told Lionel anything, for fear he'd spill it to Aunt Appie. Sarah decided she'd better change the subject. She made a deliberately erroneous observation about whom Melisande had been sitting with at the banquet, which he promptly corrected, and they went on to wrangle mildly about who else had been sitting with whom. Lionel's memory was as good as Sarah's, since all Kellings were conditioned from the cradle to keep track of their multifarious tribal connections.

The only details on which he didn't pick her up and run her down involved the early minutes of the banquet. He didn't say he'd been late entering the pavilion, but neither did he say he hadn't. When Sarah commented on the fact that some guests had straggled in long after the rest had begun to eat, and that his mother had been among the stragglers when in fact she'd been among the first, Lionel only grunted.

Probably he'd taken time out to freshen up after his strenuous workout with the morris dancers, but why couldn't he have said so? Lionel wasn't much for repressing, as a rule. Sarah gave up on him with a vague feeling of unease and went on to Hester Tolbathy.

"Why aren't you dancing?" was Hester's greeting.

"I'm a fugitive from Professor Ufford. He asked me to be his partner and I'm afraid I cut him rather short."

"How in the world did you manage that? Everyone else has been trying for years. What a pity I missed it. Where were you at the time?"

"Up on the hill. I'd gone to look for Aunt Bodie." Sarah explained about the bee in case Hester might possibly have a suspicion that needed lulling.

"That would be quite like Bodie," Hester agreed in all solemnity. "Perhaps she's still looking for the right bee. I haven't seen her around for quite some time, now that I think of it. But what was Versey doing out in the fields with nobody to talk to?"

"He claimed he'd come looking for me, which is absurd."

Hester had a genuine sterling silver chuckle. "You underrate yourself, my dear. Every man at the revel would be ravening after you if you didn't have that big, handsome husband along. Where is Max now?"

"Off talking antique cars with Bill, the last I saw of him," Sarah fudged.

"The rogue! I'll bet you anything he's wheedled his way into the car shed, which has been declared off bounds to the rest of us, though I can't think why. We've never been kept out before. Anyway, Dorothy Dork strolled up there a while back, but the gate was locked and that old handyman of the Billingsgates' was standing in front of it got up like the Lord High Executioner. Dorothy asked him to let her in, but he only growled and shook his mace at her. She thinks it was a mace. Something large and formidable, anyway."

"Really? When was this?"

"Shortly after the banquet started. Dorothy ate a big helping of frumenty right off the bat, for some odd reason, and it landed in her stomach like a ton of bricks. She said she thought she'd better joggle it down before she tackled the rest of the meal."

"How long did Dorothy stay?" Sarah wanted to know.

"She didn't stay at all," Hester replied. "Just turned around and came back. She didn't want to miss out on the peacock pie."

"Was she all right afterward?"

"I assume so. There she is now, dancing the gigue with Tom. He'll be lame tomorrow, the old roisterer."

"Dorothy was sitting with Drusilla Gaheris, wasn't she?"

"Some of the time, anyway. You know how it was, we were all flitting from table to table."

"Whom did you flit with? Aside from my handsome husband, that is?"

"Well, you had mine."

5

They laughed and compared notes for a while. "But where was Aunt Bodie all this time?" Sarah asked finally. "I'm surprised she wasn't with you."

Hester shook her amethyst-starred head. "Oh no, our crowd is far too light-minded for Bodie. She never could stand my brother-in-law, and of course we all adored Wouter. And she considers Marcia Whet flighty, and you know Marcia's my absolutely dearest friend in all the world. I don't know what Bodie thinks of me and I'm not about to ask. I assume she was with Drusilla. They always chummed around together at school. The lot of us were at Miss Chalmers's, you know, or perhaps you didn't. That was rather before your time."

The older woman laughed. "Anyway, Bodie kept in touch with Drusilla over the years far more than the rest of us did, so naturally they'd want a chance to visit now. Why don't you ask Drusilla? She's Abigail's house guest, so she's sure to be around. I've got to drag that wretched man off the dance floor and get him home while he can still walk. The air's really cold now that the sun's gone down, and we're both just over the sniffles. It's been so good to see you again, Sarah dear. Do visit us soon, and bring the baby."

"You must come to us," Sarah replied. "We're planning a housewarming as soon as we're a bit more put together."

They rubbed cheeks, then Hester gathered her purple

satin furbelows about her and went to collect her husband and find her hostess. She'd provided one important piece of information anyway. If Dorothy Dork could remember exactly when she'd gone for her walk, they'd be able to limit further the span of time during which Rufus had been killed.

Mrs. Dork could remember. She'd conscientiously tried not to nibble before the banquet, so she'd lost no time getting to the buffet. She'd taken some frumenty because she knew nobody else would and she didn't want dear Abigail's feelings to be hurt. She'd eaten it and wished she hadn't, then tried to walk it off before everybody got settled so that her coming and going wouldn't be noticed. She was sure she hadn't been gone from the pavilion more than ten minutes in all.

So she was most likely back by a quarter to four, Sarah decided. The revel had begun at high noon, there'd been the jugglers and jesters, the madrigal singing and the morris dancing, the heralds had sounded their trumpets at half-past three. An odd time to be dining according to modern custom perhaps, but a good time for Renaissance revelers, according to Professor Ufford. People who could afford two meals a day would have breakfasted shortly after sunup on meat and ale, then sat down in the latter part of the afternoon and gorged as long as the food and drink held out.

Thinking of food and drink reminded Sarah that she hadn't yet talked to the cook. She walked over the draw-bridge, through the massive front door that had been left wide open, and followed a potboy with a load of used flagons out to the kitchen. She didn't think there'd be much use questioning him or any of the other servers. As far as she could see, they'd been paying more attention to their duties and to each other's jokes than to the company. Anyway, she didn't see how she could start grilling one without starting the lot of them wondering what was going on.

Talking to the cook was another matter. It was entirely in order for a guest to pay homage to the creator of so bounteous a feast. Cook received Sarah's compliments with lofty dignity, and Sarah's apology for not knowing her name with tolerant grace.

"Cook is my title, and Cook is the manner in which I prefer to be addressed."

She was seated in a rocking chair that must have been built to her measurements. It was at least half again the regular size. She'd made no move to rise when Sarah came in, nor would Sarah have expected her to. Getting up would be a precedure not to be approached in haste by a woman of her dimensions.

"I suppose you've had a good many visitors, Cook," Sarah ventured.

"No doubt I have. On revel day, however, I concentrate so ferociously on the infinitude of details concerning the banquet that I find I retain no memory of those who come and go. Suffice it to me that they come when they're needed and go with whatever they're supposed to be taking outside. I refer of course to the potboys and wenches. As for visitors like yourself, I frankly discourage them as most of the regulars know. Not to be uncivil, Mrs. Bittersohn. You wouldn't have known, being new, and it doesn't matter now anyway because my work is over. The scullions will handle the cleanup. I myself am far spent."

"Then I mustn't spend you further," said Sarah. "Thank you for letting me come in."

Cook answered only with a kindly smile and a courteous hope that they'd meet again when her faculties had been recruited to a more sociable level. She tilted her rocking chair as far back as it would safely go, and closed her eyes. Sarah returned to the lawn.

Drusilla Gaheris, her drab gown now covered by a warm gray loden cape, was standing over by the pavilion, chatting with Young Dork and Tick Purbody. As Sarah started over toward them, the two men moved away, their dags and slitters aflutter. Both looked a trifle meaded, she thought.

"They seem to be great friends," she remarked to Mrs. Gaheris.

"Dorkie and Tick? Oh yes, they always have been. They were roommates at Princeton, Lorista tells me. Speaking of old roommates, where did Bodie go? I've been hoping for a little more time with her, but I haven't seen her for ages."

"As a matter of fact," said Sarah, "I came to ask you the same thing. Aunt Appie's worried that Aunt Bodie's arthritis may be acting up in this chilly wind."

"Then perhaps she's gone in to keep warm. I'll check the house, shall I? I'm staying with the Billingsgates, you know, until I can find a place of my own; so I know my way around pretty well. Did you want to see Bodie about anything special?"

"Just to make sure she's all right."

"If I find her, I'll come back and tell you. You weren't planning to leave just yet?"

"No, we'll be around." Sarah wondered for how long and sighed. Davy was all right with his Aunt Miriam and Grandmother Bittersohn, of course, but surely he must be missing his own mother by now. She thought wistfully of Davy at bathtime and Davy in his sleepers afterward, all three of them cuddled up together on the sofa with Max telling a bedtime story. She could take the car and go home by herself. Miriam's son Mike would be only too glad to drive it back here and pick up his uncle.

But Max would still miss Davy's bedtime, and he missed too many of them as it was. He'd asked her particularly to work with him on this unexpected job. "You know how these people think," he'd said. "I have a hell of a time figuring them out." She straightened her hennin and looked around for somebody else to tackle.

There weren't all that many left. The dancing was over, the musicians were starting to pack up their instruments. Those revelers who'd stayed to struggle through the pavane were threading their way across the now cluttered terrace to bid Abigail goodbye. The hostess was taking time between hugs and handshakes to look vexedly over her shoulder for the host. Now Bill was joining her, trying to be cordial and almost succeeding.

And here came Aunt Appie, bundled now into a lurid granny afghan, her nose the color of a flowering quince and her eyes beginning to water. "Sarah, where on earth has Bodie got to? I've been looking everywhere."

"What do you mean, everywhere?" Sarah asked in some alarm.

"Oh, around. I keep bumping into people, you know, and stopping them to ask. Then we get talking about something else, as one always does."

"So in fact you've been mostly on the terrace and in the pavilion?"

"Yes, I expect I have, now that I think of it. But I've asked and asked, and nobody's seen her."

"I expect she's gone for her four-mile walk. Don't worry, Aunt Appie."

"But Lionel's anxious to get started back, and I did want another little chat with Bodie before we go. She and I see each other so seldom."

There was a reason for that. Apollonia had been named for the patron saint of toothaches. Maybe her parents hadn't realized that, but they couldn't have chosen more aptly. Her company for any length of time was about as welcome as a root-canal job to anybody who believed in a well-ordered life. Even Boadicea's dedication to positive thinking could stretch only just so far. Sarah wouldn't have said so for worlds. She kissed her aunt and gave her a pat on the cheek.

"You run along with Lionel before you catch a chill. I'll give Aunt Bodie your love when I catch up with her."

Assuming in fact she did. Sarah was getting a little anxious about Bodie. But she was far more concerned about Max and what was happening back at the car shed.

Well she might be. Ever since Nehemiah Billingsgate had met Chief Grimpen and his attendant minion and led them to the fatal horse chestnut tree, Max Bittersohn had been a most unhappy man. The police chief refused to be impressed by the suspended corpse.

"He'd been drinking, I assume. Eh, Mr. Billingsgate?"

"A jack of nut-brown ale with his manchet and beef, I

expect, to help him feel his way into his role," Bill replied rather stiffly. "We made sure Rufus had a hearty lunch before he went on duty."

"Did you watch him eat?" Grimpen demanded.

"Hardly." Bill was getting stiffer by the second. "I was much too busy with other things. But I'd told him to be sure and stoke up well for a long afternoon, and Rufus always followed my instructions to the letter. He'd have gone into the kitchen and Cook would have given him what he wanted. We can ask her what Rufus ate if you think it's important."

Chief Grimpen decided it wasn't. "When did you last see this Rufus?"

"Shortly after noontime, here at the car shed. I brought him his costume and *Totschläger*."

"His what?"

"A mediaeval weapon he was going to carry as part of his costume. Horrid thing, actually. Somebody gave it to my great-grandfather when he built his rather fanciful house. As a joke, I suspect. Anyway, the *Totschläger's* been kicking around the place ever since, so I thought we might as well get some good out of it at last. It's a club sort of thing you flail about and hit people with. Rufus wasn't supposed to do any flailing, merely to make a feint of brandishing the weapon if anybody tried to get past his sentry box."

"Where is the *Totschläger* now?"

"I haven't the faintest idea," said Billingsgate. "Dear me, why hadn't that occurred to me sooner? Max, have you seen it?"

"No, I haven't. Unless it was strapped to his back. I didn't turn him around to look."

"Why not?" said Grimpen.

Max gave him a surprised look. "Because I assumed you wouldn't want me handling the evidence."

"Oh yes. Well, let's cut him down and have a look."

"Aren't you going to examine the rope first?"

Chief Grimpen was blond and handsome, if you liked the

type. Though he was in fact only an inch or so taller than Max, he contrived to look down as from a height of amused superiority. "They only do that sort of thing in detective novels, Mr. um er—Sergeant Myre, untie that knot."

"It's a clove hitch," said Max.

This information elicited from the chief not so much as a raised eyebrow or a sarcastic, "Do tell?" All Sergeant Myre said was, "It's kind of tight."

"It's made to tighten from the weight of the body," said Max. "You'll have to pull in some slack."

Continuing to look amusedly superior, Chief Grimpen whipped out a silver-handled jackknife and cut the rope. Max fielded the body before it could crash, and lowered what was left of the faithful old retainer gently to the ground.

Rufus was not wearing the *Totschläger*. Nor, Max was relieved for Bill's sake to notice, had the *Totschläger* been used on Rufus. Something else had, though. The noose was dug tight into the weathered flesh, but the head was not cocked at an angle suggesting a broken neck, the face was not congested, and the tongue wasn't hanging out.

"As I expected," said Chief Grimpen. "This is a most distressing affair, Mr. Billingsgate, but it's plain to see what happened. Your old fellow here, for whatever reason, formed a noose in one end of the rope and put it around his neck. He tied the other end to the tree in a clove hitch as your learned friend so kindly informed us, then climbed the tree, looped the rope over a limb, and jumped."

"Leaving no trace of scuffing from his heavy boots on the trunk of the tree, no broken twigs, no fallen leaves, and no rips or rubs on those new plush knickers he's wearing," said Max.

"Yes, he must have been quite agile for his age," Grimpen condescended to allow. "Would you wish to handle the arrangements with the mortician yourself, Mr. Billingsgate, or shall I have Sergeant Myre call the police ambulance?"

"Why, I—Max?"

"Since an autopsy will be required to determine the actual

cause of death," said Max, "you'd better call the wagon, Myre."

"With all respect, Mr. Er"—Grimpen was having a bit of a struggle with his aplomb—"it's customary for bystanders to leave such decisions to the authority in charge."

"With all respect to you, Grimpen," Max told him, "you're no authority. In my own professional opinion, you don't know your ass from your elbow. This man shows no sign of strangulation. He was killed on the ground and hauled up into the tree by means of a prearranged block and tackle device."

"What?"

"If you hadn't been too goddamn lazy to climb the tree yourself, you'd have found the rope had been threaded through two pulleys, one screwed to the tree farther up the trunk and one to the heavy branch from which he was hanging. The object of the pulleys must have been to make the job of raising the body faster and easier, and is an indication of premeditated murder. Obviously you think Mr. Billingsgate wants a cover-up, but he doesn't. He wants to know who murdered his old friend and stole his Silver Ghost."

"Stole his—" Grimpen made rather a production of turning his smartly uniformed back on Max. "Really, Mr. Billingsgate, you can hardly expect me to stand here and listen to this—"

"Mr. Bittersohn is referring to my 1908 Rolls Royce Silver Ghost, Chief Grimpen." There was an edge to Bill's voice Max hadn't ever heard before.

"Your Rolls Royce?" This should have been an embarrassing moment for Grimpen, but he managed to rise above it. "You mean one of your famous antique cars has been stolen? This does put a different complexion on the matter. I might point out that we'd have saved valuable time if you'd said so in the first place."

"I probably should have," Billingsgate answered drily, "if I didn't value a human life over an old car. I suggest we carry poor Rufe's body into the car shed until the police ambulance gets here. Some of our guests might happen to walk this way as they're leaving, and I'd hate to let them go with such a distressing last impression."

"By all means," said Grimpen, "unless Mr. Um Er—objects."

"Open the gate, Bill."

Max squatted and got a firm grip on the dead man's torso. "Mind taking his feet, Myre?"

Sergeant Myre didn't mind. At least he didn't say he did. Together, he and Max carried the old retainer into the shed and laid him on a long counter that Bill had swept clear of ribbons and trophies from antique car rallies. Bill then fetched a handsome mohair carriage robe from one of the remaining cars and spread it tenderly over his faithful servant. At last he folded his hands, bowed his head, and stood in silence. Grimpen watched in puzzlement, Max in compassion. Sergeant Myre brushed a few bits of grass off his uniform.

"Now then." Bill straightened up and spoke too briskly, to hide the fact that he was close to crying. "You'll want the details, Grimpen."

He whipped open a deep drawer under the counter and took out a bulky file. "Here's a photograph of our Ghost. As you doubtless know, the first Silver Ghost was manufactured in England in 1906 and may or may not have been the show chassis that appeared at Olympia that year. The record is not clear. That one had green upholstery and gleaming silver everywhere else, hence the name. Ours is a more conservative gray with maroon upholstery, as you can see in this color snapshot. That's Rufe at the wheel, dear fellow."

Bill quickly went back to the larger black and white photo. "A number of Silver Ghosts were built at the British works up through and shortly after World War I, though they weren't actually called by that name until after 1925. To distinguish them from the New Phantoms, you know. Our New Phantom was the first to go, I'm sad to say."

"You mean it broke down on you?" said Myre.

"No, it's been stolen, also. That was why I called Mr.

Bittersohn. New Phantoms were only made from 1925 to 1929, which would certainly make them particularly desirable to what we may call a clandestine collector. Though I must say a Silver Ghost in virtually mint condition, like ours, is probably far rarer because most of the early Ghosts were simply worked to death. They were absolutely splendid cars for the time, you know."

Bill couldn't help wincing as he restored the photograph to its file. "In fact, it would be hard to find an early Rolls Royce that isn't a rarity because there was so much swapping around of body and chassis, and so much custom work done on every car. But I'm rambling. What it boils down to, Chief Grimpen, is that my Silver Ghost was here at noontime and now it's gone. The car shed was locked and so was the gate. My trusted friend and helper was on guard outside. He's dead. I do not for one moment believe Rufe committed suicide."

6

Chief Grimpen brushed that unimportant aspect of the matter aside. "This New Phantom, when did it disappear? Myre, take down the facts."

"I first missed the Phantom this past Monday evening," said Bill.

"You didn't report the theft."

"I wasn't sure at the time there'd been a theft. My daughter, Melisande, and her husband, Tichnor Purbody, often take out one or another of the cars."

"Why, Mr. Billingsgate?"

"For a parade, an antique rally, or a little spin. We see no sense in keeping the Rollses if we don't get some fun out of them. My son-in-law might also have discovered something wrong with the Phantom and taken it to be fixed without bothering to tell me."

"Did you ask him?"

"Not then, no. He wasn't around. He and my daughter have their own place in Shrewsbury, though they're back and forth a good deal."

"Did you check with the garage?"

"It was too late in the day. Anyway, I hadn't the time. I'd barely finished my dinner when I was called out of town on urgent business. As you may know, I own a small chain of radio stations. They're unpretentious operations by and large, and some of them get along with very small staffs.

Monday evening I got a frantic call from our station in Pettibunk, Maine. The station manager, the engineer, and the chief announcer had all walked away from their jobs without so much as an hour's notice and driven off to New Brunswick because they'd heard the salmon were running on the Miramichi."

"Surely you didn't believe such a tale?"

"Why not? Maine people are like that. It's worse in the deer hunting season. Anyway, this created a crisis situation, so I hopped into the Silver Shadow and nipped on up there. Made it in time to do the ten o'clock news, as a matter of fact. Then I stayed on the job until we managed to transfer a couple of people from other stations. The upshot was that I remained stuck there till Friday."

"Did you speak to your son-in-law during this time?"

"Oh yes, but always about more pressing matters. Tick, as we call him, is my executive assistant. I stuck him with rounding up the substitutes, which meant he himself had to do some substituting at the stations he took them from. Tick's one of those multi-talented people who can put their hands to just about anything, and I must say we kept him hopping this week. He also had to rehearse the morris dancers for the revel and help my daughter with mead deliveries. Naturally they got a rush of orders just at the most awkward time."

"But weren't you worried about your Rolls Royce?" demanded Grimpen.

"No, I didn't give the New Phantom another thought until I arrived here and drove the Shadow into the car shed. Then I noticed the empty space and did begin to feel alarmed. My daughter happened to be in the house at the time, helping her mother prepare for the revel, so I asked her. She was quite sure Tick hadn't even had time to think about the New Phantom, much less take it anywhere. So I asked the Bittersohns to come along and look into the matter."

"Why them and not the police?"

"Because I still wasn't sure any crime had been committed.

The Bittersohns are private detectives whom I knew to be efficient, honest, and discreet. I could have them here without causing remark because Mrs. Bittersohn is related to several of the other guests who'd be present. You must realize, Chief Grimpen, that a good many people we know have been in and out this past couple of weeks on various errands connected with the revel. Even the workmen who put up the pavilion are old acquaintances. I thought it possible one of them might have borrowed the New Phantom without asking permission."

"Does that happen often?"

"It's never happened before, but there's always a first time. Yesterday, I was only concerned about getting my car back with a minimum of fuss. Today, with Rufus murdered and the Silver Ghost gone, too, I realize more drastic action has to be taken. Though I have to confess," Bill's tender conscience forced him to add, "that without Mr. Bittersohn's insistence, I might not have acted so promptly."

And a hell of a lot of good the urging had done, Max thought. Chief Grimpen was looking superior again, for no good reason.

"You say the cars both disappeared from inside this shed, Mr. Billingsgate. Isn't the shed kept locked?"

"Of course it is, and so is the gate. Our insurance people insist on the tightest possible security, especially now that antique Rolls Royces have appreciated so much in value."

Grimpen picked up on this point fast enough. "Can you give me some idea what your two missing cars are worth now?"

"I can tell you what they're insured for."

Bill did, and Grimpen forget all about looking superior. "That much? This is grand larceny! What are we wasting time for? Give me the photo of the Silver Ghost. What's the license and serial number? Find me a picture of the New Phantom. Full descriptions, pronto. Myre, take down the details. I'll get to them later. Where's the nearest telephone?"

"Right beside you, on the wall," Billingsgate told the chief somewhat drily. "And here's the information on the cars."

Grimpen barked masterfully into the phone, then held out his hand. "I'll keep those folders, Mr. Billingsgate."

"I'm sorry, but you can't have them. We have a strict rule that our records never leave the car shed. I can provide you with duplicate copies of the photographs, if you want them."

"Better than nothing, I suppose. Now then, Myre, the notes."

"They're in shorthand, chief."

"Then read them to me."

Myre began to read. Max and Bill wandered off. When they were out of earshot, Bill murmured, "One tries not to pass judgement, but I must say that fellow Grimpen does seem to be rather full of himself."

"He's full of something, anyway," Max conceded. "Who is he, the mayor's nephew?"

"Cherished only son of the chairman of the Board of Selectmen. I believe his burning ambition is to become Sir John Appleby. Do you think this all-points bulletin will accomplish anything?"

"Let's hope so. Routine police procedure is often highly effective. Anyway, they have the facilities for it and we don't."

Max was restless, prowling around the vast shed, examining the bare concrete walls with more interest than they appeared to warrant. "The car shed backs right up to the stone wall, does it?"

"Actually the shed is part of the wall," Bill told him. "The stonework simply comes to meet it on both sides. The iron fence on top of the wall goes across the back of the roof. If you're thinking someone climbed into the yard by way of the shed, I can only say it would be extremely difficult. The fence is electrified, I'm ashamed to admit. The insurance people insisted on that as an added precaution."

"For which you can't blame them, considering what these cars are worth on today's market," said Max. "What's behind here?"

"The road that leads out to the bee fields. Hardly more than a path, really. It's a further extension of the main drive," Bill explained.

"And where does that come out? Does it just circle around and come back?"

"No, as a matter of fact. We have a number of paths through the bee fields, but this particular one goes on to connect at the far end of our property with a town road that leads eventually to the old turnpike."

"Is this path wide enough to take a car through?"

"Just about. One would find it rough going at the far end. We leave the ruts unfilled in order to discourage outsiders from entering."

"How long is the path?" asked Max.

"Just about a mile. You're thinking the cars must have been taken out that way, aren't you?"

"Any reason why they shouldn't have been?"

"Aside from the fact that they'd be awfully visible going through the fields, I can't see why not. Especially if the driver knew how to work the drawbridge," Bill added.

"You have a second drawbridge?" Didn't everybody?

"An apology for one, anyway. It looks like the remains of an old board fence, but actually there's a steel-plate reinforcement sandwiched between two thin layers of wood. It lets down by a rather ingenious arrangement of wire cables and covers the worst of the ruts so it's possible to get a car out without too much joggling. Silly, perhaps, but we do get a good deal of fun out of the thing."

"We meaning your family?" asked Max.

"And a few of our closest friends. Except in the winter when there's snow on the ground. We couldn't plow or drive through then, of course, without leaving tracks and giving away our little secret. Other than that, we use the bee field escape, as we call it, quite a lot. It saves our having to make a wide detour to reach the turnpike. We figure we cut off anywhere from ten to twenty minutes, depending on who's driving. Tick and Melly make the run a good deal faster than Abigail and I."

"Can your wife manage the drawbridge by herself?"

"Easily. The fence is nicely balanced and counterweighted so that we can move it up or down with no effort to speak of. The only hard part's remembering where to find the end of the cable. It's quite well hidden."

"Who'd be apt to know the hiding place, aside from yourselves?"

"That's a good question. We've taken guests through the bee fields at various times over the years when they've had a plane to catch or whatever, and I suppose there's no reason why somebody from down the road couldn't have come poking around and hit upon the cable. It's not so much that we're anxious to keep the private road a secret, as that we don't want a lot of youngsters driving in with their flivvers and mopeds and getting the bees upset. It doesn't take too much to annoy a bee, you know."

"No, I don't suppose it would," said Max. "I should think the bees themselves would keep people out."

"I'm sure they're a more effective deterrent than anything else," Bill agreed. "We do have warning signs posted all around our borders, and outsiders don't seem much interested in challenging them. About the cable, let's see. The Tolbathys know, certainly. It was Wouter who rigged the drawbridge for us. He was marvelously inventive, you may remember."

Max nodded. Tom Tolbathy's late brother had been a man of almost appalling mechanical ability. Worse yet, he'd had an imagination for which *untrammeled* would have been a paltry and pitiful description.

"I didn't know Wouter ever got around to anything so mundane as a drawbridge. Wouldn't an aerial tramway held up by midget dirigibles have been more his style?"

"He did say something once about trained eagles," Billingsgate admitted, "but we were afraid we'd run into trouble with the Audubon Society. Dear old Wouter! Never shall I forget his funeral, Jem Kelling reading the eulogy with the Great Chain of the Convivial Codfish around his neck, while Tom walked up the aisle leading that fire-breathing dragon. It was so beautifully fitting. 'I am a brother to dragons and a companion to owls.' Job 30:29."

He paused a moment in fond remembrance. "Too bad Tom didn't happen to think of the owl. Wouter would have liked an owl. Max, tell me honestly, do you see any tiny gleam of light whatsoever in this dreadful situation? Will the thefts continue? I'm beginning to wonder if I should consider this a chastisement for my foolish pride in earthly possessions. Dear heaven! To think my friend Rufus may have been so foully done to death through my vanity. How could I ever atone? Shall I sell all the remaining cars and donate the money to some worthy cause?"

"This isn't the time to back down, Bill."

"I suppose not. 'No man, having put his hand to the plough, and looking back, is fit for the Kingdom of God.' Luke 9:62. Thank you, Max. The time to have sold the cars, assuming I were to do so, would have been before this horrible chain of events began. Now I have to see it through. 'Be not overcome of evil, but overcome evil with good.' Romans 12:21."

"Which means we have to isolate the evil before we can do any good," said Max. "What's this?"

He'd entered an alcove beside the changing room, about eight feet square and none too well lighted. The side walls were of smooth concrete like the rest of the shed's, but the back was oddly roughened. "Did somebody get into the wet cement?"

"Oh, that." Bill managed to work up a smile of sorts. "Another of Wouter's little whimsies. It started one weekend about five years ago. Our grandchildren were still in the pre-teen stage and so were some of the Tolbathys'. Young Dork's daughter was only a toddler then and had a nanny, so we rounded up all the kids and left them here with the nanny to run after them and Cook to feed them. Rufus went along with us and the other grownups to a big antique car rally. Since there were enough of us to drive all ten Rollses, the shed was left empty, so the children had permission to use it for a playroom."

"It would be a great place for kids to run," said Max.

"Yes, and that's what we'd assumed they'd be doing. Unfortunately, this silly girl believed in self-expression and supplied all the children with colored chalks. By the time we got back, they'd expressed themselves over every inch of the walls and floor."

"Must have been a cheerful homecoming."

"Oh, it was. I thought Rufe would go into convulsions. I'll admit I was none too pleased, myself. But anyway, Wouter offered to stay and help Rufe wash the walls, so Abigail and I went off by ourselves to another rally. In the New Phantom, as a matter of fact. When we got back, we discovered Wouter had got the rest of the place shining but he'd put a skim coat of mortar on this one wall and scratched in his own graffiti. He said he'd always had an urge to deface a wall. Even Rufe laughed. One had to, you know, at Wouter."

"So you left the wall as it was."

"Oh, we talked every so often about having it plastered over, but for one reason or another we never did. Then Wouter died and the wall became a sort of monument to his memory. I wouldn't change it now for anything. Yes, Chief Grimpen, did you want me for something?"

"Only to tell you that I'm going along now. I've accomplished everything that needs to be done here. It's perfectly obvious what happened. Your man there," he nodded at the robe-covered heap on the counter, "was in league with a well-organized gang of antique car thieves. He may have been blackmailed into it," Grimpen added out of deference for Mr. Billingsgate's feelings.

"Anyway, he let them into the car shed, helped them get the Silver Ghost away, then raked the gravel to obliterate the traces they'd left, and locked the gate behind him. At this point it must have occurred to your man that he'd put himself in an impossible position. Seeing no way out of being convicted and disgraced, he hanged himself."

"Having rigged a hoist in advance just in case he might take the notion," Max Bittersohn amplified.

"How am I supposed to know what the hoist was for? Maybe he'd planned to do some tree work."

"We have professional tree people come in for that sort of thing," said Bill. "Have you arranged for the autopsy?"

At last he'd managed to make Grimpen uncomfortable. "I—er—was just going to consult with you on that point. I assumed you'd prefer to wait until your guests were gone before we had the body removed. So as not to spoil your party," he added hopefully.

"Most considerate of you." Max hadn't thought Nehemiah Billingsgate could ever use that tone toward anybody. "Tell them to come as soon as possible, please. You'll wait for them, I expect."

"Sergeant Myre will stay. I have pressing business elsewhere, I'm afraid. Myre, you're in full charge as of now. Order the ambulance and arrange for the autopsy."

Sergeant Myre opened his mouth, then shut it with an audible snap. Grimpen turned smartly and strode from the shed. Bill went after him to unlock the gate. Max looked at Myre and shrugged.

"Who's he going to press?"

"I'd like to press him between two barn doors and run a tractor over 'em," snarled the policeman. "He knows damn well we've got the in-laws coming to supper because I told him so when we started out. My wife's going to raise hell."

"Call her and tell her you've just been promoted to acting chief."

"You tell her."

"Okay," said Max, "if you want."

For the first time since he'd arrived, Sergeant Myre's somewhat chubby face relaxed into a full-blown grin. "Thanks, but I'd better do it myself. What should I tell her?"

"Tell her your jackass of a chief has been doing his best to louse up an important investigation and you've been put in charge because you've got a lot more brains than he has."

"So does the station cat."

"Then tell her we're getting the cat in to help you. Just don't say where you are or what's happened. We don't want the word to get out any sooner than we can help, or we'll have a crowd control problem on our hands along with everything else."

7

Mrs. Myre must be a reasonable woman. The policeman came back looking relieved.

"It's all set for the autopsy and they'll have the wagon here as soon as possible. I told my wife I'm working with this big detective inspector from Boston. Was that all right, Mr. Bittersohn?"

"Sure. I'm inspecting. What do you think of this wall?"

"Bunch of kids got loose in the wet cement, huh?" Myre ran his fingers somewhat wistfully over a crude depiction of an open runabout. "I always had a hankering to do that."

"I did, once," Max confessed. "They were laying a new sidewalk outside my folks' house and I decided to leave my footprints for posterity. My father caught me and made me get a trowel and smooth them out, then he wouldn't give me any movie money for a month. I wonder what I'll do if my kid ever tries the same thing."

"How old is he?"

"Six months."

"My youngest is seven." Myre sounded deservedly smug. "Say, you know what this wall reminds me of? They had this art festival over at the park last summer and Grimpen stuck me with extra duty as usual. He doesn't dare ask the older guys, they'd spit in his eye. But anyway, there was this hunk of what they were calling folk sculpture that looked something like this. Beats me what anybody'd want of it, but I guess rich people pay big money for that far-out stuff, eh?"

"Some of them do," Max agreed, "but this was just a practical joke by a mad genius who was a friend of the family. He died a couple of years ago and the Billingsgates keep the wall as a tribute to his memory."

A beautiful light broke over Myre's countenance. "Oh jeez, I'll bet I ran into that guy once. I'm a rookie cop, see, it's my first day on the job. So Grimpen assigns me to traffic duty down at the square. It's a Monday morning. There's a little rush hour traffic and the kids going to school, then it quiets down. I help a couple of old ladies across the street and wonder if anybody's going to rob the bank today, but nobody does. So I'm standing there shining my new whistle when this 1932 Chevy coupe, black with red wooden wheels, comes zigzagging down the middle of the road doing about five miles an hour."

Myre was thoroughly happy now. "So I start waving my arms and blowing my whistle and the car stops. There's the driver up front in this dinky little coupe wearing a fancy chauffeur's uniform and in the rumble seat's a great big raccoon. The chauffeur sits there deadpan, looking straight ahead. The raccoon leans out of the rumble seat and starts giving me a hard time."

"You're kidding," said Max, knowing perfectly well he wasn't.

"So help me God! The raccoon's wearing a black felt hat pulled down over his eyes and a pink and green necktie with yellow spots on it. He's puffing on this big cigar and he talks like Jimmy Cagney. And the chauffeur's just sitting there. Finally it hits me, I'm having a fight with a raccoon. Then I catch on. It's a stuffed coon. The chauffeur's a ventriloquist and he's working its mouth and paws with wires or something. So I go up to the front window and say, Okay, wise guy, let's see your driver's license.

"So he still doesn't look at me or say a word. He just holds out his hand with a card in it. I go to take the card and the whole hand comes with it. I'm standing there looking down at this hand and thinking, Oh my God, when the Chevy takes off like a bullet and there's the raccoon leaning over the back of the rumble seat waving bye-bye. I ought to have shot the bastard's tires out, but I was laughing so hard I couldn't get my gun out. So I just waved back with his hand. I've still got the darn thing in my locker down at the station. Do you think that was him?"

"I hope so," said Max. "I'd hate to think there was another one like Wouter running around loose. Do you suppose we could get a little more light over here?"

"Sure, wait a second."

Myre nipped over to the workbench, opened a drawer, and pulled out a large battery lantern. "I figured they'd have one like this around the place. Want me to hold it for you?"

"Just set it on the floor here, if you don't mind, and see if you can find me a screwdriver or something."

"I noticed one in the drawer."

Myre brought back the tool and stood watching while Max probed gently at inch after inch of the concrete, like a dentist checking a patient's teeth for sensitive spots. "What are you hunting for, Mr. Bittersohn?"

"I don't know," Max replied. "It just strikes me that a mere slab of concrete graffiti might be a fairly tame joke for a guy who could invent a talking raccoon."

He went on peering and poking, occasionally using his pocket magnifier for a closer look at something that appeared to merit closer attention but turned out not to. At last he was down on his knees, his scholar's robe making a dark puddle around his legs and picking up dust from the floor. Wouter's literary efforts might have been amusing to those in the know, but Max was growing bored with inscriptions like JT LOVES ID, which JT couldn't possibly if JT was one of the Tolbathys' intelligent grandsons and ID was the obnoxious little Imogene Dork whom Max had last seen pouring maple syrup over her cousin James to sweeten him up at one of Aunt Appie's awful gatherings. As far as he could see, he was getting nowhere except to the end of his patience.

Down at the right-hand corner, Wouter had chosen to

finish off his cumbersome frolic with nothing more original than a lopsided heart not more than five or six inches high. Inside, Wouter must have used a nail or some small tool to print K.I. + C.K.

Max jumped to his feet, dusted off his robe, handed Sergeant Myre the screwdriver, and kicked the center of the heart. Instantly and silently, the entire back wall of the alcove swung out at a right angle to the car shed. Instead of scribbled-over concrete, the two men were looking at broad fields of green clover and a narrow bluestoned lane.

"Why, that crazy son of a bitch!"

Max's cry was from the heart. Sergeant Myre yelled, too.

"Jeez! And I thought getting stuck with a waxwork hand was something. What the hell would make him do a thing like this?"

"The mere fact that he happened to see how it could be done, I suppose. Wouter wouldn't have stopped to consider the possible side effects of putting in a door its owner didn't know he had. I wonder how you shut it."

"Maybe you just wait a while and a stuffed raccoon comes along and shuts it for you," Myre suggested.

"That's a reasonable possibility," Max conceded. "I expect, though, that Wouter was thinking in terms of a practical operation. That means the door ought to shut automatically as soon as a car's been driven past some point or other. Like for instance this big eye he's put smack in the middle of the wall with 'Here's looking at you' scratched around it. I thought there was something peculiar about that pupil, but since I didn't get any action when I waved my hand in front of it, I decided it must be only a glass bead he'd imbedded in the mortar. This must be Wouter's interpretation of an electric eye."

Max picked up a long pole intended for opening the high windows, and waved it in front of the eye. The door swung shut. Again they faced a solid concrete wall.

"How come they ever let that guy Wouter run around loose?" Myre demanded. "For Pete's sake, anybody who took the trouble to read that stuff he wrote on the wall might have figured this out ages ago."

"Anybody who could get past the locked gate and the electrified fence," Max agreed.

"Meaning friends and family, right? I don't know about you, Mr. Bittersohn, but if those had been my Rolls Royces that got stolen, I wouldn't go after any gang of professional car thieves. I'd start wondering which of my brothers-in-law was in trouble with the bookies."

"Which would be a damn sight sounder premise than the one Grimpen's working on," said Max, "but you never know. This secret door opens up a new dimension, as you might say."

"I'll say it does."

A bit sheepishly, Sergeant Myre swung his boot at the little heart. The door swung open. A woman screamed.

"What did I do?" Myre started through the opening.

Max hauled him back. "Watch it, you'll activate the electric eye and get slammed by the door. It's all right."

An electric go-cart had appeared on the bluestoned path. In it sat two women. The small one in green with the hennin was perfectly self-possessed. The tall one in the scarlet gown and the padded beige satin headdress wound with pearls was close to hysterics.

"Was it a bomb?" cried Melisande.

"No," said Max. "Come on, drive the cart inside."

Nehemiah Billingsgate's daughter obeyed, and the door closed behind the cart. "I don't believe this. What did you do?"

"Discovered one of Wouter Tolbathy's little jokes. Didn't any of you ever take a good look at his graffiti?"

"I certainly didn't." Melisande climbed out of the cart, guarding her billows of flame-colored satin. She was a sturdily built woman of forty or thereabout, fair and rosy like her parents but taller than either of them. The flamboyant Renaissance costume suited her. "What did I miss?"

"See this?" Max bent and pointed out the small heart down at the right-hand corner of the again solid wall.

"It's a heart. What about it?"

"There are initials inside," said Myre.

"I can't read them without my glasses. What does it say?"

"K.I. and C.K."

"So what? C.K. must be one of the Kellings, I suppose, but who's K.I.? Can you think of anybody, Sarah?"

"Try it without the plus sign in the middle," Sarah suggested. "Does it actually work, Max?"

"Watch."

It was so simple when one knew how. Melisande Purbody's large blue eyes opened wide and stayed that way. "Does Daddy know?"

"I'm sure he doesn't," Max replied. "Sergeant Myre here and I just discovered it."

Melisande turned to the policeman. "Oh, hi, Reggie. I'm glad it's you and not old Beanhead. How come your boss isn't here, standing around looking impressive?"

"He was but he had to go. He's in a bridge tournament at that fancy club he and his missus belong to. He left me to mind the body."

Max cocked an eyebrow at Sarah. She nodded.

"I told Melisande on the way here. I thought she ought to know."

"It's awful," said Bill's daughter. "Poor old Rufe! I'm keeping a stiff upper lip till it's all over, then I'm going back to Shrewsbury and bawl my eyes out. I suppose Grimpyboy's got the case all solved?"

"Naturally," said Myre. "Tough luck, Mel, this happening right in the midst of your party."

"Thanks, Reg, but the revel's almost over, thank goodness. The parking lot's empty, except for—" She threw a glance at Sarah. "We have another complication. Minor, I hope."

"Melisande and I have been looking for Aunt Bodie," Sarah explained. "We've asked everywhere and nobody's set eyes on her since early in the banquet. Tick's just got the bright idea of borrowing a helicopter they use at Station XBIL for doing the traffic reports. We're going to take binoculars and search the bee fields."

"What do you mean, we?" Max demanded.

"Well, the helicopter's not very big and Bodie is my aunt, after all."

"She's Lionel's aunt, too, and he doesn't have a baby at home. For God's sake, Sarah! Maybe she got a headache and left quietly so as not to break up the party."

"Lionel's already gone to take his mother home. And Davy's as much your child as mine, if you're thinking what I know you're thinking. Darling, I truly am concerned about Aunt Bodie. She's much too healthy to get headaches, and she's the last person on earth to sneak away without taking proper leave of her hostess, even if Abigail weren't a particular friend. Besides, her car's still in the parking lot."

"Are you sure that's her car?"

"Max, come on! How many beige and gray 1946 Daimlers are you likely to find on the road these days?"

"In this crowd, I wouldn't dare guess."

Melisande wasn't one to stand by in silence. "You needn't get uptight about who's going to ride in the helicopter, Max; it'll be Tick and the pilot. Tick wouldn't give up his seat to anyone on earth. He absolutely adores getting up high and looking down. I can't bear to, myself. And Sarah's quite right about Bodie Kelling. This isn't like her at all. We've asked all her friends, and nobody's caught so much as a glimpse of her since about halfway through the banquet. We've searched the house and the gardens. We've just taken a quick scoot around the bee fields in the honeybug to see if she might have gone for a long walk and sprained her ankle or something. If Tick doesn't spot her," Melisande shrugged her impressive scarlet-clad shoulders, "I don't know what to think."

"No chance she drove herself off in the Silver Ghost?" Reggie Myre ventured.

"Aunt Bodie wouldn't do that, not without getting permission from some member of the family," Sarah protested. "Besides, how could she have got into the car shed? Unless—"

She caught her breath. "Aunt Bodie did want to see the

Rollses, she said so during the morris dancing. She was coaxing Mrs. Gaheris to come with her when the heralds came out to announce the banquet, so they went into the pavilion instead."

"But she wouldn't get up and walk out in the middle of a meal," Myre protested. He himself certainly wouldn't, from the look of his beltline.

"Actually, that's something Aunt Bodie would do," Sarah replied. "She's rather a health nut, and hates the idea of people gorging themselves. She herself didn't intend to eat much, she said so, and she'd find it a bore to sit there watching a roomful of moving jaws. It would have been quite like her to get up and go for a walk, if only to set a good example to the rest of us. Don't you think, Melly?"

"Oh yes, Bodie's like that."

"And she evidently didn't know Bill wasn't letting anyone into the car shed this year or she wouldn't have suggested to Mrs. Gaheris that they go. Or else she'd have thought the rule didn't apply to her, which would also be like Aunt Bodie. So if she happened to arrive here at just the wrong moment—"

Max put his arms around Sarah to stop the shivering. "Okay, kid, take it easy. We'd better search the remaining cars, don't you think? There's always the chance she might be tied up in one of them." There were other chances, but Max didn't go into those. "Are the trunks all unlocked, Melisande?"

"I'll get the keys. Come on, Reggie."

"Sure, Mel."

Sarah took no part in the search. She'd never been particularly devoted to Boadicea Kelling, but an aunt was an aunt. If there was anything to be found here, she did not want to be the one who found it.

8

Sarah needn't have hung back, there was nothing to find. The cars were all empty. The shrubberies yielded no gruesome bundle. Tick Purbody and the helicopter pilot flew as low as they could, shining their searchlight on every inch of the bee fields, but drew a total blank. A telephone call to Boadicea's house only served to throw her housekeeper into a tizzy.

It was long after dark by now. The frazzled remnant of the Renaissance Revel were gathered around the fire in what Abigail called the castle keep, drinking hot coffee and trying to bolster each other's spirits.

"There's only one logical explanation," Bill was insisting. "Bodie must have got into the car shed somehow, discovered the secret exit, and driven away in the Silver Ghost. Chasing Rufe's murderer, I suppose."

"Never." Abigail was holding up somewhat better than her husband. "Why should Bodie rush right over and discover that crazy trick of Wouter's when the rest of us have been overlooking it for the past five years? Why would she waste time trying to start the Silver Ghost, which isn't the easiest thing in the world, as you very well know, when she could have run down the hill and got her own car in half the time?"

She spread honey on a crumpet and handed it to Bill. "Here, for goodness' sake eat something before you drop.

But why should a middle-aged woman as commonsensical as Bodie go chasing a murderer in the first place? Bodie's never taken a reckless chance in her life. She wouldn't even join in the pillow fights at school. Would she, Drusilla? I'm not saying she didn't leave the car shed in the Silver Ghost, dear. I'm only saying that if she did, it wasn't of her own free will and we might as well face it. Max, what are we going to do?"

"I've phoned a description of Mrs. Kelling to the state police," he reassured her. "They already had a bulletin out on the Silver Ghost. If she's in it, they'll find her."

"But what if she's been kidnapped by somebody else?"

"That's hardly likely. In any case, we'd just have to wait until the kidnappers get in touch."

"With whom?" Abigail fretted. "Bodie's a widow and her only son lives in Hong Kong. They'd hardly call here, I shouldn't think."

"I should think they'd call some of the Kellings," said Tick Purbody.

"Who in turn would call Max." Sarah was inclined to be waspish in more ways then one about the way her family kept dumping their problems into her husband's lap. "We'd get the word fast enough."

"But what if she's being held hostage?" Melisande suggested.

Max shook his head. "Why should she be? Look, let's quit pussyfooting around the issue. It must have occurred to everybody here by now that Rufus's murder and the theft of those two cars were almost certainly engineered by an employee, a close friend, or a member of the family."

Drusilla Gaheris was first to break the thunderous silence that followed. "I've been wondering whether anybody would get up nerve enough to say that. It does look dreadfully obvious, one has to admit. I expect what Mr. Bittersohn's getting at is that a person in any of those categories wouldn't have to take a hostage. If he, or I suppose I have to say she, should have happened to bump into Bodie at an awkward moment, he simply could have pretended he was there on some innocent errand like herself, and postpone stealing the Silver Ghost until some more opportune time."

"But suppose Bodie came along just as this person was in the act of killing Rufe?" Tick Purbody insisted.

"Then there'd have been two bodies in that tree instead of one, don't you think? You know, everywhere we went in Europe, people were aghast at what a violent lot we Americans are. I've spent years trying to convince them we're not all muggers and gunslingers, but—"

Mrs. Gaheris shrugged and set down her coffee cup. "No thanks, Abigail. I mustn't have any more or I shan't sleep a wink. Now that the conversation's getting down to the touchy part, I believe the tactful thing for me to do is say good night and slide along to bed. I am rather exhausted, as a matter of fact."

"By all means do what feels most comfortable to you, Drusilla." Abigail Billingsgate sounded as if she'd have been glad to go, too. "I'm so terribly sorry your first visit to our house has to be marred by this dreadful business."

"Please don't feel that way, Abigail. I'm just thankful I'm here to lend a bit of moral support, if I can't do anything else."

"Maybe you can," said Max. "Before you go up, Mrs. Gaheris, is there anything at all you can say that might be useful? My wife tells me you may have been among the last to talk with her aunt at the banquet."

"Perhaps I was, though I honestly don't know. Ironically enough, Bodie and I were all set to stroll off and look at the Rollses, or thought we were. I hadn't understood the car shed was to be put off limits, which was pretty stupid of me considering that I've been right here in the house all this week."

"It was a last-minute decision," Bill told her.

"I'm sure it wasn't, but thanks for helping me save face, Bill dear. Anyway, just as we were about to start, the heralds came out blowing their trumpets—that was a marvelous touch, Abigail—so naturally we went into the pavilion instead."

Mrs. Gaheris smoothed down the heavy brown skirt she was still wearing. "I'd rather taken it for granted Bodie and I would sit together, but somehow that didn't happen. My fault, I expect. I kept running into people I hadn't seen for ages and stopping to chat a bit. You know how one does. By the time I was ready to sit down, Bodie was off somewhere and Dorothy Dork was asking me to sit with them. Dot's my cousin, actually, though her children call me aunt. I think she's just a wee bit miffed because I chose to stay with Appie and Bill instead of with her and Dork; so needless to say I wasn't going to tread on her toes again. All of which is rather boring and totally unhelpful for you, Mr. Bittersohn."

Max thought so, too. He got back to business. "How did Boadicea seem when you were with her? Not preoccupied or anything?"

"Bearing in mind that this was the first time we'd been together in many years, I'd say she acted perfectly normal. Bodie was always Bodie, and she hadn't really changed a bit. I was disappointed not to have more time with her. I did look for her again, as soon as I decently could."

"Where did you go?"

"Oh, just around the terrace and the pavilion. I wasn't exactly searching, you know, merely keeping an eye out in hopes."

"Did you leave the pavilion at any time during the banquet?" Max persisted.

"Yes, I did. I have some pills I'm supposed to take at mealtimes and I'd forgotten to bring them downstairs with me. Nothing serious, Abigail, just too much foreign cooking for too many years."

Mrs. Gaheris's digestive problems also failed to capture Max Bittersohn's interest. "Were these pills in your bedroom? How long did it take you to get them?"

She seemed faintly amused at his persistence. "Yes, they were in my room. On the dressing table, to be precise, where I'd left them after breakfast when I went up to get into my costume. As to the time, it's rather hard to say. I dawdled at the dressing table a minute or so, fussing with my wimple and dabbing on a little powder for whatever good that might do. I visited the usual offices while opportunity presented itself; one learns that in the diplomatic corps. And I stood at the window a little while, admiring the front terrace and the fields out back. Oh."

"Oh what?"

"Oh nothing, I don't suppose. I just happened to recall a tiny thing that can't possibly matter a bit."

"Why don't you tell us anyway?" said Sarah.

"It's just that one of the morris dancers came along."

"Along where?" Max wanted to know. "Out of the copse?"

"No, into it. I thought he might be heading for the car shed, probably because Bodie and I had thought of going that way ourselves. There's a pretty footpath and a wooden bridge. I've strolled that way a couple of times already."

"Could you see who the dancer was?"

"No, he had his back to me and his hood up. All those red and yellow flutters did look picturesque against the masses of greenery. I was sorry to lose sight of him."

"How long would you say you stood watching him?"

"Perhaps a minute or two. Not longer. He was walking fast, almost running."

"Did you happen to notice the time?"

"No, I didn't. I do have a traveling clock on the nightstand, but I didn't bother to look at it. I was deliberately not noticing, if you want the truth, trying to imagine myself in an age where clocks didn't much matter. When one's been under a good deal of pressure for a long time and then has an opportunity to let go and drift, that's all one wants to do, I find. I'm sorry if you think it matters, but it did seem so trivial at the time. Whenever that was."

"Did you see whether the man turned toward the car shed?"

"No. There's no way I could possibly have seen that far. My view is completely blocked by some big trees. I believe you said, Bill, that the landscaping had been planned with that factor in mind."

"That's right," Billingsgate confirmed. "Security was much less an issue than privacy in my great-grandfather's day. By now, some of the trees he planted are so big that they do pose certain problems for us, but they're such magnificent specimens we can't bear to have them taken down. Sorry, Max, I didn't mean to maunder. Could you give us any inkling of who the morris dancer may have been, Drusilla? Was he tall or short, heavy or lean?"

"He was nimble on his feet, but then they all are. As to his build, that's less easy than you might think. I was looking down on him from a fair height, you know, and one gets a sort of telescope effect. He definitely wasn't fat or conspicuously broad in the shoulders, but neither was he skinny. 'Well-muscled' would be my best description."

And would fit any one of them, Sarah thought, though she refrained from saying so. The same thing must have occurred to Mrs. Gaheris, however, because she added a couple of qualifications.

"It wasn't Young Dork, I'm sure. He's too short and burly. And I think we can eliminate you, Tick, because you're so much taller than the rest."

Sarah caught her breath but again she didn't speak. Mrs. Gaheris still had the floor.

"Telling people from the back when they're all dressed alike would be a tricky business even if I knew them well, which, needless to say, I don't."

"How about you, Tick?" asked Bill. "Can you cast any light on who it might have been?"

"Short of agreeing with Drusilla that it wasn't myself, I'm afraid I can't. After we stopped dancing, I made a beeline for the bathroom, if you want to know. Then I went straight to the pavilion."

"How long were you in the bathroom, just for the record?" Max asked him.

"Only as long as was necessary. I was hungry and thirsty and I didn't want to miss any of the fun."

"And which of the bathrooms did you go to?"

"Oh. Good question. Both the downstairs ones were in use, so I ran upstairs to Melly's old room, which is the one she and I still use when we stay here. That's on the opposite side of the house from the one Drusilla's staying in, since you were no doubt intending to ask. I couldn't have seen what she saw even if I'd stopped to look, which I didn't. It's my impression that most of the other dancers were in the pavilion when I got down, but they weren't all together so I can't swear to it."

"Can you give me a list of the dancers?"

"Sure. Myself, of course, and Young Dork and Lionel Kelling. And Bunny Whet and his son Erp who did the Betty, and Buck Tolbathy and his cousin Chad."

"How come Chad was dancing instead of Sallie?" Melisande broke in. "I've been meaning to ask."

"Sal sprained his ankle this morning. He hopped out of bed and tripped over that old beagle of his, of all the rotten breaks. So he got hold of Chad and sent him along instead."

"All the way from Schenectady? How could he?"

"Sal chartered a plane by phone and alerted Buck to pick Chad up in Worcester so they wouldn't have to bother us. Darned decent of them, I thought."

"Darned convenient this guy Chad knew the dances," Max grunted.

"Chad was one of our regular performers," Tick explained, "until he got transferred to New York State. He'd have liked to keep on, but it's just too awkward trying to synchronize the rehearsals. That's why we're breaking in Erp. Let's see, where was I? Oh, and Joe Abbott and his son Monk. You can rule out the Abbotts, Max. They were due for a family wedding at three o'clock and had to leave before we finished our sets. That's why we did the eight men's morrises early and finished with the six men's morrises, which are the older and more authentically Renaissance, anyway. Versey got a bit teed off by our switching the order at the last minute, but we couldn't help that."

"Why should he object?" Sarah asked.

"Oh, Versey always goes into a tizzy if we change anything without consulting him. He likes to think he runs the revels."

"Which is not to say he's ever around when there's any real work to be done," sniffed Abigail. "Let me heat up your coffee, Max."

"No thanks, I'm fine. What happened to the Abbotts' costumes, Tick? Would they have been wearing them when they left?"

"Hardly. They were going straight from here to the church. I assume they changed in one of the bedrooms and either took their costumes with them or left them in the car here to be picked up later. Mum, you haven't happened to run across them?"

"I've had surprisingly little time to go poking around the guest rooms, Tick," his mother-in-law replied with commendable forbearance, all things considered. "If you think those costumes will help us to find Bodie, Max, I'll look for them now. If not, I'd rather wait till morning. I'm beginning to run out of steam."

That was surely a gross understatement. For the first time since the Bittersohns had met her, Abigail looked as old as she probably was. All the color had drained out of her cheeks, her eyes were halfway into her head. Sarah was surprised she could still lift the coffeepot.

"I don't suppose they matter a rap. If they don't turn up, Max or I can call up the Abbotts in the morning and ask what became of them," she assured Abigail.

If one of the costumes had been worn to the car shed, it had most likely gone off with the Silver Ghost. If either Joe Abbott or his son had kept the doublet and hose on and hidden around the house until everyone else was supposedly in the pavilion and the coast was clear to commit the crime, then the first place to check was among the guests at that wedding they'd been supposed to attend. Sarah didn't think much of the Abbotts as possible suspects, and she couldn't imagine Max did, either. They'd be far too vulnerable to having their alibis blown.

Max was thinking, too. The likeliest and nastiest explanation for Boadicea Kelling's disappearance was that she'd gone walking in the fields and spied Rufus's killer driving off in the Silver Ghost. Mrs. Gaheris was probably right in saying that if Bodie had seen the actual murder, she'd have been killed on the spot.

The Silver Ghost was an open tourer. The thief might have risked driving it away, knowing the locals were used to seeing the Billingsgates' old cars out on the roads. One of those dust coats with a driving veil or cap and goggles would have disguised the driver adequately, but how could anybody dare take a corpse along for the ride? Boadicea's body would have been hidden in the car shed, which it hadn't, or dumped in the copse or the woods down by the drawbridge, which had also been searched without result.

A meeting out in the open was a far different matter. Trying to breeze past Boadicea with a honk and a wave would have been an act of folly that didn't appear to fit very well with a crime so carefully prearranged. Inviting her to come aboard and silencing her later on, probably inside whatever hiding place had been prepared for the car, would be the safest thing to do. A big closed van somewhere handy, with an accomplice to drive it away and dispose of the excess baggage, was the most likely explanation. The original thief wouldn't have risked being away from the revel too long. The state police could cope with vans a great deal more efficiently than the Bittersohns could.

"Just let me ask you all one more question. Then I'll take my wife home and let you get some sleep," Max said. "Since you've been holding these revels as a yearly event, I expect you've found they more or less fall into a pattern. I realize this one went haywire at the end, but most of your guests probably went away thinking everything was pretty much as usual. Is that right? Aside from what happened at the car shed, were there any major surprises?"

"Well, I was pretty surprised when Chad turned up instead of Sal," said Tick.

"And I'm surprised Sarah managed to pin Versey's ears

back," Melisande giggled. "I wish I'd been a bee on a bush when that happened."

"Now, Melly," chided her father, though not without a slight twitching of his own lip, "Vercingetorix Ufford is an old and valued colleague."

"Colleague?" Sarah was surprised. "I thought he was a professor."

"That's true. He still lectures occasionally, but he also does some of the programming for our radio stations, such as choosing the music and writing the scripts for our 'Renaissance Ruminations' series. He even had a program of his own for a while, doing readings from the early poets, notably Chaucer and Spenser."

"The listeners adored it," drawled Tick, "all three of them. How did you tangle with Versey, Sarah? Was he lurking in the bushes, waiting to pounce on the first toothsome wench who came along?"

"Nothing surprising about that," said Melisande. "He always lurks."

Sarah gave her a wry smile. "Oh dear, another illusion shattered. He said he'd followed me all the way from the pavilion because none of the other women came up to his specifications."

"That's what he always says, the old beast. He said it to me the year I was eighteen. I couldn't think of a snappy comeback and got stuck for two courantes and the galliard."

"Don't be too hard on Versey, girls," said Abigail. "He does the best he can with what little he has to work with. Let's see, Max. Drusilla's being here is unusual, but that's only because she's been away so long. And it's no surprise, we'd been expecting her for the past two months. Do you know, the most surprising thing I can think of is that all the frumenty got eaten."

"Mother, you don't mean it," cried Melisande.

"I do so. They even scraped the bowl. Cook couldn't believe it when I showed her. She's terribly embarrassed at not making enough, poor dear, but how was she to know? Usually we wind up throwing most of the batch on the compost heap. Even the Sunday School children hardly touch it."

"Did your cook change the recipe this year?" Sarah asked.

"Oh no, she couldn't do that. The one we've been using ever since we started the revels is taken straight from a fourteenth-century manuscript written by the prioress of an abbey in Kent. You don't suppose this nouvelle cuisine fad has finally got around to frumenty?"

Nobody had anything to say on that question. Nehemiah Billingsgate looked around at the weary cluster of still costumed ex-revelers.

"Well, my dears, if frumenty's the most exciting thing we can come up with, I think we may as well call it a day. You and Sarah will be back in the morning then, Max?"

"Let's see what happens between now and then," Max answered. "The police may come up with something."

Saying goodbye was a bit awkward. Sarah could hardly thank her hostess for a lovely time under the circumstances. She compromised on, "Please don't worry too much, especially about Aunt Bodie. I simply can't imagine she'd stand for having anything awful happen to her. We'll be in touch."

9

"What a relief to get out of there!" Sarah released the underpinnings of her hennin, pulled the tall cone away from her head, and tossed it into the back seat of the car. "Turn up the heater, will you, dear?"

"It'll warm up once we get going. In the meantime, you could move a little closer."

"I don't want to get my draperies in the way of the gas pedal." Nevertheless, Sarah took Max up on his attractive offer, kicking her by now bedraggled train over to the far side of the passenger seat.

"I feel as if we ought to be out combing the byways for Aunt Bodie, but I know she'd be the first to say that's nonsense. What could we accomplish in the dark that the police and Tick with the helicopter haven't already done better? I'm just relieved that Abigail and Bill managed to get their company away without having police and media all over the place."

"I'm surprised Grimpen didn't go for the publicity," said Max. "I've seen cops willing to cover up a crime before, especially when somebody rich and prominent is involved, though it sometimes works the other way around. But I've never seen anybody so ready to shove the whole case under the rug after he'd arrived at a brilliant solution without even bothering to examine the evidence."

Sarah yawned. "Melly said her friend Reggie told her

Grimpen had a bridge game on at the country club. Maybe he was afraid his wife would be cross if he dallied around doing his job. Or else he stole the Ghost himself and was getting edgy."

"I'd buy that with pleasure if I thought Grimpen had brains enough to carry it off. We'll have to check him out, *Kätzele*."

"You'll have to, darling. I ought to get after Cousin Lionel about the morris dancers."

"That brings up a slightly embarrassing point," said Max.

"Yes, dear. Don't worry, I'll know in a flash if he was in on the doings. Lionel thinks he's a master of guile, but his eyes cross whenever he tries to tell a lie. Besides, he has all that money of Aunt Appie's to play with nowadays, so I hardly think he'd begin rustling Rolls Royces for kicks. Do you think Miriam will be furious with us for having stayed out so long?"

"You phoned the house and told her what was happening, didn't you?"

"Of course. She said Davy went right to sleep after his story and he's welcome to stay the night, but she knows how we feel and she'll be waiting up for us."

"Don't start feeling guilty about that. Miriam and Ira are both night owls. They'd be prowling till all hours anyway. See what's on the radio, why don't you?"

After that they didn't say much. By the time they got to Ireson Town, Sarah was actually asleep, curled up on the seat with her head in Max's lap. He had to give her a gentle nudge.

"Hey, sleepyhead. We're here."

"Here? Oh." She bounced up and opened the car door. "Brr! It's chilly. I wish I'd had sense enough to bring something warm."

But it was only a step to the Rivkins' pleasant ranch house, and Miriam had hot tea waiting.

"So you ran into big trouble?" was Ira's greeting.

"How did the houppelande work out?" was Miriam's.

Sarah answered the more important question first. "Fine.

Everyone said mine was the prettiest costume there. Didn't they, Max? Was Davy a good boy?"

"Come and see."

All four of them tiptoed into the guest room, where Miriam had set up her own son's old crib as a lure. Once assured that Davy was alive, well, and sleeping the sleep of the innocent, Sarah and Max allowed themselves to collapse around the kitchen table and unwind.

"I didn't realize I was hungry," said Sarah, gladly accepting a slice of Miriam's spicy dark prune bread. "Though except for a cup of coffee, I haven't had a thing to eat since the banquet, and that's been forever. It seems so, anyway."

"What did they serve?" Miriam wanted to know.

"Who got killed?" Ira demanded. Max and Sarah tried to answer them both, with mixed results.

"Peacock pie? How could anybody eat a peacock?"

"It was just turkey with feathers stuck in the—"

"So here's this guy up in the tree with just his feet—"

"Oddest thing was the frumenty. Nobody liked it but everybody—"

"Sounds to me like the cop." Ira had the floor to himself at last. "The hell of it is, how do you go about arresting a police chief?"

"I'll find out and let you know." Max set down his empty cup. "What do you say, Sarah? Think we ought to get the kid home?"

"He could stay with us," Miriam told them for the fifth or sixth time. "You could all stay. There's room."

"But then we'd have no clothes for the morning," Sarah reminded her. "Could I borrow an extra blanket for Davy?"

"Take one for yourself," Max suggested. "She was bitching about the cold all the way here."

"I was not," Sarah insisted. "Mainly because I was asleep a good part of the time, I have to admit. Oh, thank you, Miriam. I'll return them tomorrow."

After the usual amount of flapping around, they got themselves and the sleeping baby out to the car, made the short ride to their own house in perfect calm, and got Davy peacefully settled in his own crib. They were just laying their own heads on their respective pillows when he woke up and began to fuss.

"That's gratitude for you," Max groaned. "Shall I go?"

"No, lie still. I had that long nap in the car. He must be wet; I can't imagine he's hungry after a day with Miriam."

Sarah fumbled for her slippers and went into her formerly angelic son's nursery, sorting out the sleeves of her robe en route. "Come on, squally. Let's find you some dry pants."

Fresh diapers didn't appear to be the entire solution. Sarah carried the baby, still bawling, down to the kitchen. She warmed a bottle and settled the pair of them in the rocking chair for a feeding session. Davy took two hungry sucks, gurgled a bit, and fell asleep again with the nipple in his mouth.

"Little monster." Sarah kissed the top of his head in helpless adoration. His hair was blond and curly. Like Max's when he was a baby, Miriam said. There wasn't a peep out of him when she laid him back in his crib. Nor did she get so much as a grunt out of Max when at last she slid back in bed beside him. Like father, like son.

Sarah herself was wide awake by now. And what about Aunt Bodie, she wondered. Where was she, and what was happening to her?

It was hard to envision anything's happening to Boadicea Kelling. In her well-regulated life, events didn't simply occur. They eventuated as the result of forethought and planning. Hardly a typical Kelling trait. But then Boadicea wasn't a Kelling.

This realization came to Sarah as something of a surprise. She was so used to Kellings marrying their own distant relatives to keep the money in the family that she and most of her kin tended to lump the in-laws with the genuine Kellings regardless of what their origins had been. Max was having rather a hard time adjusting to Kellingization but Bodie had integrated easily enough, as far as Sarah knew.

Then where had Boadicea come from and why couldn't Sarah remember? Her own father had been almost obsessively involved with the family history. She'd had it served up to her three meals a day and often at afternoon tea as well, for the first eighteen years of her life. She cast her mind back among the gnarled and intertwined branches of her family tree.

Boadicea had been married to Uncle Morgan Kelling who wasn't Sarah's uncle at all but Cousin Percy's; and Percy was only her second cousin once removed. Uncle Morgan had been in wool and noils, an entirely suitable career for a Bostonian of his background; his father had been in wool and noils before him. Sarah couldn't recall much about Uncle Morgan except that she'd been taken to his funeral when she was ten as a special grown-up treat. He'd commuted from Wenham on the train every day, she remembered that.

That must be why she really knew so little about the Morgan Kellings, not because Aunt Bodie made any great secret of her doings but because they mostly took place outside the particular orbit within which Sarah had grown up. Aunt Bodie didn't like a good many of her in-laws, but that didn't make her any less a member of the family. Kellings often didn't get along with other Kellings, usually for good and sufficient reason.

Bodie had thought Great-uncle Frederick was insane, which he probably had been, and Great-aunt Matilda a menace. She'd been right on that count, too. She still considered Cousin Dolph a bore, Aunt Appie a scatterbrain, and Uncle Jem a wastrel. She'd liked Sarah's parents well enough while they were alive because they'd been sensible people. She hadn't visited them because they were too close to Aunt Caroline, whom she absolutely loathed.

Why had she been so utterly down on Aunt Caroline? Sarah was getting sleepy again. She felt like Alice falling down the hole into Wonderland, wondering whether cats ate bats or if bats ate cats. Had Boadicea rubbed Caroline the wrong way? Had Caroline antagonized Bodie? Or was it just a case of two iron wills clashing? What could it matter now that Aunt Caroline was dead and gone?

10

But it did matter. Sarah dropped off, still wondering why. She woke with the sun blazing in through the opened curtains and Max entertaining his son with an imitation of Boris Chaliapin and John McCormack singing "The Three Little Pigs" in concert.

"I know," she exclaimed for what must have seemed like no good reason. "They both came from New York."

Max finished on a high C and a low D. "Who did?"

"Aunt Bodie and Aunt Caroline, of course. Did you change him?"

"Look, that's man-to-man stuff. We don't ask you intimate personal questions, do we? Were you planning to get up today, or shall Dave and I just open a can of beans and flip a steak on the grill?"

"Why don't you both clear out of here and let me get dressed in peace? What time is it, anyway?"

"Almost eight o'clock. I've got to call Birmingham before the rates change."

"Birmingham, England, or Birmingham, Alabama?"

"Both, come to think of it. Come on, Dave. You might as well start learning the business."

Left to herself, Sarah showered and put on a fleecy blue jogging suit. She had no intention of committing athletic excesses, but the outfit was comfortable to work in and could be tossed into the washer when Davy made a mess of it as he was bound to do one way or another. She didn't bother to make the bed. Mrs. Blufert would be arriving at half-past nine on the dot.

Neither Sarah nor Max had wanted live-in help, but their strange business had made it imperative that they have a reliable person to cope with the housekeeping and, when necessary, with Davy. Mr. Lomax, who'd been caretaker at Ireson's Landing ever since Sarah could remember, had solved their problem as he did most others. His widowed niece lived just up the road a piece, liked housework and babies, and wouldn't mind earning a little something extra.

That meant she was hard up and needed a job. The Bittersohns had checked out Mrs. Blufert through Miriam's grapevine, interviewed her and liked her, and offered a generous wage to compensate for sometimes irregular hours. So far, the arrangement was working beautifully. Sarah would have liked more time for cossetting her new house, but cleaning had never been her favorite pastime and at least she got to spend plenty of time with Davy.

She'd had to curtail her long-distance traveling with Max but she was able to manage a good deal of the contact work by phone from the house, along with much of the research she loved and the paperwork Max loathed. Sarah herself rather enjoyed writing letters and keeping accounts. She'd had plenty of experience handling club reports and committee budgets during her first marriage. The late Caroline Kelling had been a tireless joiner of worthy organizations and a still more zealous delegator of the dog work.

Why did she keep thinking about the mother-in-law whom she'd always called Aunt Caroline, Sarah wondered? What was that niggling bit of family gossip she couldn't pin down about Caroline and Aunt Bodie? Instead of sitting here with one shoe on and one off, puzzling over something that probably didn't matter a rap anyway, why didn't she go down and see whether Max and Davy had managed to demolish the kitchen?

She'd misjudged her menfolk. Davy was in his high chair, gloriously happy with a spoon and a bowl of cereal. He'd got a little inside him, more on his chin, a good deal on the tray, and a few blobs on the dark red clay floor tiles. Max was talking into the wall phone, reaching over from time to time to steer his son's spoon mouthward. Sarah wiped up some of the overspill with a paper towel and measured coffee into the elegant brewing machine that had been a housewarming present from Miriam and Ira.

This house was set closer to the ocean than the old Kelling summer place had been. The North Shore offered granite ledges to build on, so they hadn't needed to worry much about erosion. From the upstairs windows, they could see all the way to Little Nibble Island and beyond to infinity. Even here in the kitchen, Sarah caught glimpses of the Atlantic as she toasted muffins and sectioned grapefruit.

The old place had been all dark corners, drafts, and mildew; this was all light and air. They'd saved none of the furnishings; Sarah had looted the old place of everything worth taking when she'd refurbished the Beacon Hill brownstone that, with the Ireson's Landing property, had been all her inheritance from her first husband. The leftovers had gone to the Goodwill before the wreckers came in. Now she had pale wood, bright colors, natural textures, the wondrous Burchfield landscape that had been Max's wedding present, and immense views of cliff and moor and forest and sea through snug-fitting, draft-free, triple-glazed windows.

The Bittersohn's usual morning's entertainment at this time of year, aside from Davy, was watching for migrating birds through the two pairs of binoculars they kept right next to the toaster. Today, they didn't have a thought for birds.

"What's on your mind?" Max asked when Sarah started to butter her muffin with her coffee spoon.

"H'm? Oh yes, I see what you mean." She put the spoon down. "It's just some probably irrelevant little thing I ought to know about Aunt Bodie and can't for the life of me remember. If Aunt Emma can't help, I may have to make the supreme sacrifice and call Cousin Mabel. And I thought I could do some discreet nosing among the Whets and

Tolbathys. If only Uncle Jem hadn't gone off on that stupid yachting party! He knows all that stuff."

"Send the coast guard after him."

"I'd love to, if I thought they'd go. You're going back to the Billingsgates', I suppose?"

"I want to check on whether Wouter installed a secret underground garage while he was about it." Max reached down to retrieve the spoon Davy had dropped and was working up to be cross about. "Here you are, tiger."

"You know, that's not such a wild idea," Sarah replied. "I wonder if the Billingsgates ever built themselves a fallout shelter. Wasn't there a craze for them back in the late forties or fifties?"

"Before people realized there wouldn't be anything left to crawl out for. Christ, Davy, I wonder what we've let you in for."

"Darling, there's always something," Sarah reminded him. "Years ago he could have died from blood poisoning, whooping cough, scarlet fever, pneumonia, or goodness knows what else, if he'd lived long enough to catch them. And he might have been motherless if he did. Do you realize it wasn't until 1843 that Oliver Wendell Holmes published his paper on the contagiousness of puerperal fever? He spent years trying to convince the eminent physicians of his day that they were killing off new mothers by not washing their hands or changing those filthy old frock coats they wore to deliver the babies. The dirtier your coat, the more successful you were supposed to be. They'd go from one patient to the next in a cloud of germs, wipe out a hundred women in a row, and put it down to the will of God. And they tore Dr. Holmes to pieces for trying to make them clean themselves up. Old poops!"

Davy babbled something that sounded very much like what Sarah had just called the eminent doctors. Max chuckled. "There, see. Teaching the kid rude language."

"Well, there are some things that can only be expressed in rude language. More coffee?"

"Just half, thanks. I've got to get rolling."

"Do give Abigail my best when you see her. Poor woman, having to clean up after a party that ended in disaster."

"It could have been worse," said Max. "None of the guests got hurt and most of them never knew anything had happened. There'd have been no point in holding them all for questioning even if that jackass Grimpen had happened to think of it. We'll know better when we get the result of the autopsy, but I'm fairly sure Rufus had been dead for at least an hour by the time I got to him. Whoever's responsible had plenty of time to cover his tracks. You probably accomplished as much as anybody could have by collecting information from the group without getting anybody stirred up."

"I can do better. We still don't know anything about that morris dancer Mrs. Gaheris described to us. Have you any ideas as to which it could have been?"

"She said he was too short to be Tick and too tall for Young Dork."

"What would you expect her to say? Young Dork's her first cousin once removed and Tick's her old school chum's son-in-law. She didn't mention Lionel, and he's at least an inch taller than Tick. I say we should check out the whole pack of them. No, Davy."

Sarah took away the empty bowl her son was trying to use for a helmet and pacified him with a big wooden spoon from the rack on the counter behind her. "If you want to know, I can't give Lionel clearance for the early part of the banquet. He didn't show up in the pavilion for almost half an hour after we went in, as far as I can make out. Aunt Appie was burbling around looking for him, and he sidestepped when I tried to find out later on where he'd been."

"I wish Mrs. Gaheris had been able to tell us exactly when she looked out the window," Max fretted.

"I know, it was terribly inconsiderate of her not to check. But why should she have?"

"To see if it was time to take her pills?"

"No, they're stomach pills. She said she takes them with

meals. Oh dear, Aunt Appie will die if it turns out Lionel's done something stupid."

"Something stupid's a pretty thin definition for killing a man and hanging his body in a tree, my love."

"Lionel might have stolen the car, but he'd never have done the actual killing. He's much too squeamish. Those brats of his must get their bloodthirsty streak from Vare's side of the family."

"So what about her?"

"She and the boys were all off rock climbing for the weekend."

"Says who?"

"Says Lionel," Sarah answered unhappily. "Darling, you don't actually believe Vare organized this outrage to give her children a richer experience of *Hill Street Blues*?"

"You know them better than I do, kid."

"That's right, throw it up to me. Can I help whom I'm related to? All right, you dreadful man, I freely concede that Vare and her hyena pack might do something really outrageous if the boys happened to think of it and Vare managed to convince herself the project would be educational. And I don't have to tell you that Vare can pressure Lionel into doing whatever she wants, except spend money recklessly."

No Kelling could do that. Even Great-uncle Serapis had died with his capital intact, although he'd managed to establish an international reputation as a millionaire playboy mainly through bluff and good management. There was something in the family genes that kept their revels from turning into routs. No matter how great their urge to chuck the dollars around, Kellings always had to stop and count their pennies first.

Another thing most of Sarah's relatives and in-laws couldn't do, though, was to refrain from airing their woes to other members of the family. She'd heard through the grapevine that Lionel's tightfistedness with his mother's money had been annoying Vare a good deal. He'd been perfectly willing to wheedle Aunt Appie into paying for the ski lodge and the thirty-eight foot auxiliary ketch. Aside from the fact that Lionel himself liked to ski and sail, these expenditures could be justified as investments. He might, should he choose, rent the lodge for income and put the yacht out to charter. Both could be sold, hypothetically at a profit, if the family tired of them.

When it came to Vare's yen for an expedition in the Andes Mountains, though, Lionel had been adamant. They might have got their money back on the llamas afterward, but overall they'd have had to operate at a substantial loss, and that was not the Kelling way. Lionel had also shot down Vare's project for sailing the ketch up the Amazon, having no faith in his boys' scheme to shoot boa constrictors along the way and smuggle the skins back into the United States for sale to handbag manufacturers. All in all, Lionel had been a sad disappointment to his wife and children of late. Would he have had the face to refuse his cooperation in what might have appeared to be an all-profit venture?

Vare and Lorista had never got along remarkably well but they were, after all, sisters. If the Dorks happened to have found out about Wouter Tolbathy's big joke in the car shed, then it was entirely possible Vare had been let in on the secret even if Lionel hadn't.

There was no real reason why Vare should have picked this particular weekend to go rock climbing with her sons. The spring semester at that glorified detention center they attended was not yet over and according to family scuttlebutt the boys themselves had been none too keen on being taken out. Jesse was in the midst of a complicated chemical experiment: preparing to blow up the lab, probably. Woody had been honing up his arithmetical skills by making book on the upcoming interscholastic soccer match. James and dear little Frank had spent most of the past week excavating a tiger pit into which they hoped to lure the headmaster as an experiment in psychology. Why hadn't Vare left her hellhounds to pursue their instructive courses and accompanied Lionel to the Renaissance Revel?

There she could have danced the *volta* and the gigue with Vercingetorix Ufford, eaten authentic fourteenth-century frumenty, and hobnobbed with her long-unseen Aunt

Drusilla. Had she not liked the idea of being just another guest while her sister queened it on the bandstand? But Vare could have brought along her sackbut and climbed on the bandstand, too. Or she could have stood around looking sympathetic and understanding whenever Lorista hit a wrong note. It was most unlike Vare to pass up the chance.

"Right, dear," said Sarah. "I'll check out Vare as well as Lionel, or would you rather do it yourself? Lorista might have some information on where they're supposed to have gone. Will you be talking to her?"

"Not if I can help it." Lorista was high on Max's list of people he could do nicely without. "Fare thee well, mine own, I'd better get cracking. Call me at the Billingsgates' if anything develops. I may not be there, but they'll know where I am."

"Is there any chance you may be in to dinner?"

"I hope so, I'll call you later on. See you later, Dave. Have a good day."

Max hunted out a relatively cereal-free spot to kiss his son goodbye, took a more comprehensive leave of his wife, and went off, leaving behind him the customary impression that he was battling his way into the teeth of a booming gale.

In fact it was overcast and blustery out. At least the Billingsgates had got the best of the fickle May weather yesterday. Sarah put the breakfast dishes in the sink for Mrs. Blufert to deal with, and flipped up the high-chair tray.

"Come on, Davy, we'd better quit lollygagging and get to work."

By the time the housekeeper arrived, Davy was cleaned up, dressed in a striped jersey and red corduroy overalls, and happy to entertain Mrs. Blufert from his playpen while she worked. Sarah said, "Let me know if he starts to fuss," and went into the office she and Max had planned for themselves. Here were three telephones: the green one they called the family phone, the white one used for business calls, and the red one that was their private hotline with a number known only to themselves and Cousin Brooks.

Cousin Brooks was in charge of the Boston office. For

years, Max had rented a dingy cubbyhole in the by now somewhat venerable Little Building on Boston's Windy Corner of Boylston and Tremont streets. He'd used it only occasionally as a mailing address or a neutral ground on which to hold interviews he preferred for one reason or another not to hold elsewhere. With typical Kelling penny-wisdom, Sarah had suggested a while back that since he was paying rent for the place anyway, he might as well get some good out of it. They'd spruced up the office with a few second-hand oddments so it wouldn't look vulgarly nouveau and installed Cousin Brooks as manager.

Brooks Kelling had been working with Max and Sarah in an unofficial capacity ever since before they were married. The keenness, daring, and almost wizardly resourcefulness which the sixtyish little man had developed during his lifetime as an ornithologist had proved equally valuable in detection. Nowadays he and Sarah handled a good deal of the local work by themselves while Max tackled the more far-flung assignments.

As soon as Sarah had checked once more with Boadicea Kelling's now distraught housekeeper, her next order of business was to get Brooks on the hotline and clue him in as to what had taken place yesterday at the Billingsgates'.

"And I've been trying to recall some bit of gossip I once heard about Aunt Bodie and Aunt Caroline," she wound up. "I can't think why it would matter at a time like this, but it keeps nagging at me."

"I wish I could help you," was Brooks's unsatisfactory reply. "My mother would no doubt have known, but she's long gone, as you know. I never did see Mother again after she took off for Switzerland with what was left of Father's money. We'd come to our personal parting of the ways some time before that, as you know. I visited Caroline a few times, but she never once mentioned Bodie that I recall. Have you spoken to Emma?"

"No, I'll try her next. It's no use asking Aunt Appie, I don't suppose."

"Not unless you care to spend the whole morning weeding out the irrelevancies. Will Max be calling in?"

"He said he would. I don't know when."

"It doesn't matter. You might mention that I have a lead on the Wilton-Rugge robbery. I'm going out and poke around a bit. In case Max tries to reach me, I'll leave a private message on the answering machine."

Max and Brooks had worked out a verbal code of amazing complexity in the Alfred Campion manner. Often they themselves couldn't decipher what they'd been trying to convey, but they forged on undaunted, inventing yet crazier convolutions. Sarah thought the whole business pretty juvenile, notwithstanding the fact that Max was ten and Brooks thirty years older than she, and refused to get involved with the code on the grounds that she heard enough gobbledegook from Davy as it was. She bade her consanguineous colleague an affectionate goodbye and looked up Aunt Emma's telephone number.

Sarah had forgotten, if she'd ever known, that this was Fire Prevention Week in Pleasaunce. Emma Kelling had been an honorary member of the Pleasaunce Fire Department ever since she'd bullied her fellow citizens into raising the money for a new ladder truck. This morning, Emma's butler told Sarah, Mrs. Kelling was off at a Women's Club breakfast demonstrating the proper way to jump into a safety net.

"Heatherstone, you're joking," Sarah gasped. "No, I suppose you aren't. What was she wearing?"

"Plus fours, a Norfolk jacket, and her Tyrolean hat. The same outfit she wore when she made that balloon ascension on behalf of the church steeple fund," Heatherstone replied.

Aunt Emma did have a knack for the appropriate costume. Sarah thanked the butler and hung up, amused but not enlightened. She thought of making the supreme sacrifice and calling Cousin Mabel, but she flinched away and rang Jeremy Kelling's Beacon Hill apartment instead, though she wasn't quite sure why.

"Hello, Egbert." Jem's *valet de chambre* and general factotum was, like Heatherstone, an old friend of Sarah's. "Any news from the briny deep?"

"Yes, as a matter of fact," Egbert replied. "It got too cold in Maine, so they're coming back down the coast. Mr. Jem phoned from Halibut Point last night. Seems to me he ought to be rounding Marblehead Light just about now."

"As near as that? The old sculpin, why didn't he call me? Are they putting in at Marblehead Harbor?"

"No, they're going straight on to Scituate, lay over at the yacht club tonight, and then going around Provincetown and down to Newport tomorrow."

"Rats! What's the name of that yacht he's on, Egbert?"

"*Maphwacha III*, Mrs. Sarah. She's a forty-five foot yawl. Mr. Jem tells me that means she has her mizzen, whatever that is, stepped aft of the wheel instead of forward as on a ketch."

"It's a mast." Sarah had learned all about yawls and ketches from Cousin Lionel. "Thank you, Egbert."

Sarah had looked forward to a morning at home with her son, but this was a chance not to be missed. "Mrs. Blufert," she called out, "where's your uncle this morning?"

11

Mr. Lomax was exactly where Sarah wanted him to be, down on the town dock mending one of the lobster pots he didn't set nowadays so often as he used to. She ran her little car as close as she could and called over to him. "How's the *Mary L.* fixed for gas, Mr. Lomax?"

"Huh? What's up, Miz Max?"

Their old caretaker had run through a gamut of names with her: plain Sarah when she'd come to Ireson's as a visiting child; Mrs. Alex when she'd married his then employer, Alexander Kelling; Mrs. Kelling when she'd become a young widow running the place with only Mr. Lomax's help. He couldn't quite bring himself to go back to plain Sarah, but he was dummed if he'd address his friend Isaac's son's wife as Mrs. Bittersohn. Miz Max was his solution, and it suited them both fine.

"I need you and the *Mary L.* right now," she told him. "She's full."

Mr. Lomax laid aside his lobster pot and tack hammer, straightened up and swayed back and forth a few times to get the kinks out, then climbed aboard the old but spruce twenty-six footer and held out his hand to help Sarah over the gunwale. It wasn't until he'd started the engine and pulled outside the breakwater that he bothered to ask, "Where we headin'?"

"Toward Marblehead. I want to intercept a forty-five foot

yawl named *Maphwacha III*. She left Halibut Point this morning sometime on her way to Scituate. She hasn't been past here yet, has she?"

"Ain't seen 'er. Here, take the wheel a minute. Keep between the channel buoys till we round the ledges."

Sarah had done a little sailing and plenty of rowing, but she'd never handled a power boat before. She might have been nervous if she'd stopped to think about what she was doing, but there was no time for that. She kept her eyes on her course and her hands on the wheel while Mr. Lomax fiddled to get his elderly radio going.

At first all he got were squawks and sizzles that suggested a hen being fried alive, then he reached somebody with whom he had a brief chat in what sounded to Sarah like Max and Brooks's secret code. Either the coast guard or the harbor master, she assumed. Then he took back the wheel from her and jerked his head toward a couple of ratty cushions on top of a locker in the tiny open-ended wheelhouse.

"I'm goin' to let 'er out. Stay under cover so's you won't get soaked with spray."

Sarah knew better than to pester him with questions. She flopped on the cushions, pulled her knees up against her chest, and sat as tight as the pitching and rolling allowed. It was amazing what a turn of speed the *Mary L.* could put on. She remembered Mr. Lomax telling Alexander six or seven years ago about the 360 cubic inch Chrysler truck motor he'd picked up second hand at a Chelsea junkyard. Alexander had liked talking about engines. She hadn't cried about Alexander for a long time.

Mr. Lomax threw her an anxious look. "Ain't gettin' seasick?"

Sarah shook her head. "How about you?"

That got a chuckle out of him. He checked his compass, tugged his filthy old swordfisherman's cap farther down over his bald spot, and chugged on.

The big waves weren't running today, but the breeze was stiff enough to raise an uncomfortable chop. The sun kept poking in and out from behind a skyful of quick-traveling clouds. Sarah wished she'd brought her sunglasses and windbreaker but she hadn't, so there was nothing she could do but stick it out.

Forever, it felt like. She still wasn't seasick but she was getting awfully sick of the eternal up and down, to and fro, of the noise of the engine and the mingled smells of exhaust and bygone fish. Were they lost? Had they missed the yawl? They'd spotted a couple of fishing boats and one yacht, but she was a schooner. Surely they must have failed to catch *Maphwacha III*.

No, they hadn't. There she was. Sarah almost panicked.

"Mr. Lomax, what shall we do? Wave our arms and holler?"

"Good a scheme as any, I guess. Stand astern an' let 'em see you."

He handed her a battered megaphone. She picked her way aft and braced herself against the gunwale. Lomax knew better than to kill his engine, but he slowed down and steered straight for *Maphwacha's* bow, shooting off his flare gun while Sarah waved and shouted through the megaphone.

"Heave to! Heave to! Stop, you idiots!"

"What the hell?" roared someone from the bridge. "Get out of the way."

"No! Stop!"

It was either heave to or run them down. Mercifully, the yawl came up into the wind and dropped her mainsail. By now half a dozen curious faces could be seen along the rail. To Sarah's unbounded relief, Jeremy Kelling's was among them.

"Uncle Jem," she shrieked.

"Sarah! Good God, is that you?"

"Of course. We came to get you."

"What's the matter? Not Egbert?"

By this time, the old tires that served the *Mary L.* for fenders were smack up against *Maphwacha III's* sleek white hull and a man in captain's uniform was having thirteen kitten fits. Sarah was not to be put off by a tantrum.

"Stop yelling and throw us a rope. We need Jem Kelling on urgent business."

"What business?" demanded the captain.

She looked across at the gaping faces, half of them slightly glassy-eyed although the sun was nowhere near the yard-arm and wouldn't be for hours yet. Jem looked to be cold sober, thank God.

"Top secret," she snapped.

"What's this? What's this?" The passengers were all agog. "God, Jem, you're not a CIA agent?"

"No comment." This was a glorious moment for Jeremy Kelling. His face grew as hard and inscrutable as its surrounding chins would permit. "Get me aboard. Pronto."

Transferring an elderly, overweight, and none too nimble gentleman wearing a natty blue blazer and white flannel slacks from a forty-five foot yacht to a twenty-six foot fishing boat in open sea is not accomplished without some discomfort to the man and dire peril to the white flannels. However, Jem was eager to bear himself manfully in the face of this unexpected notoriety and Mr. Lomax was a capable seaman even if one or two of those aboard *Maphwacha III* were something he muttered under his breath and Sarah didn't quite catch. Egbert might go into convulsions when he saw the flannels, but Jeremy Kelling was relatively unscathed and insufferably proud of himself by the time they'd got him into the cockpit of the *Mary L*.

"Will you be rejoining us, Jem?" the yacht's owner called down in a more respectful tone than he'd used hitherto.

Jem looked at his niece. Sarah shrugged.

"If you want to. I could probably run you down to Scituate later on. Can you reach them by telephone if necessary?"

After a fair amount of backing and forthing, it was determined that Jem could. The phone number, written on paper adorned with signal flags and headed "Memo from *Maphwacha*," was sent across in a pink plastic bucket. Jem saluted smartly, Mr. Lomax gunned his engine, and they were off.

"What's this all about?" Jem roared as soon as they were under way, but the noise level was so high that Sarah only screamed back, "Tell you when we get ashore," so Jem leaned back on the cushions and practiced his inscrutability.

The trip back was only half as long as the trip out, as is ever the case. Sarah was agreeably surprised to see by her car's clock that it was only a quarter to twelve when they'd tied up at the Ireson's Landing dock, thanked Mr. Lomax and persuaded him to accept reimbursement for his gas, and headed back to the house. On the way, she gave her uncle a quick fill-in on what had taken place at the Renaissance Revel.

"So that's why we need you, Uncle Jem. You know the Billingsgates' crowd, you've got the memory of an elephant. What I want you to do is start remembering. For all we know, Aunt Bodie's life may depend on you."

Jem chuckled. "Let's hope it doesn't. Bodie would never get over the chagrin of having to be grateful to a dissolute rogue like me."

They reached the house just in time to embarrass Mrs. Blufert for not having quite finished the dusting. Sarah parked Jem in the living room with a martini and the morning paper. She seized the opportunity to give Davy a few quick hugs and settle him in his high chair with a pilot biscuit to work on. Mrs. Blufert would have to feed him his lunch; Uncle Jem was not spiritually attuned to teething babies. She put a pot of chowder on to heat and fixed Jem another martini.

"Take this to my uncle and talk to him for a minute, would you please, Mrs. Blufert? I want to call my husband."

Max wasn't in the house, Abigail told her, but he and Bill were around the place somewhere. She'd give him the message. Sarah hung up and went to open a bottle of chablis she'd been giving a quick chill in the freezer. Jem wouldn't be crass enough to drink martinis at the table, but he'd expect to be given something other than water. As she was giving the chowder a final stir, one of the phones rang, a shrill bleep that could only be the private hotline. She clapped the lid on the pot, shoved the chowder off the heat, and ran to pick up the red handset.

"Hi, what's new?" was Max's greeting.

"Jem's here," she told him. "We're about to have lunch."

"Jem? I thought he was in Newport. How the hell did you get him off that yacht?"

"Mr. Lomax picked him up in the *Mary L.*" Sarah thought perhaps she wouldn't go into details just now. "What's new at the Billingsgates'?"

"Bill got the results of the autopsy."

"So?"

"Tranquilizer gun. They found the dart in Rufus's jerkin."

"What? Max, do you mean one of those things they shoot into animals on the *National Geographic* programs? Isn't that awfully," Sarah floundered for a word and came up with "inappropriate?"

"Awfully," Max agreed. "The pathologist figures Rufus got a dose big enough to stop a rhinoceros."

"You don't suppose Gerry Whet brought one back from Nairobi?"

"I assume you mean the gun, not the rhinoceros." Max didn't sound particularly struck by his wife's suggestion. "It's a thought. On the other hand, you might ask Jem which member of the party has a cousin who works in a zoo. Tranquilizer guns are more common in this country than you might think. Lots of people use them: game wardens, animal control officers, researchers, vets."

"What do they look like?"

"Pretty much like an air rifle, and they're used the same way. They have a spring mechanism that shoots a hollow dart. The principle's the same as an overgrown hypodermic syringe."

"How close would you have to be to hit anything with one?"

"Maybe fifty yards, if you were a first-rate marksman."

"Then Rufus could have been shot from the edge of the copse."

"Quite likely. The gun could have been stashed there in advance, then hidden again while the killer ran forward to hoist Rufe's body out of the way. Again minimizing the risk of getting caught, you see. If the killer was unlucky enough to be seen crossing that strip of lawn, he could have claimed he'd seen Rufus fall and was hurrying over to see what was wrong with him."

"Has the gun been found?"

"Not yet. Grimpen's got his men messing around in the pond now. My guess is they'll find it and it won't tell us a damned thing."

"I must say there appears to have been some efficient planning." It flashed into Sarah's mind that Boadicea Kelling herself couldn't have organized the matter more efficiently. All she said was, "Anything new on Aunt Bodie?"

"Not a yip so far. What's with Jem?"

"I haven't had a chance to talk with him yet. He's still catching his breath."

"Acquiring one, you mean. How's Davy?"

"Eating his lunch. Have you had any?"

"Plenty."

Max's carelessness about regular meals worried Sarah sometimes, but she might have known there'd be no problem about that today. A person would have an awfully hard time starving around Abigail Billingsgate. She explained about promising to take Jem to meet the yacht, broke off reluctantly, and went to give her uncle his lunch.

Being a Formerly Exalted Chowderhead of the Comrades of the Convivial Codfish, Jeremy Kelling took his chowder seriously. Sarah waited until her uncle had a pint or so aboard before she broached the business of the meeting.

"Max just told me they've found out Rufus was killed by a dart from a tranquilizer gun, Uncle Jem. Do you know who might have been able to get hold of such a thing?"

"Wouter Tolbathy made one once."

Sarah groaned. "I might have known. Whatever happened to it?"

"Don't ask me. The only time I ever saw the gun was at a

farewell party Tom gave for Gerry Whet. Gerry's always tootling off to Kenya, you know. Generally it's to buy bug powder, but this time he was taking his son, Bunny, and his two sons-in-law on safari."

"Who are the sons-in-law?"

"Joe Abbott and Buck Tolbathy. Joe married Gerry's daughter Lilias and Buck married Primula."

"And all three are in the morris dance group," said Sarah.

"Well, naturally. Joe and Buck are cousins, the whole tribe have always been close. Ski together, sail together, all that. Anyway, Wouter had made this great big hippo out of some revolting plastic stuff and painted it in a tasteful melange of fuchsia, chartreuse, and turquoise, as Wouter would naturally have done. We were all supposed to plug away at the hippo with the tranquilizer gun. If you happened to hit it in a certain spot, the beast would begin to snore."

"Clever," said Sarah. "But you don't remember who got to keep the gun, Uncle Jem?"

"I haven't the dimmest recollection. Most likely Wouter kept it himself, or else Tom took it and locked it up somewhere. It wasn't the type of thing they'd want the grandchildren to get hold of."

"Did the gun shoot real tranquilizer darts?"

"What would have been the point if it hadn't? Wouter didn't put real tranquilizing juice in them, I don't suppose. Probably lemonade or some such abomination. He was loading the darts in and the rest of us were shooting them out, that's all I can tell you."

"Can you find out from Tom what happend to the gun, Uncle Jem? If you don't, the police will have to."

Jem spluttered into his napkin. "Confound it, Sarah, hasn't Tom had troubles enough from Wouter's inventions?"

"I'm afraid he's in for more when he learns what's been happening with that insane garage door Wouter installed in Bill's car shed. Did you know anything about that?"

"Not a yip, on my word of honor, and I was as close to Wouter as any man alive except Tom. Old Wout could be closed as a clam when he was working up to one of his more spectacular effects. It would surprise me if he told anybody at all except his accomplices."

"What accomplices, for goodness' sake?"

"In this case, I'd say Rollo, that old coot who works for the Tolbathys, and Rufus."

"Rufus?" cried Sarah.

"Oh yes. Rufus and Rollo were great cronies, and they both pretty much worshipped the ground Wouter walked on. Maybe you don't realize what an odd old cuss Rufus was. He was born and brought up right there on the Billingsgate estate, to begin with."

"Yes, I do know that. Bill told us yesterday."

"Rufus fancied himself as a kind of seneschal of the castle, but he also had a streak of court jester in him. Most people didn't know that because he was careful to keep it under cover most of the time. Anyway, Rufe was also a dab hand at lots of odd jobs, so Wouter used to get him to help with projects he and Rollo couldn't handle by themselves. I should think a blasted great concrete wall might well fall into that category."

"Uncle Jem!" Sarah put down her chowder spoon. "That puts the whole case in a new light. Rufus must have been killed not just because he was in the car thief's way but because he knew how the cars were being got out of the shed. But why was he allowed to live until the second robbery? Why didn't he tell the Billingsgates about the secret door as soon as the New Phantom disappeared?"

"He well might have if he'd got the chance," Jeremy Kelling replied. "According to what you told me in the car, Bill got home, found the Phantom gone, turned around, and rushed off to Maine without even stopping to tip his hat to the queen bee. He didn't get back till Saturday morning, by which time everybody was flapping around in all directions getting ready for the revel."

"Abigail was at home the whole time," Sarah argued. "Rufus could have told her, couldn't he?"

"He could, I grant you, but he wouldn't have. Rufe liked the mistress well enough, but his fealty was to the lord of the manor. He'd have waited until such time as he could crave an audience at his master's pleasure."

"Rufus sounds a trifle batty to me."

"Ah, you modern women," Jem replied tolerantly. "You're too young to understand the workings of the feudal mind, that's all. I was about to add, Sarah, that Rufe might have received a message purportedly from one of the lads, say Bunny Whet, for instance, that he intended to appear as a knight in shining armor and had borrowed the Phantom with the intention of disguising it as a richly caparisoned steed. This is only one hypothesis, of course, but it's one Rufe would inevitably have fallen for. He tended to think of Bill as King Arthur and the rest of us as Knights of the Table Round."

Sarah glanced across the table. Like her son, Jeremy Kelling had a round, rosy face. Like Davy when last seen, he had a red checkered napkin tucked under his extra chin. As Davy would do were he here, Jem was regarding her with an expression of guileless innocence.

"No comment," said Sarah.

12

Sarah did have a question, though. "Uncle Jem, why did you mention Bunny Whet?"

Jem's face turned a shade rosier. "Dash it, Sarah, how do I know? Why do women have to pounce on a man every time he dares to open his mouth? I mentioned Bunny Whet because we were talking about the Whets just now, I suppose."

"We were talking about other people, too. What are you squirming for? Come on, Uncle Jem, this is not the time for your Boys of the Old Brigade routine. Rufus's death was no practical joke; it was cold, calculated, and very well planned murder. For all we know, Aunt Bodie may have been murdered, too, and she's one of your own relatives."

"I beg to differ. Boadicea Van Brunt was a member of an aristocratic New York family said to have been descended directly from the Headless Horseman. Her forbears made their fortune selling pickled pigs' feet to Hessian soldiers during the Revolution, though Bodie would be the last to tell you so."

"All right then, what else do you know about her? Why were she and Aunt Caroline so down on each other?"

"Would you by chance be referring to the circumstance that before she married Uncle Gilbert, Caroline jilted Bodie's brother Lancelot?"

"Is that what it was? You mean Bodie held a broken

engagement against her all that time? Was it because Aunt Caroline thought Uncle Gilbert a better catch?"

"No, I believe Lancelot had got his walking papers before Gilbert ever came on the scene. Bodie's and Caroline's people belonged to the same set in New York, naturally. Caroline was by some years the elder of the two; she came out while Bodie was still a youngster. Lancelot showed up at the debutante cotillion and as Caroline was no doubt the reigning beauty, he proceeded to give her a big rush. He'd been educated abroad and I expect his continental line was a bit slicker than the New York boys'. Anyway, by the end of the season, they were engaged."

"Lancelot doesn't sound much like Aunt Bodie, I must say," Sarah remarked, thinking of the velvet toque.

"Oh no," said Jem, "those two were as different as chalk and cheese. However, Bodie adored her big brother, probably because she hadn't seen much of him growing up. Lancelot had been shipped off to Switzerland after various private schools in the States had chucked him out and the rest had got the word not to take him in. Mabel says Lancelot was the handsomest thing she ever laid eyes on, not that Mabel had much opportunity for comparison. Anyway, needless to say, once Caroline's father began checking on his prospective son-in-law, the engagement was abruptly terminated."

"I'm surprised Aunt Caroline let it happen. Being thwarted was never her favorite thing, you know." Sarah spoke with feeling. For seven long years Caroline Kelling, actually only the wife of her father's distant cousin, had been her mother-in-law.*

"I also know Caroline liked her creature comforts," Jem Kelling reminded his niece. "I shouldn't be surprised if giving Lancelot the shove had been as much her idea as it was her parents'. In any event, his people accepted the situation more or less philosophically. I daresay they were honest enough to admit they'd have done the same if the shoe had been on the other foot. But Bodie, I understand, was furious. She claimed the wild stories about Lancelot were all a pack of lies put about by jealous rivals."

"Poor Aunt Bodie! One can hardly blame her for defending her own brother. Is there any chance she may have been right?"

"None whatsoever," Jem replied. "Lancelot Van Brunt was a man of whom it can truly be said that he was more sinning than sinned against. As a young fellow, he specialized in rubber checks and fraudulent impersonations. When his father got sick of paying his bills and turned off the supplies, Lancelot would pull one of his confidence tricks, usually on some woman who'd be reluctant to prosecute. Eventually he got involved with the mob, I've been told. Don't ask me what mob or why, but it all sounded more than a bit scurrilous."

"What finally happened to him? Is he still alive?"

"No, he got rubbed out, as the saying goes. At least the New York police dredged up a block of cement from the East River that had a certain indefinable *espièglerie* about it, so they assumed that must have been Lancelot. Bodie always held Caroline responsible. She claimed if Caroline hadn't broken her brother's heart by handing him his hat, he wouldn't have thrown his life away, as she rather melodramatically expressed it."

"I've never heard her express it," said Sarah.

"No, I don't suppose you have. This all happened somewhat more than half a century ago, you know. Lancelot's never been considered a subject for dinner table discussion when Bodie's around and I don't suppose anybody ever thinks of him when she isn't. None of us ever knew him anyway so we'd have to go on hearsay, which is no fun except for Mabel."

"Whoever would have thought it?" Sarah mused. "Aunt Bodie having a brother who got bumped off by the mob. She's always been such a pillar of righteousness, herself. Though under these circumstances she'd almost have to be, wouldn't she? Was there a dreadful scandal?"

"I'm afraid I can't answer that one. Gangsters had a fad for shooting each other in tastelessly flamboyant ways back during the thirties, but I think Lancelot died quietly. He may have been a scoundrel, but I never heard he stooped to vulgarity. Somebody once told me he'd been killed, that's all, and I can't even remember who it was. I hope my brain isn't starting to curdle."

"Well, quick, before you fall apart," Sarah told him practically, "let's have your rundown on the morris dancers. Cousin Lionel first, please. He's not in trouble of any kind, is he?"

"Unless you call being married to that Freud-spouting virago and fathering a troop of baboons trouble," Jem drawled. "Not to mention having Appie for a mother."

"But nothing specific that you know of?"

"Lionel does not confide in me. On October 27, 1949, at approximately 5:15 P.M., I yielded to Appie's importunities and permitted her to place the little blister, as he then was, on my knee. He wiped his jammy hands all over my shirt and tie, drummed his heels on my shins, committed a nuisance in my lap, and bit my finger when I tried to pry him off. Since that time, relations between us have not been warm."

"But you know all his friends," Sarah argued. "Don't they tell you things?"

"More specifically, I know the fathers of his friends. However, I concede that I do get along well enough with the sons. Why don't you ask Tick Purbody about Lionel? He's head of the jingle and stomp brigade, isn't he?"

"He was yesterday. He said that as leader he had to dance every set. Is that what happens?"

"Sarah, I know rather less about morris dancing than I do about herding buffalo. If Tick says he was dancing—" Jem hesitated in the act of buttering another pilot biscuit. "Anyway, you were watching him the whole time, weren't you?"

"Well, hardly. I didn't even know who he was until Max pointed him out to me. The dancers were dressed alike in distractingly busy costumes, so it was easy to mix them up even if I had known them all. Not that it signifies whether he danced all the time or not, because Dorothy Dork says she saw Rufus still alive and on guard after the banquet had started. Is she reliable?"

"Dorothy? Oh yes, I should say so. Yes, Dorothy's reliable enough."

"What are you hedging for? What's the matter with Tick?"

"Sarah, I am not hedging."

Jem gripped the handle of his butter knife in his fist and held it out at arm's length, eyed the blade suspiciously, then laid it back on his plate. "There's nothing the matter with Tick, so far as I know. It's just that he has a well-deserved reputation as a puller of practical jokes and narrator of wild tales. Tick's a mere beginner compared to dear old Wouter, I hasten to say, but one does tend to look for the symbolic whoopee cushion under the chair seat before swallowing anything he says."

"Surely he wouldn't have joked about what happened yesterday?"

"Dash it, Sarah, how do I know what Tick Purbody would do under stress? It's not unheard-of for a person to take refuge in japery when reality becomes too painful. Anyway, Tick shouldn't be too hard for you to check up on, should he?"

"Harder than you might think. You've been to those revels, you know what they're like. Everyone kept going up to the buffet and wandering around among the tables to chat with this one and that. And the dancers were bobbing up all over the place. One couldn't miss seeing them, they were so garishly dressed. For all I know, they were milling around on purpose."

Jem scowled. "Why should they?"

"To keep the rest of us from realizing Tick wasn't among them, perhaps? They're his friends, aren't they? Wouldn't they try to cover up for him if they thought he was about to pull one of his practical jokes?"

"What sort of joke?"

"No joke at all. Uncle Jem, you're just being wilfully obtuse. Tick Purbody serves as Bill's right hand. That means he's involved with both the radio stations and the meading business. He also is curator of the Rolls Royce collection. Therefore he must spend a fair amount of time in the car shed and could easily have discovered that trick wall Wouter installed. It's obvious enough if one stops to consider what sort of mind Wouter had. Bill's too high-minded and Abigail too practical to think in those terms, but you say Tick operates pretty much on Wouter's wavelength. He's probably known right along and kept quiet until he could think of a really spectacular way to use the secret door."

"Namely to steal his in-laws' cars? Confound it, Sarah, why should he? Tick's had free use of the entire collection ever since he married Melisande. If he's pinched the Phantom and and the Silver Ghost, he can hardly go swanking around in them any more the way he's been doing all this time."

"No, but he can sell them. A 1937 Phantom III went for over a hundred thousand dollars at auction not too long ago."

"Pah! How could Tick get away with peddling Bill's cars? They're always being exhibited here and there. Everybody and his grandfather would recognize at once whose they were."

"Everybody around here might know," Sarah conceded, "but what if he had them shipped across country? Tick travels a good deal on business for Bill, doesn't he? Couldn't he invent an errand in California?"

Jem snorted. "Not on Bill's money he couldn't. The fact that Bill tends to tootle around loving his neighbor as himself doesn't make him a blithering imbecile, you know. He has some esoteric theory about being a good steward."

"Does that mean he keeps Tick short of ready cash?"

"Of course it doesn't. Not short according to Bill's definition of short, anyway. I don't know how Tick and Melisande interpret shortness."

"Did Melisande get a generous marriage settlement from her parents or from anybody else?" Sarah pressed. "And what about Tick? Has he any money of his own?"

"I don't know whether Melly gets an allowance or not. She does get the profits out of the mead business, I know. And as the only child, she'll naturally scoop the pot when Bill and Abigail go. As for Tick, he's no doubt inherited capital but it can't be much. Old Purbody took a beating on that shrinkage in the wool market before he died. He'd been heavily into noils. The maternal grandmother left a sizeable estate, but with thirty-seven living heirs to divide it among, none of them got rich on her."

"Does Tick gamble?"

"Not to my knowledge. Bridge at a cent a point or a few hands of poker with the lads like the rest of us, I suppose."

"Any expensive hobbies?"

"None that Bill and Abigail aren't ready to finance," Jem replied somewhat drily. "I grant you Tick's a logical suspect from the angle of opportunity, Sarah, but when it comes to motive I don't see how you can make a case."

"You'd be surprised what I can do. How about other women? He's awfully good-looking."

Jem remained unimpressed. "If you can show me how Tick Purbody would conceivably find the time to conduct a clandestine amour, I might be able to give some credence to that suggestion. The Billingsgates keep him in a constant ferment of wholesome activity as far as I can see. Furthermore, Tick simply isn't the type. If I ever caught him eyeing an attractive woman in a speculative manner, I'd naturally assume his thoughts were bent not on seduction but on the most expeditious way to drop an ice cube down her back. However, I suppose anything's possible. I'll nose around a bit, much as I detest prying into other people's affairs."

That was nonsense, of course. Jem was about as incurious as Rikki-Tikki-Tavi, and a regular Mrs. Bennett for gossip. Sarah kept her face straight.

"I'd appreciate that, Uncle Jem. Now tell me about Bunny

Whet and his son. How old is Erp, and why on earth do they call him that?"

"Erp's about seventeen and I haven't the remotest idea why they call him Erp. I don't know why Bunny's known as Bunny either, in case you were warming up to ask. Nor do I consider either question germane to the issue at hand."

Jem puffed out his cheeks and allowed them to deflate slowly. "Let me cogitate. As to profession, Bunny's a research chemist specializing in environmental problems. Again don't ask me to elaborate. All I know is that he's affiliated with M.I.T. in some arcane manner and putters around his father's bug juice factory in his spare time. As you doubtless know, the Whets manufacture organic insect-control powders and potions and do rather well out of the worms and weevils. Gerry's always rushing off to Nairobi for another boatload of that ill-smelling weed they powder the beetles with. Not that it would matter much if they ran out; Gerry and Marcia both inherited enough to keep them in modest comfort."

Sarah knew all about the Whets' modest comfort; she'd visited both their Beacon Hill town house and their summer place at Seal Harbor. "So Bunny manages to eke out a living?"

"He gets by. Aside from what Gerry pays him, he has his salary from M.I.T. and a house in Milton that his grandparents left him. A good-sized trust fund came with it, but Gerry tells me Bunny's recently begun donating all the interest from that to some ecological project in which he's become involved."

13

"That sounds like rather a major involvement," Sarah observed. "Does he plan to involve himself further?"

Jeremy Kelling's pink little mouth drew up in a pucker. "He's been after Gerry to help him break the trust so he can get at the principal."

"Oh my! Is Gerry helping?"

"No, he thinks it would be unfair to Erp and his sisters. Gerry did give a substantial donation out of his own pocket to show Bunny he's not taking a wholly negative stand on the project, but evidently it was just a drop in the bucket compared to what Bunny hoped to raise. Elizabeth, Bunny's wife, is organizing a fund drive. You might like to help, Sarah."

"Not on your life, and don't you dare volunteer me. So what it amounts to is that you think Bunny may have tried a different way of raising money."

"Dash it," Jem sputtered, "this is turning into a singularly unpleasant conversation."

"You might bear in mind that your friend Bill isn't having too pleasant a time right now, either. I do most sincerely hope Bunny Whet hasn't let his enthusiasm get out of hand, but you know perfectly well these things have to come out if we're going to get anywhere."

Sarah didn't add that Bunny Whet would match Drusilla

Gaheris's description of the morris dancer as well as any and better than some. She didn't remind her uncle of certain Kellings who'd allowed their interest in good works to turn into something almost like fanaticism. Almost but never quite. Was that the case with Bunny? Would he rather sell the Billingsgates' family heirlooms than his own grandparents' house, for instance? Why not? His wife and children needed a place to live, but nobody really needed ten antique Rolls Royces.

Bunny's wife had been in Lorista's consort yesterday, playing the serpent. Sarah recalled Elizabeth clearly: one of those thinnish, tallish, intense women who oozed intellect even in a starched ruff and a steeple hat. Radcliffe, no doubt. She'd be sympathetic to Bunny's ecological urges, but probably not to the extent of mortgaging her children's future. Jem was right, this was not agreeable mealtime conversation. That didn't mean Sarah was going to change the subject.

"Does Erp share his father's interests?"

"In morris dancing? Certainly, or he wouldn't do it," Jem replied with some acerbity. "Sarah, you're not toying with the notion that Bunny Whet would rope his own son into helping him kill his friend's servant and steal his friend's cars on a matter of principle?"

"John Brown got his sons to help him raid Harper's Ferry on a matter of principle."

"John Brown was what some people today might call a terrorist and his sons didn't go to a rather strict boarding school. You might check with Erp's housemaster about the period during which the New Phantom was taken."

"Thank you, I expect I will. Now what about Young Dork?"

"Young Dork is a model of filial virture. He's kind to his parents and dutiful to his in-laws. He's taken over his grandfather's business, which was the manufacture of hoe handles, and managed it so expertly that Dork hoe handles have become a status symbol and are widely purchased even by upwardly mobile New Yorkers who have no hoes to put them on. He's generally assumed to have married that ghastly sister-in-law of Lionel's as an act of penance, although nobody knows what he'd have to be penitent about. Furthermore, he's remained faithful to Lorista and has even been heard to say he likes her."

"If you say so, Uncle Jem. Are he and Lionel particularly chummy, do you know?"

"Being married to sisters, they'd almost have to be, wouldn't they? Sarah, you ought to understand that all these chaps have known each other forever. They grew up together, went to school together, married the girls they learned to dance with when they were ten years old. If they're not actually related to each other, they're connected by marriage or simply by force of habit. I can't tell you whether Young Dork sees more of Lionel than he does of Buck Tolbathy or Joe Abbott. I know he does see a good deal of Melly and Tick because they all go to automobile rallies together. Young Dork's an expert driver and thoroughly familiar with the Billingsgates' cars. He'd be as well qualified as anybody to steal a couple. I cannot for the life of me imagine him doing so. Unless Tick put him up to it as a practical joke," Jem added reluctantly.

"Which of course is nonsense," Sarah retorted. "Young Dork would have to be feebleminded to involve himself in anything like that. Tell me about Buck and Chad Tolbathy," she added quickly because Jem was starting to make frog faces.

"Chadwick is not a Tolbathy but an Ogham. You may remember that Hester Tolbathy, Buck's mother, is connected to the Oghams, though I don't personally hold it against her. Chad used to dance with Tick's group, but he doesn't any more because he's moved to Schenectady. You must mean Salmon Tolbathy, Buck's brother."

"Perhaps I mean both of them. According to Tick, Sal had intended to dance yesterday but he sprained his ankle getting out of bed. Sal then called Chad, who flew in from

Schenectady by chartered plane and took his place. Does that sound plausible to you?"

"It has to, doesn't it, if Chad was there and Sal wasn't? Anybody can sprain an ankle. I sprained mine once reaching for an olive. That's why I take my martinis plain."

"You've led a hard life, Uncle Jem. Is there any way we can make sure Sal's sprain was authentic? Does he have a wife and family?"

"Yes, but they're not with him at the moment. Sal has just the one daughter. She's one of those whiz kids and has been given a chance to appear on some television series, flaunting her IQ to no good purpose that I can see. The filming's being done in California and since the girl's only fifteen and quite pretty, all things considered, they naturally wouldn't let her go alone. Sal's wife is with her and he's batching it for the duration at their house in Dover."

Jem wiped his lips in a somewhat perturbed manner. "This could be a bit of a sticker, Sarah. Sal and Tabitha have no live-in servant, to the best of my knowledge. Unless the sprain was bad enough to require medical treatment, which they usually aren't because there's not much you can do anyway, I don't know how you'd go about proving Sal was genuinely incapacitated."

"He works with his brother in the family's importing business, doesn't he?"

"Oh yes, ever since he left Harvard. And during his school holidays before that, I believe. Neither Sal nor Buck ever wanted to do anything else. They run the whole show nowadays. Tom hadn't been all that active for some time, and since Wouter died he's pretty much bowed out."

"Is Salmon having any money problems that you know of?" Sarah asked him. "Maintaining his wife and daughter in Hollywood must be costing him plenty, I should think."

"No doubt it would, if Sal were paying. The child's being given some ridiculous sum to toss her curls and flash her intellect. Anyway, Tabitha has something of her own and Sal and Buck inherited Wouter's share of the Tolbathy money."

"Is there any chance they've run the firm into hot water and don't dare let their father know?"

"To the best of my knowledge, they're still contributing quite successfully to the country's foreign trade imbalance," Jeremy Kelling replied testily. "I expect you could check on that issue through *Dun and Bradstreet* or somewhere, assuming you'd stoop to anything so sordid."

"I don't see where solving a murder is any more sordid than committing one, Uncle Jem. You say Chadwick's an Ogham, but he's still the Tolbathys' relative. He didn't have anything to do with their business before he moved, did he?"

"No, he's in electronics, on the managerial side, whatever that may mean. Chad was something fairly important here in Massachusetts, but his wife got something even more important in Schenectady, so they transferred. She's one of those high-powered career women. A trifle too high-powered for Chad, in my personal opinion. It's generally assumed she married him for his connections."

"She evidently didn't come with him to the revel," said Sarah. "At least I don't remember meeting her."

Jeremy shook his head. "No, Parthenia wouldn't have gone. She'd be off somewhere at a conference."

Assuming she wasn't waiting at the far end of Abigail Billingsgate's bee fields with a large closed van, Sarah thought. "Did Chad ever lend his electronic expertise to any of Wouter's free private enterprises?"

"I doubt whether Wouter would have asked. Wouter was fairly well up on that sort of thing himself. He used to hang around the Radio Shack and such places, checking out the latest gadgets. That electric eye door, for instance, can't you just go out and buy the doings?"

"Oh yes," said Sarah. "Lionel bought a kit somewhere and installed one for Aunt Appie. He says anybody could do it. Even you," she added somewhat doubtfully.

"Madam, you jest. Anyway, Wouter could surely have done it with Rufe's help. As for Chad, it's my understanding he's in no way involved with the widgets and thingumbobs in his business. And if you're thinking he'd be the type to mess around in wet cement for a chuckle, abandon the notion. Chad carries a Mark Cross attaché case with solid gold corners."

"But he goes morris dancing in a green leotard," Sarah protested. "He must let his hair down sometimes."

"There's a nuance here, Sarah, as you must realize. I shall be blunt. Chad Ogham is not my favorite person, nor my next favorite. He's a bore and a stuffed shirt. I should have no qualms about fingering him, if that's the proper terminology. Aside from the problem of opportunity, however, I can't believe Chad would have the motive, the brains, or the guts."

Jem drained the last of his chablis and set down the glass with a small thump. "Is that the lot?"

"Let's see," said Sarah. "We've already touched on the Abbots. They seem to be out of it because they had to leave early and show up at a wedding."

"Joe's niece," the oracle replied at once. "She's an orphan, so Joe was going to give her away and Monk was one of the ushers. Lilias planned to duck the ceremony and show up later at the reception in her kirtle."

"Oh. Bill didn't mention the details. That does seem to make Joe's and Monk's alibis fairly ironclad. We'll still have to check, I suppose. I should imagine, though, that we'll find the Abbots a complete waste of time, shouldn't you?"

"I never imagine, Sarah. I always stick to facts."

Since Jeremy was held in high regard by some of the relatives and in abhorrence by the rest as the most accomplished liar ever to somersault from Kelling loins, Sarah took this declaration for what it was worth.

"Yes, Uncle Jem. Just for the record, is there anything else I ought to know about the Abbots?"

"They see their dentist twice a year and eat high-fiber cereal for breakfast," her uncle replied nastily. "Joe teaches Shakespeare at some academy for brainy females, Lilias runs a hand weaving shop, and Monk's working on a degree in anthropology, God knows why. They appear to be healthy and contented with their lot, as well they might be considering that Joe has a thumping trust fund to fall back on and Lilias didn't exactly go to him empty-handed. This obviously means they're all guilty as sin. What does a man have to do to get a cup of coffee around here?"

14

"'**W**hom the Lord loveth, He chastiseth.' I keep remind-ing myself of that, Max, but I have to confess that lately I've been feeling somewhat excessively beloved."

Nehemiah Billingsgate managed a wry smile. "Sorry about that. I must be making you feel like Bildad the Shuhite."

Max Bittersohn protested that he didn't feel a bit like Bildad the Shuhite. "And you're saying every one of these crazy foul-ups has happened within the past month."

"Yes, it's been positively uncanny. We've jogged along so comfortably year after year, and now all of a sudden it's just one calamity after another. Equipment breaking down, tapes mysteriously erased, irreplaceable old phonograph records turning up scratched or broken, and nobody ever knows why. We've had our little troubles from time to time, naturally, but never a string of them like this."

Bill's hands were trembling, Max noticed. What a hell of a position for a man his age to be in!

"But what's truly appalling," Billingsgate went on, "is the attrition in our staff. People who've been with us for years and years, who've demonstrated their dedication to our stations over and over, who've struggled through floods and blizzards sometimes to keep us on the air, people I've considered my close friends, just putting on their coats and walking off the job without so much as a backward look. I can't understand it, Max. I truly cannot understand it."

"Any chance some union's trying to organize you the hard way?"

"I thought of that, of course, but there's no evidence it's happening and no reason why it should. Radio personnel don't get paid at the level of television anchormen, I freely admit, but we do pay better than most other stations in our category. We have a yearly profit-sharing program in which everybody benefits proportionately. We have an excellent pension plan, maximum health insurance at no cost to the employee, and we're the only chain in the communications industry that keeps every member of its staff supplied with home-gathered honey."

"Then I don't understand it either, Bill. Have you spoken to any of your remaining employees about what's happening?"

"They've spoken to me, that's the most incomprehensible part of all. We've had to do a good deal in the way of borrowing equipment and shifting personnel around from one station to another, you know, to fill in the gaps. Naturally I've had to explain what's happened. Always there's the same outcry: What on earth is the matter with so-and-so? How could he do such a thing? What's happened to company loyalty? The indignation and astonishment have been genuine, Max, I swear they have. And yet the last person to inveigh against the one who just left is as often as not the next to leave without warning."

"There's been no sign of threats or harassment?"

"Max, our people know and trust me. At least I've assumed they did. I've always been ready to discuss any problem relating either to their work or to their private lives; they know that, or ought to by now. Over the years, we've had plenty of frank interchanges and straightened out many a difficulty, with the Lord's help. Surely if some outsider were going around terrorizing the various staffs, at least one of them would have had the nerve to come and tell me. But they don't act frightened, any of them. They're quite matter-of-fact about what they're doing, according to the people who've seen them go. Like lemmings deciding, well, we've hung around here long enough. Let's march down to the sea and hurl ourselves in," Billingsgate concluded bitterly.

"How many have you lost so far?"

"Eleven, mostly announcers. That may not seem like many to you, but bear in mind that we have only ten stations in our little chain, and most of them run with a handful of personnel. Losing even one key member out of the whole chain would have been enough to throw us into a tizzy ordinarily. Having to cover eleven in a single month is almost more than we've been able to cope with. If one more person walks out on us, I honestly don't see how we're going to manage."

Max shrugged. "Then I guess what it boils down to is, who's trying to buy you out?"

"Nobody." Billingsgate was positive. "Why should anybody want us? We don't make any money, you know. The fees we get from our advertisers pay our operating expenses and leave some over for the profit-sharing bonuses I mentioned. Once those are paid, we're cleaned out and we start over. My personal involvement is purely a labor of love. I don't take a cent of the receipts and I pay my chief assistant out of my own pocket."

"Is that Tick or Ufford?"

Bill was surprised at the question. "Oh, Tick. Yes, Tick's been a great blessing. He's fully in sympathy with our efforts and quite content with his modest stipend. Of course he and Melly also get the rather substantial profits from our Apian Way mead and honey enterprise, which they richly deserve since they do most of the work. And they each have dividends coming in periodically from inherited trust funds, so they manage comfortably enough."

Maybe Bill knew his son-in-law better than Lionel Kelling did. Max didn't say anything.

Bill thrust his hands into the pockets of the tweed jacket he was wearing. "I know there's a fashion for takeovers just now, but we're such a puny target, Max. Anyway, takeovers aren't usually achieved by employees who sabotage the equipment and walk off their steady, well-paid, and not too terribly arduous jobs, are they? They say everybody has his price, but assuming that's true, which I find hard to swallow, the bribes would have to be far greater than the kind of profit anyone could possibly hope to make out of the stations. Don't think Tick and I haven't thrashed this out before. We're not quite the starry-eyed dreamers some people think we are."

Max nodded. "I know you're not, Bill. But damn it, there's got to be something. This may sound crazy, but have you any enemies? Is there anybody alive who hates your guts enough to want to ruin you?"

"How can I answer that? I could give you a fairly long list of people who think I'm either a crank or a fool or both, but as to actual hatred—a vicious urge to destroy what amounts to my life's work—Max, I don't know what to say. We have had a barrage of letters from Ironclad Rockbound, a fundamentalist preacher who finds our little ecumenical homilies dangerously thought-provoking. It's not idle hands so much as closed minds for which the devil finds work, in my opinion. I beg your pardon, Max. Here I am getting off on my hobbyhorse while you're wanting to know who's out to ruin me."

Nehemiah Billingsgate thought a moment, then shook his head. "Nobody is. I'm not that important. Unless a deranged listener has taken a dislike to me for some unlikely reason that I don't know about."

"I don't think I can buy that, Bill. If it's a listener, he or she knows far more about your domestic arrangements than seems credible. Okay, let's drop it for now. Maybe something will come to you. I wonder if they've found that tranquilizer gun yet."

Aside from a brief and unrewarding visit to the elder Tolbathys and Dorks, Max hadn't been able to accomplish much so far except to eat an excellent lunch of leftovers from the banquet. He was still in what Sarah had officially labeled the poking-around stage, hoping he'd find something useful and know it when he saw it, trying to avoid anything like a confrontation with the police.

Captain Grimpen had shown up in jodhpurs and boots today but without a horse, displaying yet again his keen grasp of the nonessentials. He'd been all set to organize a band of scuba divers to search the pond. Nehemiah Billingsgate had mildly pointed out that the pond was nowhere more than three feet deep and that what they usually employed to clean it out were a couple of long-handled rakes. Bill had then brought out the rakes and offered to teach Chief Grimpen how to use them, to the amusement of everybody except Grimpen.

So far, the rakers had come up with the remains of a toy submarine, a disgruntled mud turtle, several biggish rocks, and a good deal of sodden vegetable matter that Bill had claimed for the compost heap and Grimpen wouldn't let him have, suspecting some dark machination. When Abigail had come out with a hamper of sandwiches for the policemen and an invitation for Max to join herself, Drusilla Gaheris, and Bill in the dining room, he'd been glad to leave the cops in the copse and go back to the house with the others.

It hadn't been a lively meal. Bill had got another message of doom from one of his already stricken radio stations. Abigail was depressed at having had to cancel the Sunday School picnic and instead spend part of the morning on the phone to the undertakers, planning Rufus's funeral. All of them were increasingly worried about the still unheard-from Boadicea Kelling. Mrs. Gaheris had made a few commendable attempts at inconsequential table talk, then let her unanswered comments lie where they fell and finished her cold beef and salad in silence.

Being a houseguest in a situation like this must be a difficult position, but Mrs. Gaheris was doing her diplomatic best to cope. She'd invited Max to her bedroom so he could see for himself exactly how much of a view she had. She'd even put on a red cardigan and yellow head scarf, borrowed from Abigail since her own wardrobe seemed to be all in shades of brown, and impersonated the morris dancer.

Max had timed her, as she strode briskly across the lawn

and slipped into the copse, where her vivid garb did become invisible as soon as the dense green shrubbery closed in behind her. One minute and forty-seven seconds. An agile man unhampered by anything more than a few dags and slitters could no doubt have cut half a minute or more off the middle-aged widow's time.

Lunch over, Mrs. Gaheris had gone to help Abigail and Cook finish packing up the rest of the leftovers and take them to a soup kitchen in a mill town not far away from the affluent suburb. Max and Bill had wandered out to the terrace. Perhaps it was the empty pavilion and the trampled grass, unhappy reminders of yesterday's gaiety, that had prompted Bill to open up about the problem that was bothering him far more than the loss of his two cars, perhaps even more than the frightful death of his old retainer. It was near the pavilion that Abigail found the men.

"Max, you just got a phone call from Sarah. She'd like you to give her a ring if you can spare the time. I thought Sarah mentioned that Jem was with her, but my hearing's not what it used to be and I must have got it wrong. Jem's yachting with Harry Bellrope's crowd, isn't he?"

Without stopping to answer, Max dashed for the house and dialed his own number. "Hi, what's new?"

As they talked, he scribbled fast in the little black looseleaf notebook that was his indispensable vademecum. "Is that the lot?" he asked her at last.

"For the moment. He may think of something else along the way."

"What time will you be back?"

"Fiveish, I hope, depending on the traffic. What about you?"

"Hard to say. You've done better than I, so far."

Max would have liked to prolong the conversation, but Sarah had her guest to feed, and he had his own job to do. He'd better get back to Bill.

As it happened, Bill came looking for him. "Max, I heard some shouting just now."

"I'll bet the police have found the gun. Come on."

Sure enough, when they got to the pond, they found Grimpen, still natty in his shiny boots and bulging breeches, Myre living up to his name, and a couple of other policemen also muddied to the eyeballs, all clustered around a silt-covered object on the bank.

"Can you identify this, Mr. Billingsgate?" barked the chief.

"I might be able to if we rinsed the mud off," Bill told him.

"Myre!"

The man thus roughly addressed took the object by its smaller end and sloshed it around in the murky water, then presented it for Bill's inspection. He nodded.

"That must be the tranquilizer gun Wouter Tolbathy made."

"No snap judgments, please," ordered the chief. "Examine it closely, Mr. Billingsgate."

"Chief Grimpen," Bill replied none too gently. "I am not a frivolous-minded man and I do not make snap judgments. As it happens, I was not at the going-away party where the dart gun was introduced so I've never actually seen it before. I have no hesitation in making the identification, however, because I know such a gun existed and because I can't imagine who else than Wouter Tolbathy would have carved the stock in the shape of a crocodile and painted it chartreuse with magenta trimmings."

Grimpen wouldn't accept this without being filled in on the details. After he'd got them, which took some time, he said they were irrelevant, which no doubt they were. Finally he demanded with surprising relevance, "Who had the gun last?"

Bill didn't know. "I should suppose Wouter himself held on to it after the party, but he could have passed it on to somebody else later. It could have been stolen, for that matter. The party took place about five years ago, if my memory serves me. The gun could have changed hands several times since then, for all I know."

"Or it might have been lying right here at the bottom of this pond the whole time," Grimpen added with ill-concealed scorn. "Before we waste any more valuable time investigating a red herring, we must determine whether this allegedly homemade weapon is still capable of being fired, and specifically of firing the dart that was found, as I predicted, in your late servant's clothing."

Nobody asked when he'd made the prediction. Billingsgate glanced at Max, then nodded.

"Whatever you think best, Chief Grimpen. I can't authorize you to take the gun because it doesn't belong to me, but I suppose you're entitled to confiscate it as evidence."

"Possible evidence," Grimpen amended. "Come along, men, there's nothing more to be learned here. This gun must be rushed to the state ballistics laboratory *instanter.*"

"Where do we put the rakes, Mr. Billingsgate?" asked Sergeant Myre.

"Leave them," ordered Grimpen. "You're a police officer, Myre, not a hired man."

Unaware that he'd just uttered the words setting off a chain of events that would by the end of the present calendar year place Sergeant Myre at the head of the local police force and himself on the bottom rung of the ladder in his uncle's cough drop factory, Chief Grimpen strode manfully from the copse, followed by his oozy minions. Max and his employer exchanged shrugs.

"What now?" asked Bill.

"I know the police have been all over the grounds this morning," Max replied, "but if you don't mind, I'd like to look around myself. Sarah raised an interesting question last night. Since nobody's yet found any evidence that the Silver Ghost was either driven away or taken in a van, she suggested that might be because the car wasn't taken far enough to notice. She wondered whether you or one of your neighbors might have a disused air raid shelter or something of that sort. Any chance?"

"Good heavens, Max, that's one possibility that never crossed my mind. Let me think. We have none here, certainly. Our neighbor Eric Hohnser built one years ago when it was rather the going thing to do. The shelter was a sort of underground tank, as I remember it, with something like a submarine's conning tower on top. There was a heavy steel door that worked on some kind of lever, with a long ladder leading down inside. The whole thing reminded me ludicrously of a gigantic in-the-ground garbage pail. I went down just once and came straight up again. It was a ghastly feeling, like being buried alive. Hohnser's quite embarrassed about the shelter nowadays, I understand. He's covered over the opening and planted Peace roses on top, which was surely the more sensible thing to do."

"How are the roses doing?"

"Beautifully, I'm sure. Hohnser always has magnificent roses. We can drop over and take a look if it will set your mind at rest. I shouldn't go poking around much, though. Hohnser takes his mulch very seriously, and I'm not his favorite person anyway."

"It wouldn't take more than a glance to see whether the ground's been disturbed recently."

"But naturally the ground would have been disturbed. Everybody always forks up and fertilizes his flower beds in the spring," said Bill with the naive confidence of the wealthy landowner who has somebody else to do it for him. "But that porthole wasn't much more than four feet across, as I recall, and it was a straight drop of about twenty feet to the bottom of the tank."

"Oh well, it was just a thought," said Max. "Can you think of a hiding place where the car wouldn't have to be dismantled and dropped down piece by piece?"

"Not offhand. But if you want to look over the grounds, let's go in the honeybug. Sometimes I get ideas while I'm driving."

That seemed as good an idea as any. Max walked with Bill down to the gardener's shed and climbed aboard the screened-in electric cart. He'd never ridden in one of these things before. It reminded him of the Dodgems at Revere Beach amusement park when he was a kid. How soon would Davy be ready to ride the Dodgems?

15

As they turned off the main drive into the bee fields, Max said, "Tell me some more about Ufford, Bill. How long have you known him?"

"Versey? Dear me, it must be upward of thirty years by now. Not precisely a boyhood friendship, but certainly a long-standing acquaintance. Why, Max? Surely you don't suspect poor Versey?"

"I'm curious about him. You may recall that he accosted my wife up on the hill, not far from the car shed. You might also remember he was wearing bright green hose with that otherwise authentic costume, although the ones in the Arnolfini portrait are either black or some very dark color. I checked last night in a book I have at home. The exact shade was hard to make out from the reproduction, but they sure as hell weren't emerald green."

"Is that important?"

"It might be, if under that loose surcoat he happened to be wearing a red doublet and had a yellow hood slung down his back."

"Are you suggesting Vercingetorix Ufford was Drusilla's wandering morris dancer?"

"Go ahead, make me a liar."

Bill sighed and shook his head. "Tick did say something about Versey's being annoyed because they'd had to change the order of the dances, but surely—"

"Tick said the sets that required fewer dancers were originally scheduled to come first in the program. That could mean somebody in a dancer's costume strolling around the grounds by himself would be less apt to attract attention, mightn't it?"

"Unless one were to count the men remaining on the dancing green, find them all present, and wonder where the odd one came from," Bill replied cautiously. "Then there's the Betty, who doesn't always appear. Betty's a sort of clown, you know, who doesn't dance with the rest but cavorts around the edges in that absurd farthingale. Not that I'm accusing young Erp, you understand."

"Erp seems to be clear," Max assured his employer. "I checked him out with the Dorks and the Tolbathys this morning. He's hoping to start a morris dance group of his own at school, and stayed right there every minute of the time to pick up pointers. When he wasn't doing the Betty, he filled in for one or another of the men who wanted a break."

Hester Tolbathy had commented spontaneously on Erp's keenness, with a footnote to the effect that she wished her own grandsons would show a similar interest. So far, Monk Abbott was the only other member of the third generation who showed any inclination to follow in his father's jangly footsteps. Because their Buck was dancing, she and Tom had watched most of the sets and claimed not to have noticed anything untoward.

The Dorks, with both a son and a daughter-in-law performing, had also stayed close to the dancing green. Dorothy had particularly mentioned how easily Erp had been able to drop his Betty costume, just a rudely contrived hoopskirt framework with a wide swatch of red material draped over it, and leap in doublet, hose, and hood into the set with the rest. It turned out by a happy coincidence that she herself had devised the rig.

Both Dorks and Tolbathys had been of the opinion that all dancers had remained with the group whether they were dancing or not, except for quick trips to the pavilion for refueling. The only ones who'd left early were the Abbotts, as expected. They in fact had not gone as soon as they ought to have. They'd wound up running for their car in their costumes with loud outcries and lamentations. Lilias had had to abandon her plan of staying for the banquet and drive the car so that her husband and son could change their clothes en route. Lilias in her kirtle would surely have outshone the bride, but she'd appeared when last seen to be bearing up bravely under that expectation.

So that solved the question of what the Abbotts had done with their costumes and why Vercingetorix Ufford's bright green hose were now interesting Max Bittersohn. Nehemiah Billingsgate wasn't being particularly helpful as yet.

"I don't quite know what to tell you, Max. I suppose when you come down to it, I don't know Versey all that well, myself."

"After thirty years?"

"It does sound absurd, I know. But I expect you yourself have acquaintances of long standing whom you don't exactly count as friends. The sad fact is that Versey isn't the sort one warms up to."

"He's hard to get along with?"

"I shouldn't call him contumacious. It's more that gently condescending manner of his that gets under one's skin. Versey does know a great deal, but he tends to take it for granted nobody else knows anything at all. You must admit it's hard to get close to someone who's giving the impression he thinks you're a nitwit. I don't suppose he really thinks anything of the sort, poor fellow, but there it is. Am I being uncharitable, Max?"

"Not by me, Bill. I never got to talk with him yesterday, but I don't feel all that charitable toward him, myself. Sarah had some trouble with him, as she mentioned last night."

"Yes, I'm afraid that's another of Versey's problems. He fancies himself a ladies' man, and that can become tiresome. We don't have him out as often as we might for that very reason. However, the Renaissance Revel is one event from which we couldn't possibly exclude him, considering how much he's done to help us get started and keep them going."

"Like what, for instance?"

"Planning the music and the menus, advising on costumes, coaching the morris dancers, helping Lorista assemble and equip her consort. How many people, for instance, would have known just where to put their hands on a cittern or a pandora?"

"I thought Pandora was a girl who opened the wrong box," said Max.

"So did I," Bill replied, "but thanks to Versey, I've learned it can have other meanings. That peculiar-looking guitar Tick's niece Alison played yesterday for the minstrelsy was a pandora. Or bandore, if you prefer."

Max had no particular choice in the matter. "Alison was the pretty one in the Burne-Jones getup who looked as if she'd just ridden her palfrey in from Camelot?"

"Yes, Alison is quite lovely, we think. She's another who has little use for Versey, you can imagine why."

"How does a guy like him manage to teach? By staying away from coed schools?"

"Oh, Versey hasn't taught much for years. He's a visiting lecturer, which is to say he spends a little time at one place or another delivering a series of talks on Renaissance dancing, which is really his specialty; but he never stays anywhere long, so I suppose he manages to control himself for the duration."

"On the other hand, that may be why he never stays," said Max. "How's he fixed for money?"

"Adequately, as far as I know. There's some family money, I believe, as well as whatever Versey gets for his writing and lecturing. The pittance we pay him would hardly count, but he does enjoy the work, and it apparently gives him some kudos in academic circles."

"So he's got enough to live on, anyway?"

"Oh yes, though not lavishly." Bill shook his head. "I shouldn't say that; I have no idea how he lives when he's abroad. But he lives rather frugally here. He has an apartment in somebody's attic, from the way he describes it. He doesn't even run a car. That's a nuisance for us because it means he's always having to be fetched and carried, but I don't suppose he'd get enough use out of one to justify the cost of keeping it on the road. Versey does seem to spend a fair amount on recordings and sound equipment, from what he tells me, but I suppose he can write all that off as business expenses. His only other extravagance that I know of is clothes. Versey's a dapper fellow. But he buys his things in Italy where they may not cost so much."

"Why Italy in particular?"

"Because that's where he spends at least half his time. Versey has a place in Venice. I can't tell you what it's like because I've never seen it. I do have the address, should you need that for any reason. Melly claims he keeps a mistress there who cleans the house and cooks the fettucine, and carries on an amorous dalliance with a fat gondolier when Versey isn't around. Melly and Tick are rather given to rude conjecture on the subject of Versey's love life, I'm ashamed to say."

Bill didn't look ashamed, he looked mildly amused for the first time since he'd learned about Rufus. Max waited until the smile began to fade before he remarked, "This is quite a spread you've got here. I never did get to see much of the grounds yesterday. What are all those big pink things over in the distance?"

"Crab apple trees in full bloom. There aren't too many garden flowers this time of year, so we rely a good deal on flowering trees and shrubs to keep our bees busy. We plant them far away from the house because we don't want the bees bothering people. That's a point we really have to consider, because if one happened to swat at a bee and got stung, the whole swarm might attack."

"Thanks for telling me," said Max, glancing around to make sure the screens over the cab were securely in place. "What's that building over there?"

The low brick structure was so well camouflaged by spreading evergreens that someone with less acute vision might not have noticed it at all. Bill obliged by steering the electric cart toward it, but said there wasn't anything to see, really.

"That's what we call the honey shed, where we take the honey from the hives to be extracted and bottled. We also use it to store a lot of the paraphernalia. There's so much stuff one needs: bee veils, smokers, frames for the combs, crates of empty jars and bottles—Abigail could tell you better than I. The mead is brewed and aged in the cellars back at the house, and also shipped from there, so we try to keep all the extraneous clutter out here in the shed."

"Is the door locked?"

"I hope so. There's nothing inside of value except to ourselves, but we have that problem about the insurance, so we just make a rule to keep everything locked and then we don't forget."

"Would you mind showing me inside?"

"Not at all, though I'm afraid you won't find it very interesting." Bill stopped the cart so he could reach into his pocket. "Oh dear, I was afraid I'd left my keys at the house, and I have. It's been such a bewildering morning." He fished some more. "I don't have my wallet, either, or my pocket Testament. I suppose they're all on the dresser in our bedroom. Old age sneaking up on me, Max. I spend half my time lately wondering where I've put things. We can turn right here and go straight back to the house, if you can spare an extra few minutes."

"My time is your time."

As they made the turn, Max kept his eyes on the shed, but its camouflage was so good that before they'd gone fifty yards down the other path, it was completely invisible. Bill didn't show any interest, but concentrated on steering the cart toward a small side door of the big house that looked as if it ought to admit them to the dungeon.

Instead, they climbed a few stairs, passed through a short hallway, and came upon a small sitting room where Abigail and Drusilla were sitting in front of an open fire, each with a piece of needlework in her lap. Except for their tweed skirts and knitted cardigans, they might have been a pair of mediaeval ladies whiling away the time until their absent lords wended their respective ways home from the geste.

"Well, you two have made yourselves cozy," Bill remarked, stepping nimbly between a hassock and a sewing basket to give his wife a peck on the cheek. "I expect a spot of cozy is what you both need just now. No, Drusilla, don't move. Max and I are merely passing through. Or rather, I'm passing. Why don't you stay here and enjoy the fire, Max, while I run upstairs? I shan't be two minutes."

"My pleasure." Max took the other end of the sofa on which Drusilla Gaheris was sitting and stretched his legs toward the fender. "It's nippy out there. Quite a change from yesterday."

"What have you been doing?" Abigail asked him.

"Riding around in your electric cart, mostly."

Max didn't feel like bringing up the unpleasant subject of the tranquilizer gun just now. He'd let Bill tell them later on. "Those carts are fun, aren't they? I wouldn't mind getting one for Sarah, but I suspect they're not much good on rough ground. Our land is mostly up and down."

"Do you have a big place, Mr. Bittersohn?" asked Mrs. Gaheris.

"Thirty acres, now that we've sold off the far corner. Not much compared to this."

"Bill's grandfather laid out an eighteen-hole golf course on this property, did you know that, Drusilla?" said Abigail. "But it was a dreadful nuisance to keep up, and Bill never cared much for the game anyway. After his father died, we got interested in beekeeping, or rather I did and Bill, bless his heart, went along with me. As the swarms multiplied, we kept plowing up hole after hole and planting more clover and so forth, until we'd eliminated the entire course. We've rather got our eyes on the tennis court now, but Melly and Tick like to play and so do the grandchildren. Anyway, there's not enough space to do much with, so I expect we'll leave it alone. Did you play much tennis while you were abroad? Drusilla used to be our school champion," she explained to Max.

"That was a great many years ago." Mrs. Gaheris snipped off her thread and reached into her workbox for a skein of a different color. "I can't remember when I played last, to be honest with you. Diplomatic tennis isn't much fun, you know. One has to be so careful not to outplay the wrong opponent. My husband and I did try mountain climbing in an unambitious sort of way when we first went to Switzerland; but as time went on we had to settle for short walks and long rides."

"Up and down the Alps?" Abigail cried to cover the moment's embarrassment they must all have felt at being reminded of Mrs. Gaheris's recent widowhood. "I should call that quite ambitious, myself."

"Not really. It's rather fun once one gets used to driving with one's heart in one's mouth."

"And it's surely given you excellent training for driving in Massachusetts. We do that all the time here. We can also arrange some nonthreatening tennis if you like, Drusilla."

"Don't bother. I've decided to take up the recorder instead. They're easy to carry about and nobody ever asks one to play."

"Ah, but we shall, my dear. We adore recorder music. Now that you're going to settle here, you ought to join Lorista's consort."

"Not I. I'll never be good enough. Besides, I don't know the first thing about Renaissance music."

"Get Ufford to teach you," Max suggested.

"But I don't know Professor Ufford, either." Mrs. Gaheris got her needle threaded to her satisfaction and took up her work again. "Not well enough to ask a favor, anyway."

"Nonsense," said Abigail. "Versey would love to have you as a pupil."

"Perhaps, if I were forty years younger and as attractive as Mrs. Bittersohn. But even then I'm afraid we'd never have clicked. I was a brunette and Versey prefers blondes." She took a neat stitch. "Or so Melisande claims, and I gather from what she said last night that Melly has reason to know. She did look absolutely gorgeous yesterday, Abby."

Mrs. Gaheris took another stitch. "By the way, Mr. Bittersohn, what color is your wife's hair? She had it all covered up and I never did get to see."

"It's brown." For some reason, Max found the question annoying. He was relieved when Bill stuck his head in at the door.

"Can I tear you away, Max?"

"Wouldn't you both like a cup of tea to warm you up before you go?" Abigail offered.

"Thanks," said Max, "but I'd like to do as much as possible outdoors before it rains, if that's what it's getting ready to do."

The day that had started out so fair was now overcast. He hoped Sarah wouldn't get caught in a storm on the way back from Scituate. Driving the South Shore highways was lousy at the best of times.

The fields must be positively cobwebbed with paths. Bill took yet a different route back to the shed Max wanted to see.

"This one doesn't get used a great deal," he remarked when they'd gone a fair distance into the fields. "It has a tricky dip that Abigail doesn't like out near the honey shed. I don't know why we've never got around to having it filled in. Always too many other things to be done first, I suppose. Max, is this motor making a lot more noise than when we started out? I hope it's not going to act up on us."

"That's not the cart, Bill." The electric motor was still purring along at about the decibel level of a well-stroked cat. "The noise is coming from up ahead somewhere. Would anyone be using a chain saw?"

"They'd better not be on our side of the road."

Bill put on an angry burst of speed. Max hoped he'd simmer down before they got to that tricky dip in the path. The noise grew louder, a throbbing buzz more like half a dozen distant saws than one. But not quite. Abruptly, the driver stopped the cart to listen.

"That's bees, Max. But why should they be swarming

now? And why here? We'll have to check this out. Stay in the cart and don't open the screen, whatever you do."

Bill eased the cart forward. The buzzing grew louder, more insistent. Max didn't like it a bit. When he caught sight of the bees, he turned sick.

They were blocking the path at the bottom of the dip, a great pulsing clot of brown workers, tumbling over each other to get at what lay beneath them. The shape of the mass was horribly suggestive, but all the men in the cart could see for the covering bees was one well-polished black loafer shoe with a chic little gold-beaded tassel at the toe.

"Great God in heaven," whispered Nehemiah Billingsgate. "How did this happen?"

"Who is it?" Max demanded. "Do you know?"

"I'm afraid so."

Swerving recklessly around the dreadful obstacle in their path, Bill opened the motor as wide as possible and sped toward the honey shed. "We've got to have smokers and bee veils; otherwise they'll be after us, too. Thank God we went back for the key."

He ran the cart up to the shed, unlocked the front door, and hustled Max inside. "Here, put these on quickly."

"These" were a tan coverall with velcro fastenings at neck, sleeves, and ankles, a wide-brimmed hat with a netting that hung to the shoulders, and heavy gauntlet gloves. A ludicrous outfit, but Max was glad to wear it. Bill donned its mate, got four smokers working, handed two to Max, and took the others himself. "Just squeeze the bellows gently and point the nozzle at the bees. Smoke stupefies them. Come on."

"Is there any chance he may still be alive?" Max asked as the cart bucketed them back down the path.

"I don't dare hope so, but we must do what we can. Max, I cannot understand what went wrong. Abigail's been keeping bees for thirty-seven years and we've never had any trouble before. Our bees are quite amiable as bees go, and I should have thought they'd be heading back to the hives now that it's turned so dark and cold. Dear Lord, what a thing to happen today, on top of everything else. Have your smokers ready. Normally we'd just use one, but this—"

Bill stopped the cart, threw open the screened door, and ran toward the hideous buzzing, Max at his heels.

It seemed to take an incredibly long time. The two men were enveloped in smoke, choking, gasping, clawing with their clumsy gloves at the stupefied bees, desperate to get at their victim in case there might yet be a spark to fan.

There wasn't. Vercingetorix Ufford was dead as a doornail.

16

"'Lord, into Thy hands we commend the soul of this Thy servant.' Poor Versey, I thought it must be he. Those fancy tassels on the shoes, you know. Max, we must get out of here before those bees wake up."

"What will they do?"

"Die, poor things, if they've lost their stingers. But there must be a good many that weren't able to get at him. Can you take his head?"

Max knew he ought to insist the body be left where it lay until the death could be investigated. He also knew he wasn't going to hang around here once the smoke cleared away. He bent over the body, trying not to look at the swollen mass that had been a face. "Okay, Bill. Shall we slide him on the cart?"

"Yes, on the back." A boxlike arrangement had been fitted to the vehicle as a means of carrying equipment to and from the bee fields. They laid the body across the top as best they could, and Max steadied while Bill drove. That meant having to keep the screen open, and Max was extremely relieved when they reached the shed without hearing that buzz again.

"We'd better make sure we don't carry any bees inside with us, or we'll be in trouble again," Bill fussed. "Here, Max, let me brush you off. Then you'd better fetch another smoker just in case. Good Lord, poor Versey's clothes are full of them. I'm afraid we'll have to strip him and leave the things outside. Ghastly!"

It was all that and then some. Ufford had been wearing a high-necked black cashmere pullover and matching slacks. The garments were of beautiful quality and ought to have been soft to the touch, but felt stiff and clung unpleasantly to their gauntlets.

"Sticky," said Max. "Had he been robbing the honeycombs?"

"I can't imagine why he should. There wouldn't be enough to bother with at this time of year. Anyway, Abigail gave him honey a few weeks ago, and he knew he could always have more for the asking. Ugh, I hope I never see anything like this again."

The bees had got through the sweater and up Ufford's pant legs. They were even inside his fine black lisle socks. A few were still active in there where the smoke hadn't got at them.

"One might think they'd leave him alone now that he's dead," Billingsgate half sobbed.

"They might be after something," said Max. "See those shiny patches on his skin? It looks to me as if he might have been doused with a sweet liquid that's soaked through the clothes and got on his body. Have you any idea what it would be?"

"Why, yes, I expect I do. Since we take away most of the honey that would be their natural winter food, we give them supplemental feeding of a sugar and water solution. That was how we helped to keep the bees out here in the back fields yesterday, as a matter of fact. We set a number of the collecting trays around and poured syrup into them. With netting over the tops, of course, so the bees could get at it without drowning themselves."

"What happened to the trays?"

"I expect they must be where we left them. Rufus had been delegated to bring them in after dark, when the bees had gone back to the hives for the night." Bill grimaced. "I don't suppose anybody gave them a thought. I'm sure I didn't. Look, Max, you must be right about the syrup. The bees are going at Versey's clothes."

As they'd taken the garments off, they'd thrown them aside, out of the smoke they were still using to repel any further assault on the naked, horridly disfigured body. Now some of the bees they'd chased off Ufford and themselves were recovering and beginning to crawl over the slacks and sweater, even the underwear. Bill stood up and watched them, sighing.

"In a way, Max, I'm relieved. At least it shows they weren't just being vindictive. I suppose they went after the sweetness and Versey panicked. He began swatting at them, and they panicked, too. It does take considerable strength of mind to stand still when they start coming at you, I have to admit. Poor fellow."

He sighed again. "I suppose Grimpen will have to know about this. He'll want to pass it off as another accident, no doubt."

"Is there a chance he might be right, Bill?"

"Anything's possible, I suppose, but Versey'd been around here often enough over the years to know one doesn't go strolling through the bee fields without taking reasonable precautions. He was rather leery of the bees, in fact. I can't imagine what he was doing here at all, let alone how he got into the syrup. I suppose he might possibly have tripped and fallen on one of the trays, but they're shallow things, only about two feet square. It would have taken a bit of doing to soak both his trousers and his jersey."

"Speaking of trousers, where did he get these clothes? Did he change into his costume here?"

"No, I'm quite sure he didn't. The Whets picked him up and brought him, I know, and it was my understanding they were going to take him back. They were all in costume when they came; I distinctly remember what an effective picture they made as they walked across the drawbridge to the pavilion."

Max wondered for a second whether Bill was starting to pray again, but the older man came out of his silence. "Why should he have changed? Nobody else did. As to what he was doing out here today, I cannot imagine. He can't have come about Rufe, I shouldn't think. We haven't told any-body. Unless Grimpen blabbed to the press."

"Have you had any reporters out here? Any phone calls, people wanting to know what happened?"

"No, just friends calling to thank us for yesterday, the usual thing."

"Then it hasn't hit the media. Grimpen must be doing some fancy footwork to keep it quiet. I wonder why. Unless he's afraid of looking like a fool in spite of his big talk. And you say Ufford didn't have a car. Is there a bus or anything he could have come here in?"

"Not conveniently, no. I'm afraid it's generally assumed in a place like this that everyone is able to provide his own transport. Versey could have taken a taxi, but it would have cost him a good deal. What he usually did if he needed to get somewhere was simply call and ask to be picked up. He was quite arrogant about cadging rides, if that's not too unkind a word. And you know, Max, I don't understand those clothes."

"What do you mean by that, Bill?"

"The—the ambience of them, as it were. If he'd wanted to see me on business, he'd have worn a business suit. If he'd come for an informal visit, he might conceivably have shown up in tweed knickerbockers and a Norfolk jacket. The country gentleman look, you know. Versey didn't mind being a trifle eccentric in his dress, but never inappropriately eccentric, if you follow me. As for this all-black getup, maybe I'm behind the times, but it strikes me as being out of place here. Too modern and sophisticated, I suppose is what I'm trying to say."

"Do you think they were somebody else's clothes?"

"Oh no, I don't think that. They look like clothes Versey might wear someplace where that sort of thing was being worn. Good quality, well-fitting, and somewhat on the spiffy side. Abigail could probably be more coherent on the subject than I. Oh dear, I do dread having to tell her about Versey."

"Was she fond of him?"

Bill had to think that one over. "She found him exasperating at times. We all did, I'm afraid. But we'd known him so long, and to have him killed by her own bees—Max, has it struck you there's a diabolical mind at work here?"

"I can't say it has, Bill. I'd call it more a practical mind, and damned little human feeling. The impression I get is that whoever's responsible for these killings doesn't care about anything but getting the job done with a minimum of risk and whatever weapon comes handiest. If you call a swarm of bees a weapon. I don't know how we're ever going to prove Ufford didn't mess himself up in the bee syrup and get stung to death by accident."

"Mightn't this be a case similar to Rufe's? Couldn't he have been shot with Wouter's dart gun and had the syrup poured over him afterwards?"

"If he was already dead, how would he have annoyed the bees into stinging him? And would they have raised those God-awful welts if they did?"

"I'm sure I don't know, Max," Bill replied humbly.

"Well, the medical examiner can straighten us out on that one. The biggest question in my mind right now is how Grimpen's men managed not to find him, if they searched the grounds as thoroughly as he claims they did. Unless they heard the bees buzzing and chickened out."

"People do," said Bill. "I might have, myself, if we'd come upon an infuriated swarm without any protection. But Grimpen could at least have gone up to the house and told us what was happening. We might even have saved Versey, if we'd got to him in time. How long do you think he's been dead, Max?"

"In a situation like this, I don't even want to guess. The autopsy will show, though you may have to throw some more weight to get Grimpen to order one."

"I shall throw whatever is necessary, you may rest assured of that. Let's get the poor chap covered up. There ought to be some clean sheets around here somewhere. I wonder where Melly keeps them."

While Bill puttered around, opening drawers and muttering to himself, Max exercised the curiosity that had sent them back for the keys in the first place. During their earlier approach he'd caught sight of what looked like a concrete ramp behind the junipers, and he saw no opening here to which it might have led. The back of the room he was in appeared to be filled solid with crates of honey jars, but reason told him there must be more than this. He edged around behind the crates, and found another inside door.

Stuck to the door with sticky tape was a sign printed with a heavy marking pen on Apian Way Bee Farm stationary. It read, THIS ROOM HAS BEEN STERILIZED. KEEP OUT UNTIL NEEDED.

The door, Max noticed, was steel-faced and fitted tightly into its jam. A piece of heavy weather stripping had been fastened across the bottom. For extra protection against any germs that might be strolling by, he assumed. Casting prophylaxis to the winds, Max turned the white porcelain knob and pushed. It was as he'd hoped.

"Got a minute, Bill?" he called.

"Eh? What is it, Max?"

"I've found your cars."

"In the honey room? Great Scott, the one place we never thought to look because it was so ridiculously obvious."

He hurried in. "Yes, there they are, right beside the centrifuges. The Phantom and the Ghost. There's some balm in Gilead, at any rate."

There was more than Max had expected. From the open back seat of the ancient Silver Ghost poked up a not quite tidy gray head surmounted by an out-of-date velvet toque.

"Well, Bill. I've been wondering when you were going to show up."

"Bodie! What on earth are you doing here?"

"Trying to get my feet untied," was her matter-of-fact reply. "My hands gave me a good deal of trouble and the circulation doesn't yet seem to be fully restored. Perhaps you or—who is that man? Do I know you, sir?"

"I'm Max Bittersohn. You were calling me Max yesterday."

"Was I? How unlike me. What time does the rally start, Bill? I suppose the reason that silly fellow tied me up was that he wanted to drive instead of me. Stupid and discourteous, and I'll thank you to tell him so."

"Tell whom, Bodie? Who tied you up?"

"Bill, whatever are you talking about? You make no sense whatsoever. You know, I still feel a trifle woozy. It must have been the mead."

"It's more than that," Max told her. "I think you've been drugged. Your eyeballs look funny."

"So will yours when you're as old as I am. Nonsense, young man, I never touch any of that muck. Not even aspirin. A brisk four-mile walk every day, a balanced diet, and a large glass of water before breakfast to promote regularity, that's all anybody needs. Have you untied me? I can't feel anything in my feet."

"Rub her ankles, will you, Bill?" said Max. "We'd better get her back to the house as fast as we can and get a doctor to check her out."

"If by 'her' you mean me, why don't you address me directly?" snapped Boadicea Kelling. "I don't want a doctor. A cup of hot tea and a wash, and I'll be fine."

She probably would, the old termagant. Nevertheless, Max wanted her examined.

"Listen to me, Boadicea. Bill's going to drive you back to the house in the electric cart. He'll telephone the state police and ask them to send somebody out here as fast as he can. There are things to be checked over that Chief Grimpen probably wouldn't have the equipment for, even if he had brains enough to use it. Bill will also ask a doctor to examine you. If there's nobody available, you'll have to be taken to the nearest hospital as quickly as possible."

"I shall allow no such liberty!"

"Oh yes, you will," Max told her. "You've been the victim of an assault, and your condition has to go on the record."

If by any chance Boadicea Kelling had not been the victim of an assault, that ought to go on the record, too, even if she was Sarah's aunt. Or whatever. Sarah wouldn't take it amiss;

she hadn't gone into that spate of genealogy on the phone just to make conversation.

Fortunately there was the expected side door to the ramp, so Bill was able to bring his cart around instead of having to steer Boadicea past that sheet-covered form in the front room. Between them, he and Bill supported her out to the cart and got her aboard.

"Are you coming with us, Max?" asked Bill.

He and Boadicea were already taking up the cart's only two seats, but Max forbore to point that fact out. "No, I'd better stay here in case somebody happens along. You can manage all right, can't you?"

Boadicea did her best to freeze him with a look, though the result was not one of her better efforts. "Drive on, Wilberforce," she ordered.

She wasn't likely to fall out of the screened cart unless she got funny with the door handle; still, Max didn't envy Bill the ride back to the house. He strolled around to the front of the shed and stood looking up the path at the small heap of clothing they'd taken off the dead man. Bees were still crawling over the lush fabrics, brown againt dull black, brown against glossy. Ufford had even been wearing black silk underwear, the old sybarite. Bill had been right about that outfit. It might be just the ticket for a coke-snorting party on the Lido or for lounging around one's sumptuously decadent apartment sipping absinthe and reading *Les Fleurs du Mal*, but it sure as hell didn't fit into the Billingsgate ambience.

What it suggested to Max was that Versey had emerged from his Giovanni Arnolfini period and decided to take a whack at being Raffles the Gentleman Burglar. Raffles would have known black would make him stick out like a sore thumb in the clover fields, but perhaps Ufford hadn't thought of that. Or perhaps he'd come in the night and planned to be gone by daybreak. If so, what had kept him? Would the bees have attacked in the dark? And would they have stayed with their victim all this time? Or had new ones kept coming? Those flowering trees were a good deal closer

:o the honey shed than they were to the house. Max went back inside and shut the door against that nerve-wracking buzz.

There was no dearth of sugar here, certainly. Two fifty-pound sacks were lying under the bench he and Bill had preempted for a mortuary slab. A gap between them suggested that there'd been other sacks, used up during the winter feeding. The stainless steel sink on the wall beside the bench must be where they mixed the sugar and water.

Did they keep any syrup already mixed? Yes, a plastic bucket was standing under the sink. Its lid was ajar; Max could see the receptacle was only half full. Grainy dribbles down the outside struck an incongruous note in this impeccably maintained place. Somebody'd been in a hurry.

Not much would have been needed to douse a man. Anybody who'd ever dumped a cup of hot coffee into his lap would have known how far even a small amount of liquid could go toward achieving total saturation. Half a pailful would have been more than plenty.

If Ufford had got his lethal baptism inside the honey shed, though, there ought to be more of a mess around than these few dribbles. Max got down on hands and knees and crawled around the concrete floor, feeling for a sticky patch and not finding any. Then, most reluctantly, he uncovered the corpse's head and touched the hair. That pageboy coiffure he'd supposed yesterday to be a wig had, after all, been Ufford's own hair. Every strand of it was stiff and sticky.

So the syrup had probably come from this bucket, but had been poured over Ufford somewhere else. That was not to say Ufford hadn't been inside the shed. Boadicea Kelling had alluded to a silly fellow who'd tied her up; no doubt she'd have thought the black turtleneck jersey and the Prince Valiant hairdo stagy and affected. That would have had to be before Ufford got into the syrup, though. Surely if he'd been anywhere near this big, deep sink at the time, he'd have stuck his head under the faucet and tried to wash himself clean. Unless whoever soaked him had marched him at gunpoint out to where the bees could get at him.

That would seem to have been an unnecessarily complicated and melodramatic procedure for a practical-minded killer to go through. Max decided that in the unlikely event he himself had decided to commit such an inhuman act, he'd have filled one of those quart-size honey jars with syrup, screwed the lid down tight so the bees wouldn't get a premature whiff, and followed Ufford out into the pathway. When he was close enough to be sure of his aim, he'd have opened the jar and thrown the syrup over his victim, being darned careful not to spill even a drop on himself. Then he'd have heaved the jar as far as he could, and run like hell.

A paper cup dispenser was clamped to the wall beside the sink. One of those cups would have made a dipper adequate to fill a jar from the bucket without too much mess. A few of them lay in the trash container below, along with some crumpled-up paper towels. It was too much to hope there'd be a cup that was sticky on the inside and had a nice set of fingerprints on the outside, but Grimpen might as well have the fun of hunting for it, if the chief ever got through having the dart gun authenticated. He'd let Grimpen hunt for that hypothetical container in the field, too.

The chief ought to be sore when he found out Ufford's body had been moved, but he probably wouldn't have sense enough to know it should have been left where it fell. Anyway, he'd have hated squashing those dashing jodphurs under a bee suit. Why the hell did Grimpen have to go tootling off like that, anyway? He might at least have left Myre. One thing Max hated about jobs like this was the waiting around for people to show up. Especially when they were people he didn't like having to work with in the first place.

17

At least Max didn't have to wait long for Bill to get back. He was wandering around the back room, looking over the two Rolls Royces and shaking his head, when the electric cart poked its nose up the ramp.

"I didn't feel like passing those clothes of Versey's, so I came around this way," Bill remarked. "Do you suppose we ought to go and bring them in? I got hold of Sergeant Myre and he says he'll try to get some of the men moving as fast as he can. They've been having an educational tour of the police laboratory. From his tone, I don't think Myre enjoyed it much."

"Grimpen ought to be stuffed and mounted," Max grunted. "We'd better leave the clothes for him to deal with if he ever gets around it. Technically we could be in trouble already for having stripped and moved the body. Did you get hold of a doctor?"

"Yes, I had better luck there. Our friend Maude Addams has a practice downtown and she's going to pop over right away. She was having office hours, but the two doctors she's in with are going to cover for her."

"Great. Did Boadicea say anything that made sense on your way to the house?"

"Only that she was hungry and thirsty and wanted a bath, which didn't surprise me. Abigail and Drusilla are attending to her creature comforts now. The rest of Bodie's talk was

147

mostly about that imaginary car rally. She's driven with us a few times, so I suppose she got the notion from waking up in the Silver Ghost. Reasonable enough, as delusions go. I didn't tell them about Versey, Max. I just couldn't, with Bodie in such a state. They were upset enough as it was. To think of her being right here in the shed all that time, and we never thought to look! I blame myself bitterly."

"Why yourself more than anybody else?" Max pointed out. "This is Abigail's end of the business, why didn't she think of it? Why didn't your daughter, when she and Sarah were riding around here in the cart yesterday? Why didn't Tick? Why didn't the helicopter pilot? They must have seen the shed from the air."

"I suppose they each thought somebody else had searched it," sighed Bill. "Thank you, Max. You have a good heart. I'll save the sackcloth and ashes for when there's nothing more urgent to do. Getting back to what Bodie might have said, I didn't try to question her. I thought it was probably wiser to wait until after Maude has had a chance to look her over. Was I wrong?"

"No, you were being sensible. You could have sent her off the deep end, the shape she's in. Or she might have told you something that sounded rational enough but sent us off on a false trail. What are these things for?" Max asked, mostly to change the subject.

He was talking about a couple of stainless steel machines that sat along the wall behind the New Phantom.

"They're used to extract the honey from the combs," Bill explained. "The honey then either gets bottled as it is or taken in buckets down to the house for the meading."

"And what happens to the beeswax? Wait, don't tell me. Are those things candle molds?"

"That's right. Years back, we'd mold the wax into little cakes and sell it to cobblers. To wax their threads, you know. But now synthetics seem to have replaced the old linen thread and there aren't all that many cobblers around. So we make pure beeswax candles for churches as an act of piety."

"Nice of you," Max grunted. "Look, Bill, if the police don't show pretty soon, I'll have to take off. There are several things that ought to be done as soon as possible. For one thing, I suspect Grimpen's going to give Tom Tolbathy a thorough overhauling about that gun of Wouter's and it would be better if Tom heard about it from us first, don't you think? He's already pretty upset about that door in the car shed."

Bill nodded. "Tom minds so terribly about losing Wouter. It's a further blow to him, I'm afraid, learning that his dead brother's pranks have embroiled old friends like us in this dreadful situation."

"I don't think it was Wouter's pranks that did the embroiling, Bill. I have a hunch his secret door and hippopotamus gun were used only because they happened to be available. If they hadn't been, something else would have served the purpose."

"But what is the purpose?"

"I'll tell you when I know myself," was the best Max had to offer. "Tell me, Bill, what happened to those records that were played over the air yesterday at the banquet? Do you still have them?"

"We never did have them, more's the pity. That was one of the services Versey performed for us. He taped the complete two-hour program from his personal collection of Renaissance music recordings."

"Is that so?" said Max. "Where would he have done the taping?"

"In his own apartment. He had one room fitted up as a recording studio. Versey was quite a capable sound engineer and over the years he'd acquired some first-rate equipment. He could do all sorts of things. For instance, he got hold of a few original Edison cylinders and a machine to play them on, don't ask me where. Somebody's attic, I suppose. Anyway, he taped the sound and filtered out the squeaks and squawks so that the result sounded far better than the original. Which still isn't saying much, I'll grant you. But some of the old 33's and 78's gave truly exceptional results by the time Versey got through tinkering with the tapes."

"Other than yesterday's broadcast," Max asked him, "did you use many of Ufford's tapes in your stations?"

"Oh yes, a great many," Bill replied. "Versey was awfully good at finding the right theme song to introduce a program, for instance, and supplying us with background music for our little homilies. He also made tapes of a good many commercials that Melly and Tick worked out—quite entertaining, some of them. They really have a flair for that sort of thing. Most importantly, every one of our regular weekly programs of Renaissance music for the past fifteen years has been taped in Versey's studio. He did all the announcing himself. He'd put in snippets of interesting information about the different composers and the historical context within which they worked, and hand us the tapes as a fait accompli. All we had to do was play them."

"How did that work?" Max wanted to know. "Did you pass the tapes along from one station to the next, or have some kind of inter-station hookup?"

"Neither. Versey always made a separate copy for each station, meticulously labeled as to which was for whom."

"Why should that matter, if they were all alike?"

"Ah, but they might not be," Bill explained. "They probably would be if Versey was off on one of his periodic stays in Italy because he'd have taped a series of programs in advance. If he was around, however, he'd read announcements of coming events or local news that Renaissance music devotees might want to know about. Like most stations, we got a good many publicity notices sent in. We do try to air as many as possible, but not all of them are of earthshaking importance to our entire network. If Lorista and her consort are putting on a recital in Wayland, for instance, we probably announce it over our Natick station, but not in Maine or Vermont."

"I see." Max wouldn't have announced Lorista's recital in Maine or Vermont, either.

"I don't know how we're going to manage the Renaissance music programs now," Bill went on ruefully. "We can repeat some of the old ones for the time being, I suppose, but losing

Versey is going to mean another big hole in our operation. It's disgusting to be fretting about my own problems at a time like this, but when I think of the years of loving effort that have gone into our organization, and now to see it crumbling away from one day to the next—" Bill had to stop and recover himself. "It's almost as if the Lord's telling me it's time to fold up and quit."

"I'd suggest you make very sure it's the Lord who's talking before you put yourself off the air," said Max. "Do you have any of Ufford's program tapes that haven't yet been played?"

"Yes, one. Our Oxbridge station postponed the Renaissance Revel so they could do live, on-the-spot coverage of their annual quilting bee and forsythia festival yesterday. They're planning to air the tape at four o'clock this afternoon. Unless, heaven forbid, something goes wrong between now and then. That's the one station we haven't yet had any trouble with."

Until today. Max was getting fidgety. He pushed the button that controlled the overhead door from the ramp, and it slid back into place. It wasn't a huge door, just wide enough to let one car squeeze through.

"Somebody knows how to drive," he remarked. "Getting both these cars into a room just about big enough to hold them and parking them so neatly side by side wouldn't have been a job for an amateur."

"No, I don't suppose it was." Billingsgate didn't sound much interested. "I'm so used to expert driving in our own circle that the point hadn't occurred to me."

The implication of what he'd just said didn't appear to have occurred to Bill, either, Max thought. "You told me Ufford didn't keep a car," he remarked, "but did he know how to drive one?"

"I haven't the faintest idea," Billingsgate replied. "If he did, he never told us. He certainly never drove one of ours, though he did ride in them at various times. What Versey enjoyed most, it always seemed to me, was the dressing up. Cap and goggles and the long dust coat, you know. And sitting in the back seat pretending to be J. Pierpont Morgan while somebody else chauffeured, as Melly once unkindly observed."

He walked around the Silver Ghost, shaking his head. "Max, I'm even more bewildered now than I was before. Why should both Rufus and Versey have had to be killed in such gruesome ways merely so that two cars could be moved from one shed to the other?"

"Good question," said Max. "Legally, of course, the cars haven't been stolen since they haven't been removed from your grounds. If Rufus's death had been accepted as suicide, which it would have been if you'd gone along with Grimpen, and Ufford's as an accident with the bees, which it may still be, then no crime would presumably have been committed. Maybe the object was not to steal the cars but to harass you further."

"Then the object has been achieved, God knows. But it's so crazy, Max!"

"What still strikes me as slightly insane, if you'll forgive my saying so, is that none of you thought to look here sooner. It's so obvious, a nice concrete ramp, plenty of hiding space, and an automatic door for a quick run in. How would you operate the door from the outside, by the way? You'd need one of those hand-held remote control switches, right?"

"Or someone to poke the button from the inside," Bill replied. "There's just the one control switch, as far as I know. It's kept clipped to the honeybug's panel and one gives it a poke as one approaches the ramp. As to why none of us thought to search the honey shed, I suppose one reason was that we couldn't imagine anybody would go to such lengths to steal the cars, then hide them so close to the house. Another's what I expect that Skinner fellow would call conditioning. You must have noticed that KEEP OUT sign on the door from the storeroom?"

"Yes, I did."

"That's Abigail's doing. She has to be terribly fussy about

keeping this room clean because it's where we bottle the honey. She makes Melly and Tick spread old sheets on the floor to drive the cart over when they come in with loads of combs. They take off their shoes and put on washable slippers and coveralls. She hasn't got as far as surgical masks yet, but one does have to wear an absurd stockinette cap so that no hairs fall into the extractors. That's assuming one has hair to drop."

Bill himself was so thin on top that his scalp showed through the white peach fuzz almost as pink as his face. "The last thing they do in the fall, after all the honey is spun and taken away, is to scrub the entire room: floor, walls, ceiling, every nook and cranny. They sterilize the extractors and other equipment, then seal the room until it's needed again in the spring. You'll notice I said they, not I. I always manage to have urgent appointments elsewhere at scrub-up time. Melly and Tick do the heavy scrubbing. Abigail's chief bottle washer and goader-on."

"Rufus and Bob wouldn't normally help?"

"No, but the grandchildren take a hand if they're free. Young people always get so booked up, expecially when there's any hard work going. They're as bad as I am," Bill added with a quickly suppressed chuckle.

"The bees have been Abigail's hobby from the start, you see," he went on, "and she likes to keep it a family affair. Tick's inclined to feel we ought to face up to the fact that it's evolved into a fair-sized commercial venture and go along with the expansion. I must say I see the force of his argument, but the bees are still Abigail's babies, so I don't take sides. Anyway, what I started to say was that we're all so conditioned to putting the honey room off limits and knowing what we'll be letting ourselves in for if we break the seal out of season that I suppose we automatically assumed nobody else would trespass, either. And now the cleaning will all have to be done over. One more drop in our bucket of horrors."

"Think of it as a test of faith, Bill," said Max. "Tell me,

who'd have had access to that door opener? Is it synchronized to this door alone, or to the shed down below?"

"Actually it's sychronized to Melly's garage in Shrewsbury, absurd as that may sound. It's just that Melly kept mistaking one control gadget for the other and getting herself into pickles because they wouldn't work where she wanted them to. After she'd locked herself out a few times, Tick fiddled the switches so that she could use either and be right no matter what."

"Great idea." Max didn't really think so at all. "Where are Tick and Melly today?"

"Still dealing with our latest crisis over at the Natick station. Tick's trying to get the turntables repaired and Melly's filling in with music and a few inspirational readings. She has quite a knack for playing and singing what she calls the golden oldies. Things like "Hurrah for Baffin's Bay" and "My Sweetheart's the Man in the Moon," you know. We've had her on a number of times before, and always get calls and letters from listeners asking for more. Melly'd rather like to do a regular program and we'd adore to have her, but with her own house and family to care for and Abigail's needing her to help with Apian Way, there's simply not the time."

"Too bad," said Max. This time, he meant it. "What will she and Tick do after they've finished at the station? Do they have to go home and feed the kids?"

"No, the children are all off at school. I expect Melly and Tick will come here to catch up on how we're doing. They'll be glad to know Bodie and the cars are safe, but naturally distressed about poor Versey. Not to mention finding out they'll have to clean the honey room again. Can we move the cars back to their own shed, do you think, or should we leave them where they are?"

"I think you ought to let the police have a look at them, assuming they ever show up. Bill, I'm sorry but I can't hang around here any longer. Tell Grimpen I'll be available for questioning later on if he wants me. Right now, I'm leaving for Oxbridge. Can you give me directions to the station, and some kind of introduction?"

"Surely. Come out to the other room."

Bill didn't stop to ask why Max was going to Oxbridge, he simply found a piece of Apian Way stationery and wrote on it, *Please give Mr. Bittersohn all the help you can. N. Billingsgate.* "There, that should suffice. Have them phone me here if there's any problem. As for directions, you go down 495 and cut across Route G5. Go straight on till you come to the mill, then take a left. We're the little green shingled building just around the corner. You'll see the XBIX sign out in front. Er, were you planning to take off that bee suit before you go?"

Max hesitated. "I've got to commit a minor felony first. Unless you happen to have a spare key to Ufford's apartment?"

"Why, yes, as a matter of fact I do. There have been a couple of times in the past that we've had to get into the studio while he was away. It's right here on my key ring, though I haven't used it in years."

"Ufford hasn't had the locks changed, by any chance?"

"I can't imagine that he would. He'd have had to pay for the job himself, you see."

Bill handed over the key. With considerable relief, Max took off the bee suit.

18

"**I**'ll be gum-swizzled!"

The manager of Station XBIX, Oxbridge, Massachusetts, glanced nervously at Max Bittersohn. "Don't tell Mr. Billingsgate I said that, will you? He doesn't go much for vain oaths."

"Too damn bad," said Max. "So what are you going to do?"

"Well, obviously we can't run this tape. Heavens to Elizabeth, we'd have the FCC jumping down our throats in no time flat. I've never heard such filth before in all my born days."

"How much would have got aired if you'd put it on?"

"The whole reel, pretty much. That's the appalling part. You see, this is one program that needs no attention whatsoever from us, because Professor Ufford records the whole thing from start to finish, even the community service announcements. We have a backup arrangement that if the tape should break, our alternative turntable would switch immediately to *Tales from the Vienna Woods*. But that's never happened so far, so as soon as we start the theme song and see that the tape's running smoothly, Ed and I generally nip over to the inn and have ourselves a little restorative."

"Ed being your head man in charge of tapes?" asked Max.

"Ed being my head man, period," the manager answered.

156

'The two of us do pretty much what needs to be done around here, at this time of day."

"So I don't suppose you get all that many chances to go out together. Does anybody know you're both in the habit of taking a break while Ufford's on?"

"Oh sure, we wouldn't do anything underhanded. Mr. Billingsgate knows, and Mr. Purbody. They understand. They know we work a long day and need an occasional break. In fact, Tick—Mr. Purbody, I should say—usually hoists one with us if he happens to be around. He's about as big a fan of Renaissance music as Ed and I are. But this tape—maybe it's authentic mediaeval revelry, but I can't imagine why Professor Ufford thought we could get away with it. There's some of that garbage I don't know myself what they're talking about. Can you think where he got hold of such stuff, Mr. Bittersohn?"

"As a guess, I'd say Ufford just bought a bunch of so-called party records and picked out the raunchiest parts he could find. It wouldn't have been hard to put a tape together that way, if he could keep from vomiting into his equipment."

"Whatever he did, the old coot sure landed us in a fine kettle of fish," moaned the station manager, throwing verbal decorum to the four winds. "Now what the flaming blue blazes am I going to run in its place? We can't have empty air, you know, that's the unpardonable sin in our business. You wouldn't happen to have brought a shawm or a doodlesack with you, by any chance? Or even a kazoo?"

"Sorry." But Max was reflecting. If Melisande Purbody could interrupt her meading to sing "Up in a Balloon, Boys" to the listening multitudes, who was he to feign bashfulness in time of crisis? "Would you settle for a talk on how to steal a Renaissance painting?"

"You're not an art thief, are you?"

"No, I'm a detective who catches them. Sometimes."

Over the hitherto doleful countenance of the station manager a great light was dawning. "You—you're not—you couldn't be *Max* Bittersohn?"

"Ask my mother."

"Praise God from Whom all blessings flow! My daughter Belinda heard you speak last year at Boston University and she's been raving about you ever since. I've had to keep telling her you're most likely a married man."

"I am. With a son six months old," Max added proudly.

"I'll remind Belinda that these things are sent to test us. Now we'd better get you set up. Let's see, I don't suppose you'll need a podium. A glass of water? A stopwatch?"

"Why don't we just have an informal conversation? You ask questions and get me talking. When we run out of time, give me the high sign and I'll shut up."

"But how shall I know what to ask?"

"Ask whatever comes into your head. Remember the audience isn't going to know any more than you do, so yours will be the kinds of questions they'd want to ask, themselves."

"True enough. The more ignorant I sound, the more complacent they'll feel. Now, if you don't mind, we have to wait just a few minutes till Ed finishes reading the homily and plays "Under His Wings I Am Safely Abiding." Then I do the weather and the Apian Way commercial, and go straight to the introduction. You sit right here, please, and talk straight into the microphone."

Thus it was that something less than an hour later, driving back from Scituate, Mrs. Max Bittersohn happened to twiddle the knob of her car radio and get the shock of her life. Why on earth hadn't Max told her he was going to be on a talk show this afternoon?

Because he hadn't known until it happened, of course. There'd been another crisis in the Billingsgate network and Max had been hurled into the breach. She'd better find a telephone fast. It would be nice to know what was going on.

It would be a relief to get off this beastly highway, too. Sarah winced as yet another enormous tractor-trailer whizzed past her little car, its hubcaps about on a level with her ears. She'd hoped to avoid the rush hour traffic, but she might have known getting Jem delivered to his cronies would take at least twice as long as she'd estimated. At least she wasn't far from an exit, according to the signs. Route 28 led into Milton. She could cope with Milton, assuming this idiot dithering beside her would make up his mind what to do and get out of her way.

As soon as she turned on her right-hand blinker, the other car darted straight across in front of her and, after a hair-raising moment, left her free to turn. "Stinker," she hissed aloud. Of all the stupid—good heavens, that looked like Cousin Lionel.

It was Lionel, and he was cutting her off again, turning into a parking lot belonging to a convenience store that had a pay phone outside. Much as she'd rather avoid him, she'd better stop there, too. Her clock read almost five, which meant the program would be through, the station's call letters announced, and she'd know where to reach Max, assuming she could get her call through before he took off.

The instant she heard "This is Station XBIX, Oxbridge, Massachusetts," she was out of the car and racing toward that lone telephone booth. By now, Lionel was coming out of the store, peeling the wrapper from a chocolate bar and heading for the phone, too. She beat him by a whisker.

Lionel had always been a rotten loser. "Blast you, Sarah," he yowled, "give me that phone. I have to call Vare. You know what she's like if I don't check in."

Sarah knew and didn't care. Ignoring his caterwauls, she dialed Information. Lionel would scarcely resort to bodily violence in full view of the road. She had to invest fifty cents before she could get Max on the wire, but it was worth every nickel to hear his voice.

He was as delighted as she. "How did you track me here, for God's sake?"

"Divine guidance," she told him. "What's up? More sabotage?"

Max explained at some length while Lionel danced around the booth and pointed to his watch. Sarah listened almost without speaking until her husband had finished telling her how Bodie had been found and given a somewhat toned-down account of Ufford's death. All she said then was, "I'm glad Aunt Bodie's all right. Did you find the bicycle?"

"What bicycle?"

Lionel had stomped off now to buy another chocolate bar, and Sarah could talk without his hearing. "Darling, Professor Ufford was a tall man. To pour the syrup over his head, one would have had to take him by surprise, be high enough up not to douse one's self in the process, and make a fast getaway before the bees started coming. A bicycle's fast and silent, its tracks probably wouldn't show on those bluestone paths, it would give the rider a boost up, and it could even have a little carrier on the handlebars to keep the syrup handy. A bicycle also isn't hard to ditch. I'd look in those woods down by the hidden drawbridge, myself."

"Damn," said Max, "I never thought of a bicycle."

"I don't suppose I should have, either," Sarah admitted, "if Uncle Jem hadn't been telling me on the way down about the tricycle Wouter Tolbathy rigged up for Abigail when she first started keeping bees. It was shaped like a giant beehive, one of those old-fashioned conical straw ones. Abigail was supposed to sit inside with her head and arms and legs sticking out, wearing a black and yellow striped leotard and a fuzzy black hat with little antennae sticking up and a yellow bee veil with big goggly plastic eyes set into it."

"Simple, tasteful, and practical in the true Tolbathy tradition. Is the thing still around?"

"No, it got wrecked ages ago when the Convivial Codfish crowd were having one of their quiet little get-togethers at the Billingsgates'. They were taking turns riding around in the beehive wearing the bee headdress and somebody got the bright idea of doing wheelies. Uncle Jem wouldn't say who it was, so I suspect the worst. Anyway, that finished the beehive, but it's worth considering, don't you think?"

"I certainly do. I'd better call the Billingsgates right away and see if that jackass Grimpen ever came back. Unless you'd rather give them a ring yourself?"

"No, I wouldn't. I'm at a pay phone in Milton. I was on my way home from delivering Uncle Jem back to his yachting party when I happened to catch you on the radio. I assume there's been another blowup, but don't tell me now because I'm running out of change and Lionel's champing at the bit to use the phone. Don't ask me what he's doing here, unless he's been over in the Blue Hills communing with the rattlesnakes. About dinner, darling—"

"Forget it, kid. You've still got a long drive ahead of you and I'd better get back to the Billingsgates. Why don't you find yourself a decent restaurant and wait out the traffic? Davy's okay, isn't he?"

"Yes, I called Mrs. Blufert from the yacht club to tell her I was running late and she said not to worry. She'll stay as long as we need her and there's plenty to eat in the fridge. Oh, Max! Would you believe Young Dork just drove in? I've got to find out what this is all about. Take care, dear. See you soon, I hope."

She'd have turned the phone over to Lionel but he was with Young Dork now, trying to put aside his frenzy and act genial. Young Dork, though he barely knew Sarah, was far the more affable of the two.

"Nice to see you again so soon, Sarah. On your way to the great celebration, too, are you?"

"Actually I'm on my way home," Sarah told him. "I just stopped to phone my husband. What are you celebrating?"

"Haven't you heard? Bunny hit the lottery."

"Bunny Whet? Do you mean that state lottery that's always getting written up in the papers? How much did he win?"

"A bundle," said Young Dork reverently. "Something like three million dollars, didn't they say, Lionel?"

Now Sarah knew why her cousin was in so foul a mood. Bunny Whet had won a bundle and Lionel Kelling hadn't. She rubbed it in for all it was worth.

"What an utterly fantastic stroke of luck for Bunny. Some people just seem to have all the luck, don't they, Lionel? You must be thrilled to pieces for him. So you and Young Dork are giving Bunny a surprise party?"

"We are like hell." Lionel had run out of geniality. "With a windfall that size falling into his lap, Bunny can damned well afford to give us one."

"Actually it's Elizabeth who's giving the party," Young Dork explained. "Come on, Sarah, I know she and Bunny would love to have you. Follow me if you don't know the way."

"But I can't go barging in without an invitation."

"Of course you can, the more the merrier. Elizabeth said we should drag along any of the crowd she hadn't been able to reach."

Sarah shrugged. She wasn't one of the crowd and she didn't want to be, but it would be a chance to do some more nosing around. When Lionel added his own invitation, for Lionel could be hospitable when somebody else was footing the bills, she capitulated.

"Just tell me where to go and I'll find the house. I want to run into the store for a minute first." A Kelling might arrive both uninvited and empty-handed, but a Bittersohn surely wouldn't. She had a new set of standards to maintain along with the old.

Her cheese and crackers were well received, and so was she. "This is a nice surprise, Sarah," said Bunny Whet.

"It's a surprise for me, too," she told him. "I was on my way home from ferrying Uncle Jem to meet some of his friends at Scituate Harbor. I stopped to phone Max, bumped into Lionel and Young Dork, and here I am. I mustn't stay long, but I simply had to offer my congratulations. This must be one of the most exciting days you've ever spent, isn't it?"

"Actually it's been a week since I won the lottery," he confessed. "But Father and I were at an organic pest control convention in Philadelphia and didn't get home till late Monday night because we'd stopped to have dinner with Aunt Lucy. You wouldn't know her, I don't suppose. But anyway, that put me behind with my work and Elizabeth and I were both up to our ears in rehearsals for the revel, so I bunged my winning ticket into a safe-deposit box and didn't get around to turning it in until today. I knew the money was safe, you know. I expect I should have let it sit for another few days, since Monday's hardly the best day for a party, but I have to admit I was just too itchy. As it was, the lottery people seemed to find my lack of haste a trifle odd."

Sarah could see why they might have.

"But how was I to know the customary procedure?" said Bunny. "I've never bought one of the things before, I don't know what possessed me to buy this one. I'm not usually given to reckless impulses."

"It was only a dollar," Elizabeth argued in extenuation. "And we did so want a nice, big chunk of money for the Bat Fund. Are you familiar with Bunny's pet project, Sarah?"

Sarah was about to be, that was clear. Bunny was off and running.

"Bats are grossly underappreciated natural insect controllers. And what's happening to their natural urban habitat? I ask you, Sarah." But he gave her no time to answer. "Look at all those wonderful old stone churches we used to have. Getting their steeples lopped off, being turned into condominiums. What's a bat without a belfry, answer me that?"

She didn't get a chance on that one, either. Bunny's normally unimpassioned face was alight with enthusiasm. "So what we're doing is constructing a series of artificial belfries in suitably insect-rife environments where bats will find congenial living quarters, ample food supplies, and, we hope, fruitful association with other bats."

At last Sarah got a word in. "Do you have bells in your belfries, too?"

"Bells are a frill we've had to dispense with for reasons of economy," Bunny confessed, "but the bats are adjusting nicely. We do install streetlights at strategic places, to draw the night-flying lepidoptera."

"Yes, I can see where you'd need to do that."

"Honestly, Sarah, you ought to go out to one of our bat sanctuaries and see the little beggars flitting around those lights on a balmy summer evening, snapping up moths and mosquitoes. It's sheer poetry in motion. Isn't it, Elizabeth?"

"There is an aesthetic quality one learns to appreciate," Elizabeth agreed, a trifle wearily.

"I'd appreciate the three million dollars a damn sight more," Lionel told her crassly. "You must be pretty sick about losing out to a bunch of flying bug-snappers."

"Not at all." Bunny's wife was loyal to the core. "The income tax would have been horrendous. This way we'll get a magnificent write-off for the next twenty years because they dole it out to you on the installment plan. Besides, it lets Mother Whet and me out of having to run a fund drive."

It would let them out of having to fight Bunny over that trust fund, too, Sarah thought. It also wiped out Bunny's motive for having stolen the New Phantom even if he'd had the opportunity, which it now appeared he hadn't.

Salmon Tolbathy was another washout. Tom and Hester had brought their younger son with them to Milton because he still couldn't drive his own car and his brother Buck was tied up with a shipment of anchovies. Sal's problem had turned out to be no mere sprain but a torn ligament. He was on crutches and could hardly move without wincing. His incapacity was beyond question.

The male Abbotts hadn't been able to come. Monk was back at school and Joe had a meeting of some sort. Joe's wife, the lovely Lilias, had shown up with her parents, though, and was getting a good deal of ribbing about her kirtle from some people who hadn't been at the Renaissance Revel but had attended the wedding. They were loudly expressing their disappointment that Joe and Monk had insisted on doing their respective stints in conventional clothing instead of their dags and slitters.

That let the Abbotts out of stealing the Silver Ghost, at any rate. So far, though, Sarah hadn't been able to give anybody a solid alibi for both the revel and the day the New Phantom had been taken. Was it possible the morris dancers had worked in shifts? Sarah shook her head, both at the glass of champagne somebody was offering her and at the idea of so much organized malfeasance to so little purpose, and went back to Young Dork.

He'd spent last Monday at Station XBIG in Gibbon, New Hampshire, doing Tick a favor. They'd had problems with a broken cable. That meant they couldn't play their tapes or records, so he'd taken Lorista and her dulcimer along to do a live program of folk songs. As if one disaster hadn't been enough, Sarah thought unkindly.

"Done much bike riding lately?" she asked in desperation.

"Who, me?" Young Dork thought the question over and decided Sarah must be joking, so he laughed. "I'll take one of the Billingsgates' Rolls Royces over a bicycle any day of the week, myself. Your cousin Lionel's the boy for the bikes."

"Yes, I know Lionel rides a lot." He'd biked all the way from Cambridge to Ireson's Landing only last week as part of his, or rather Vare's, relentless keep-fit program. Even fully clothed, Lionel was no great beauty; the sight of him in shorts and a fluorescent green bicycle helmet had been enough to set Davy wailing in mortal terror. Sarah had had all she could do to refrain from climbing into the playpen and adding her wails to Davy's. "But don't the rest of you ride, too?" she said doggedly.

"We all used to when we were kids," Young Dork conceded, "but I don't recall our ever making a big thing of it. Except Lionel, of course, and Tick Purbody. Too bad Tick and Melly couldn't come tonight but they're both tied up. Anyway, Tick was really hot there for a while. He even entered a couple of six-day bicycle races, but Melly put her foot down on that once they were married. Sure I can't get you some champagne?"

"Not just now, thanks," said Sarah. "I want to talk to Hester and Tom."

The elder Tolbathys were sitting together on a straight-backed settee, neither of them looking particularly festive. Sarah could understand why, knowing what Max must have told them during his morning visit. At least she had one piece of cheerful news to impart.

"You'll be glad to know Aunt Bodie's turned up."

That brightened their mood a bit. "I'm so relieved!" said Hester. "We've been awfully worried about her. Where was she, do you know?"

"She'd managed somehow to get locked in the honey shed."

"But that's incredible! Bodie, of all people. However did she get into a fix like that?"

"Apparently she'd gone exploring." Sarah didn't feel this was the time or place to go into specifics. "The room had been sterilized and sealed off ever since last honey-gathering time, whenever that was, so naturally it was the one place nobody thought to look. But anyway, she's all right. Somewhat frayed around the edges, of course. The last I heard, Abigail and Drusilla had her tucked up in one of the guest rooms, taking turns playing Florence Nightingale."

Hester even managed to smile. "It's funny hearing you say that. I never think of Drusilla as playing anything that didn't involve a stick and a ball. She used to have the most spectacular tennis serve, though I have to admit it never landed quite where she meant it to."

"I suppose you found her a great deal changed."

"No, not really. Goodness knows what she thought of me."

"She thought you were absolutely ravishing, naturally. How could she possibly not?"

"How dear of you, Sarah. Anyway, I'm glad she's there to lend a hand. I called Abigail early this morning to see how things were going, and she sounded absolutely exhausted."

"Not surprisingly, all things considered," Tom grunted.

Sarah might have said more, but Lionel was at her shoulder.

"If you people want another drink, you'd better get it now. Elizabeth's making noises about shutting the bar and serving some food."

"That's fine with me. I don't want any more," said Sarah.

Her cousin glared at her. "Well, can't you take one anyway and pass it along to me?"

"Honestly, Lionel, you are the living end!"

Sarah wished she herself could end this weary visit, but she still didn't have a line on who that morris dancer in the copse could have been. Max couldn't have had any better luck than she, or he'd have said. He hadn't said anything about Rufus's *Totschläger*, either, and that worried her.

There were too many things they hadn't been able to pin down yet. But at least they'd found Aunt Bodie alive and kicking, and the Silver Ghost and the New Phantom. She couldn't let herself think about Vercingetorix Ufford now, not while she still must grill Cousin Lionel about that half-hour gap at the banquet and still must face Elizabeth Whet's high-minded version of a buffet supper.

19

"That's what I said, Bill, a bicycle. Sarah thinks there ought to be one. Why won't you allow them on the place? Oh, so the kids don't get to racing through the fields and stirring up the bees. Yes, I understand, but have Grimpen keep an eye out for one anyway, will you? He's been trying to convince you Ufford's death was an accident, eh? That figures. No, you're under no obligation to talk to reporters. If they get too pushy just lower the portcullis, raise the drawbridge, and unleash the bees."

It would have been too much to hope the news media could be kept at bay forever. Poor Bill, as if he and Abigail didn't have troubles enough already. Half of him must be longing to scoop the others and get the story on his own stations first, and the other half praying nobody would run it at all. Fat chance. Max checked the address he'd obtained, shook hands with his new friends at XBIX, sent his kindest personal regards to the station manager's daughter, and went on to the next stop.

Vercingetorix Ufford's aerie didn't take much finding. It was up among the gables and cupolas of an immense Victorian house on a sedate side road in West Newton. The house was three high-ceilinged stories tall, painted lemon yellow with a layer of chocolate in the middle and vanilla trimmings under the eaves. Ufford's was a private entrance on the side. A flossy brass plaque screwed to the door proclaimed that this was indeed the place. Max turned the key Bill had lent him and it worked.

."Quite a pad," he murmured as he reached the top of the stairs and switched on a light.

Ufford must have dreamt that he dwelt in marble halls. The plastered walls of what he'd probably dubbed his *salotto* had been painted over in a white travertine *faux marbre*, broken here and there by *trompe l'oeil* pilasters and pedestals in green serpentine, the latter surmounted by what looked to Max like funerary urns in *rosso antico*. Deep green velvet draperies dripping with gold fringe were caught back by heavy gold ropes to reveal glass curtains in shimmering cloth of gold.

To Max's trained eye, the furniture and accessories were all reproduction, but what they reproduced were the wildest excesses of the Italian Renaissance. There was enough gold here to have stripped the hypothetical mines of Golconda if Versey's gildings hadn't been equally hypothetical. True or false, the decorating must have cost him a bundle. Taste this bad didn't come cheap.

The bedroom would make a grandiose setting for a really spectacular nightmare. An immense tester bed, also gilded, had purple velvet hanging everywhere velvet could be hung, plus a fake polar bear rug thrown over the foot. And that was only the beginning. Max wasted little time straining his aesthetic sensibilities but went on into the recording studio.

Here, he was grateful to see not a fleck of spurious gold anywhere. Bill hadn't exaggerated about the equipment, there was a lot of it. Max hadn't the technical expertise to judge how good it all was, but he recognized some internationally famous brand names. Everything appeared to have been well cared for and efficiently arranged. Wall racks held thousands of recordings, all filed and labeled according to some elaborate system. There were drawers for cassettes and for what Max decided must be professional broadcasting tapes on large reels. He was beginning to feel depressed by the magnitude of Ufford's collection when he discovered one rack marked "Experimental Tapes."

Once he'd figured out how to play them, Ufford's experiments proved well worth the trip. It was Ufford himself who'd made them; Max all too easily identified that pompous, overprecise articulation he'd heard so much of at the revel. One of the professor's recorded messages was quite a little Renaissance drama in itself:

"Amaline Pettigrass, you are a slave to those turntables. For years you have stood here watching the turntables go around and around. They have hypnotized you. They hold you in their power. They are your enemies. You must destroy the turntables. You must break their evil spell. Take their cruel arms, Amaline Pettigrass. Bend them back and twist. Do it now, Amaline. Then forget what you did. You will remember nothing. You will only know the turntables don't work. You won't know why. Do it, Amaline. Break the arms and forget. Now, Amaline. Now."

This must have been one of Ufford's earlier attempts at recording a subliminal message. He'd kept the tapes, one in which he'd tried to meld the words with a bouncy jingle for a restaurant called Francine's Fritter Factory, one with what must be the theme song for some of Bill's little homilies. The first efforts were jumbled, but there was another tape where words and music must have been blended into an undistinguishable whole. Max couldn't hear the hidden message at all, but Amaline Pettigrass's subconscious mind would have sorted it out. Both the advertisement and the theme song would have been played again and again, probably several times a day over a period of weeks or even months. It would have taken plenty of urging to make a loyal employee sabotage expensive equipment for no apparent reason.

There were others, some suggesting that a named person nick a stylus or sever a cable, or hide a nice, big magnet next to where the tapes were stored, so that when the time came to play them there'd be nothing left to play. Some were less subtle, like the one that said, "Joseph Bunce, get out of here. Joseph Bunce, we don't want you here. Joseph Bunce, you stink. Joseph Bunce, get out of here right this minute." And there was a tape that repeated over and over, and over, 'Revelers, eat the frumenty. Revelers, eat the frumenty. Revelers, eat the frumenty."

Max wasn't a bit surprised. He'd suspected something of the sort ever since he'd given himself heartburn eating the stuff and wondering why.

This could have been Ufford's first experiment in instant mass manipulation. The choice of command had been a clever one. Being ordered to eat something that was perfectly wholesome if not particularly interesting would have aroused no strong resistance in guests who'd probably have taken a dab of the stuff anyway, simply because their hostess always made such a big deal of her genuine fourteenth-century recipe. Once some of the more suggestible revelers had begun attacking that massive silver bowl with unaccustomed gusto, the old follow-the-leader instinct would have incited others to dip in.

Max felt a stab of annoyance. Was he really that gullible? Obviously, yes. But had Ufford been that keen a psychologist? Had he been the real instigator of the trick or only the technician? Max wasted no more time playing the experimental tapes, but went back to the hunt.

Ufford was a systematic rogue, all right. In a neat little card file underneath the tape rack, Max found a bundle of index cards, filed under the various station call letters. Amaline Pettigrass was there; Ufford had meticulously entered the day on which she'd first have heard her specially tailored message, the number of times it would be broadcast, and the date on which the turntables had ceased to function. Joseph Bunce had his card showing the date on which he'd got his marching orders and when he'd finally marched. Ufford had even made up a card for the frumenty, the finicking old bastard.

He'd been here last night, presumably to update his files and change his clothes. Max found the Arnolfini costume in the bedroom closet, neatly zipped inside a plastic garment bag. The hat was on the shelf above, also swathed in plastic. The bright green tights were in the laundry hamper.

Of anything resembling the morris dancer's costume, though, Max could find no sign. It wasn't in the small coat closet outside the *salotto;* it almost certainly wouldn't be anywhere else in the apartment. If Ufford had been cocky enough not to bother hiding his tapes and file cards, he must have considered himself totally above suspicion. Egomania was an easy kind of craziness to manipulate.

Max wasn't feeling any too cocky himself, though. Why hadn't Ufford's landlady been up here already, wanting to know who he was and why he was in her house? Maybe she'd called the cops and was just lying low until they got here. He'd better hit the road before his luck ran out; he wasn't sure how well an argument that he was here on business for her tenant's boss would stand up now that Ufford was known to be dead. Taking the experimental tapes and file cards out of the apartment was a risk, but it would have been riskier to leave them here. Bill had better go through them all tonight and make sure there weren't still a few uncompleted experiments floating around the stations.

It was irritating that Ufford had stopped short of leaving any clues as to who'd been piping the tune to which he'd danced his final gigue. Max hadn't been able to find a thing except a whopping phone bill that was made up mostly of calls to one particular number in Busto Arsizio in Italy. Max knew his geography pretty well, and Busto Arsizio was nowhere near Venice. Perhaps it was a mountain climber and not a gondolier with whom the Italian mistress was carrying on her extracurricular *ventura amorosa.* Max copied down the number in his little black book before he went out past the fake marble and picked his way silently down the stairs.

Sarah must be in some Milton restaurant by now, he thought as he unlocked his car and laid the tapes on the seat beside him. No, it was too late for that, she'd already have eaten. She'd be back at their house, giving Davy his bath and telling him his bedtime story because the kid's father was too busy burgling a dead man's apartment. The clock on the dashboard said seventeen minutes to eight. Max hadn't realized he'd spent so much time at Ufford's.

He ought to stop for a bite somewhere, himself. He ought to quit running the roads and get home to his wife and child. But how could he knock off now? What if Boadicea was awake and talking? What if she was saying the wrong thing to the wrong person? He leaned on the gas pedal, remembered he was a family man, and eased off to within the posted speed limit. Barely within. Damn it, he did want to get home sometime or other.

Maybe he ought to phone Bill about the tapes. If there were no facilities to play them at the house, Bill might prefer to meet him at whichever radio station was handiest. He managed to find a drugstore with a pay phone, and dialed.

It was Abigail who answered. "Oh, Max, I'm so glad you called. Sarah wants you to pick her up at the Tolbathys'."

Oh God, what now? "What's happened?" He had to grit his teeth to keep from yelling into the phone. "Did she have an accident?"

"Nothing to worry about. It's just that she went to Bunny Whet's party and somebody who was leaving backed into her car and smashed one of the headlights. The garage was closed and she couldn't very well drive all the way home with just one light, so she left her car at the Whets' and came on with Tom and Hester. She didn't explain why she chose them particularly; perhaps they needed help with Sal. He's still on crutches, you know."

Max hadn't known and right now he didn't give a damn. Why should she help Sal Tolbathy? Why wasn't she home taking care of her own child? For a moment, Max felt a surge of old-fashioned male chauvinist ire. But he was an honest man. He'd brought Sarah into this affair because he wanted her with him and because she was good. He didn't know how she'd got to Bunny Whet's, but he could guess it was because she'd happened to bump into Lionel and Young Dork. She'd seen her chance to plug some of the gaps and gone along with them. He'd have done the same. He'd better make up his mind what kind of wife he wanted.

Ah, the hell with it. He wanted Sarah any way she wanted to be, and he was gladder than anybody would ever know that he'd be seeing her in fifteen minutes or so instead of God knew when. He got squared away with Bill about the tapes, bought himself a packet of cheese crackers at the soda fountain, and went back to the car.

When Max got to the Tolbathys', he found Sarah waiting for him with her coat on. "Abigail phoned to say you'd called them and were on your way," Tom explained. "You're welcome to stay and visit a while," he added rather wistfully, "but I know they're anxious to see you. And we did have a good talk with Sarah."

Once they were in the car, Sarah made her report. Buck Tolbathy had dropped in at his parents' house after they got back, to get a report on Bunny's bonanza and offer whatever help Sal might need getting ready for bed. Sarah had managed to steer the conversation back to the morris dancers and pick up a few more nuggets about who'd been where at the crucial time during the revel

"The Abbotts did go to that wedding, so they're out. Sam Tolbathy pulled a ligament and had to get a neighbor to take him to the emergency room at the hospital, so he's out. Buck came straight from the dancing green into the pavilion and stayed there all through the banquet. So did Young Dork and they both have different witnesses to prove they did. Erp and Monk were frisking around with the serving wenches a good deal, and Hester was keeping a sharp eye on them because one of her granddaughters brought an absolutely adorable friend who's only fourteen years old and a bit precocious. That Ogham man from Schenectady sat and pigged out for two hours straight, according to Buck. He hadn't had a chance to get any breakfast before he got on the plane, then he had to come straight to the Billingsgates' and get into his dancing clothes, so he was starving."

"So that leaves Tick and Lionel," said Max.

"I know, dear. I tried everything I knew, but I couldn't get any real line on either of them. Tick was here, there, and everywhere; they all agreed on that but nobody could offer anything definite. That man must have absolutely boundless energy. As for Lionel, when I asked him about it at the Whets', he tried to make me believe he was right there in the pavilion. But I don't buy it, Max, and none of the Tolbathys could vouch for him. I don't know what to think. He's such a pipsqueak!"

"You know him better than I do," was the safest reply Max could think of. "What about the costumes? Did you get any line on them?"

"Yes, I did. I thought Lorista must have made them, but it turns out Professor Ufford borrowed them from some folk dancing group he was affiliated with. Normally the men wear more conventional costumes of black knee pants and red waistcoats with white shirts and stockings, and black straw hats they trim with flowers or ribbons or whatever, according to the season. They didn't think much of the doublet and hose getup. Buck Tolbathy said it made him feel like a jack in the box."

"I can imagine. So what happened to the costumes afterward?"

"Lorista picked them up Saturday from the woman who takes care of them for the folk dancers. She and Young Dork brought them to the Billingsgates' Sunday morning about half-past ten so the dancers could change into them as they arrived. There wasn't an extra one; I asked. The men kept their costumes on for the banquet and the dancing afterward, but changed back before they went home. All but the Abbotts, who had to leave early and change in the car, as you know. Buck said he helped Young Dork carry them out to Dork's station wagon, and there were seven because he counted them to make sure. Lorista collected the remaining two from Lilias Abbott this morning and returned all nine to the woman she'd gotten them from, along with a check to pay for the dry cleaning. She counted them again when she got there to make sure she wasn't overpaying. So that's that, as far as I can see. Max, you don't suppose Lionel was knocked out and had his costume taken off him, then put back on? That could explain the temporary amnesia about where he was at the start of the banquet."

"It's the only possible explanation."

"All right, darling, you don't have to get nasty. Did they find the bicycle?"

"I passed the word along from the radio station right after you called me but I don't know what's happened, if anything. When Abigail gave me your message I just said, 'I'll see you later' and came straight to the Tolbathys'. What was this party you went to?"

"Remember I told you about bumping into Lionel and Young Dork at that store I phoned you from?"

"Yes, quite a coincidence."

"I thought so, too, but it really wasn't. The Kellings know scads of people in Milton. I suppose I was bound to run into somebody or other during rush hour at such a handy stopping-off place. Anyway, it turned out Bunny Whet had won three million dollars in the state lottery and Elizabeth felt like celebrating because now they won't have to keep on turning over their dividend checks from the trust fund to Bunny's bat preserves."

"Sarah!"

"I know, dear. But you'll be relieved to know he hasn't been putting any bells in the belfries. He says the bats don't seem to notice. Did you manage to get any dinner?"

"Not yet. I'm going to throw myself on Abigail's mercy, which means we'll never have the gall to send them a bill. How about you?"

"Elizabeth served soup and sandwiches."

The soup had been canned tomato, slightly overwatered. The sandwiches had been single slices of processed cheese on spongy white bread. Sarah didn't tell Max because she knew what he'd say. After all, Elizabeth had been fairly heroic about Bunny's giving his three million dollars to the bats.

Nevertheless, she didn't say no when they got to the Billingsgates' and were pressed to partake of a light collation. They couldn't see Boadicea Kelling yet because Dr.

Maude was with her. Drusilla was standing by to let them know when to come up. Meanwhile, though the peacock pie had gone to the deserving poor, there was plenty of roast capon and Cook had made fresh baking powder biscuits. For once, Abigail wasn't offering them any honey.

At the table, Sarah chatted about Bunny Whet's windfall and the people she'd seen at the party while Abigail and Bill made sociable noises and Max ate pretty much in silence. As soon as the plates were cleared, though, she got down to business.

"Did the police find the bicycle?"

Bill shook his head. "I believe they've given it up as a bad job. Grimpen stopped by about half-past six to say they were knocking off for the night. They did find a plastic container that had evidently been used to hold the syrup."

"What kind of plastic container?" Max wanted to know.

"The ordinary sort that gets used in a kitchen," Abigail told him. "Squarish, with a colored plastic top. You can buy them in any supermarket. We have a bunch of them around. I expect you do, too."

"Oh yes," Sarah agreed. "They're handy for leftovers and freezing things. Or bringing soup to the afflicted." Both Miriam and Mother Bittersohn were fairly big on plastic containers. "Where did they find it, Bill?"

"In among the clover, not far from where—" Bill hesitated.

Abigail squeezed his hand. "Sarah and I aren't squeamish, dear. Naturally it would be near Versey's body. You couldn't throw one of those things very far because they're too light to pick up any momentum. But what's all this about a bicycle, Sarah? We haven't had one of those on the place since Melly was a little girl. She fell off and broke her collarbone and we decided to go into beekeeping instead."

"It's just a hunch I have. And I'll bet I know one place where Grimpen didn't think to look. Would you excuse me, please?"

"But don't you want to see Bodie?"

"Yes, of course, but this will only take a minute. Has Cook gone home?"

"I believe so. If you're concerned about helping with th
dishes—"

"No, they can wait. Coming, Max?"

"Sure, kid." He was on his feet and they were out th
door. "Where to?"

"Down there."

"You don't mean that other shed where the garden
keeps his mowers? Grimpen can't have been dumb enoug
to overlook that."

"I expect he could have been if he'd tried hard enough, bt
that's not what I had in mind. Can't you think of anoth
place on this estate that must have been tacitly put out c
bounds for the time being?"

Max gave her a startled look. "Yes, I can. Okay, let's have
look."

20

Cook and Bob were both at home. Both put on a decent show of being pleased to see them. Cook didn't get out of her oversized rocking chair, they wouldn't have expected that, but she did vouchsafe them a gracious nod.

"I hope you got enough to eat up at the house? I made extra biscuits just in case."

"Thank you, yes," Sarah replied. "I must beg you for your recipe when we don't have more pressing business at hand."

"Ah, but it's not merely the recipe, it's the frame of mind. Biscuits require tranquility. I have a special mantra I keep for biscuits. For deviled eggs, on the other hand, I really have to work myself up. Fortunately Mr. and Mrs. Billingsgate aren't overly fond of deviled eggs. It's mostly when the grandchildren come and want a picnic lunch. Not that I mind, you understand, but those deviled eggs do take a lot out of me. Green tomato mincemeat's the worst, though. Melisande always loved my green tomato mincemeat. She was at me last fall to put some up for the holidays, but I had to tell her flat out: 'Melisande,' I said, 'I simply cannot risk total destruction of my equanimity. I'm not so young as I was, Melisande,' I said. 'I don't bounce back the way I used to.'"

"Happens to us all sooner or later," Max sympathized.

Cook was gathering her forces for further remark, but Sarah had had enough small talk that evening to last her a while. "Cook," she said, "have you been in Rufus's bedroom today?"

Cook managed a quarter turn of her head and the raising of an eyebrow, which probably raised hob with her equanimity. "I have not."

"Have you, Bob?"

"Not me," said the gardener. "See, Monday's my regular day for Mr. Hohnser and I'd promised him I'd work with him today on his roses. Mr. Hohnser's got this big rose garden, see, with over a hundred different varieties, some of them rare specimens. As you might expect, he's pretty fussy about who takes care of it. So anyway, I'd promised him definitely that I'd be with him all day today, rain or shine, the revel notwithstanding. Mr. Billingsgate said I'd better go as usual because we were trying to maintain the illusion that there was nothing wrong here, as you know."

"So you were gone all last Monday and all day today?"

"I was. And the week before and the one before that and so on back into March, as soon as it got so we could work outside. I leave here at a quarter past eight in the morning and don't get home till a quarter to seven at night. They give me my meals over there, and coffee breaks and all that. It's not as if he worked me like a dog, as you might think. We do put in a full day, I'm not saying we don't, but what takes me so long is that Mr. Hohnser doesn't just like to grow roses, he likes to talk about roses."

"Mr. Hohnser is a fund of information on roses," said Cook.

"He is that," her husband confirmed. "I'm primarily a dahlia man myself, but roses are a fascinating subject, as you no doubt well know. We can't grow them here except for a few ramblers down back that don't offer much scope for horticultural finesse, so when Mr. Hohnser wants to talk roses, I'm perfectly happy to listen."

"My husband is an excellent listener," Cook further exerted herself to remark.

"I may say the same of yourself, my dear," Bob replied courteously. "Anyway, Mrs. Bittersohn, what I'm getting at in my circumlocutious way is that I wouldn't have had time to go into Rufe's bedroom even if I'd had the inclination, which frankly I didn't. It would seem like an intrusion, if you see what I mean. I'd never have gone without being invited while he was alive, so why should I take the liberty now? I grant you the notion is emotional rather than rational and I expect I'll feel different once he's properly planted, but there it is."

"What about you, Cook?" Sarah asked. "I was thinking perhaps someone from the house asked you to choose the clothes to lay him out in."

"Mrs. Billingsgate did consult with me in the matter. I told her, 'Mrs. Billingsgate,' I said, 'Rufe never had any clothes except his working clothes and that old tweed jacket with the elbows out. Why don't we bury him in that suit you made him for the revel? That's what Rufe would have wanted, Mrs. Billingsgate,' I said. 'He was proud of that suit. It touched him, Mrs. Billingsgate,' I said, 'you going to all that work of making him a suit with your own two hands.' Rufe was talking of it Saturday night in this very room," she added with a decorously suppressed sniffle.

"He was," Bob confirmed. "And I made a jocose remark, I'm ashamed to admit. And Rufe said, and I honored him for it, 'It's what she wants,' he said, 'and it's what he wants.' Meaning Mr. Billingsgate, you understand. 'Mine not to question why, mine but to do or die.' I thought that was putting it a little steep over a fancy vest and a pair of velveteen bloomers, myself, which just goes to show how little we know. All flesh is as grass. It cometh up and somebody gets stuck with mowing it down, though I suppose I shouldn't digress into shoptalk at so solemn a time. Anything else you'd like to know, sir and madam?"

"Yes," said Sarah. "We'd like to know which room was Rufus's. And we'd like to take a look inside. Under Mr. Billingsgate's orders," she added in deference to the feudal system.

Bob said Mr. Billingsgate's wish was his command. Cook compressed her chins in willing acquiescence. Thereupon, the gardener showed Sarah and Max through the immaculate kitchen to a room at the back of the house.

"This used to be Rufe's bedroom when his folks were alive," Bob told them, "and he kept it for himself when the wife and I moved in. It's got a separate outside door, as you see, which made things handier all around."

"I'm sure it did." Sarah bent over and lifted one edge of the patchwork quilt that had served the old retainer for a bedspread. "What's that bicycle doing here?"

Bob was flabbergasted, and said so. "That can't have been Rufe's. He knew Mrs. Billingsgate didn't want bikes around on account of the kids. So where the heck did it come from?"

"Let's have a look." Max took hold of the wheels by their spokes and eased the bicycle out from under the bed. It was a spidery foreign ten-speed model painted a particularly unpleasant shade of olive green, and it had a small wire carrier strapped to the handlebar. "Whose was it, Sarah?"

"Professor Ufford's, don't you think? He had no car, he can't always have been able to cadge rides, and Bill says he hated spending money on taxis. In Italy, everybody uses a bicycle for getting around, so I suppose Ufford picked up the habit. He rode it out here during the early hours, I should say, wearing that all-black outfit so he wouldn't be noticed, which would be theatrical and stupid and sounds just like him."

"I'll buy that," said Max. "He'd have gone straight to the honey shed, I expect. Your aunt was talking about some silly fellow in black who tied her up. I shouldn't be surprised if Ufford spent the rest of the night in the shed with her."

"Sleeping in the New Phantom," Sarah agreed. "Then his accomplice came along, sent him out into the bee fields on foot for some reason, and rode the bike after him to douse him with the syrup."

"How come Professor Ufford let the other guy ride the bike?" Bob wanted to know.

"I don't suppose he realized what the accomplice had in mind. Whoever it was must have taken an awful chance, bringing the bicycle back here in broad daylight."

"Not if the rider took the direct path from the honey shed," said Max. "I noticed today that it goes through the hedgerow all the way. Bob, you'd better lock both doors to this room and make sure nobody touches the bicycle until we can get it checked for possible fingerprints."

"Sure, Mr. Bittersohn. Say, you don't think my wife and I had anything to do with this?"

"I don't see how you could, Bob. Your wife was at the other house all day and you were with Mr. Hohnser. Somebody knew you'd both be gone, knew there was a back entrance to Rufe's room, and figured this would be a safe place to dump the bike for the time being. I'm sure you can produce witnesses who saw you at Hohnser's."

"Well, there was Mr. Hohnser and the woman who keeps house for him. Porterfield, her name is. She brought out the coffee and served lunch and came a few times to see what was going on. And some guys from Perkins Nurseries were bringing loads of pine bark mulch and spreading it around the paths most of the day. As for my wife," words failed him.

"Cook has Mrs. Billingsgate and Mrs. Gaheris to vouch for her," said Sarah, trying not to think of Cook on an Italian racing bicycle. "Thanks for your help, Bob. We're sorry we had to bother you."

"It was no bother. Rufe was a friend of ours."

The four exchanged good nights with some ceremony. When Sarah and Max got back to the big house, they found Tick and Melly there, being briefed on the latest horrors.

"Howdy, folks. Another big day at the OK Corral, eh?" was Tick's greeting.

"You might say that," Max replied. "How did your program go, Melisande?"

"Quite well, I think. We had people phoning in with requests. Only I think I sprained a tonsil on "Don't Go in the Lion's Cage Tonight, Mother Darling." I got a bit carried away doing the growls. Ordinarily I'd take hot lemon and honey, but—" Melisande shuddered and took another sip of plain tea.

"She knocked 'em dead and she knows it," said Tick.

"Sorry, that was a poor choice of words. But honestly, the phone was ringing off the hook. We've really got to give Melly her own program, Dad, right now. We need her to plug the gap Versey's death will leave. Maybe we can even get our help back now that we can demonstrate the filthy tricks that old reptile played on them. So help me Hannah, if I'd found out about those tapes before the bees got him, I'd have—"

"Tick, please," his father-in-law interrupted. "No vain oaths, I beg you."

"Vain oaths be—sure, Dad. But when I think of all the times I had to drag that old bag of bones around in my car because he was too cheap to buy one of his own, listening to him rattle on about how much smarter he was than anybody else—" Tick swallowed what might have been another vain oath. "I always thought Versey was crazy as a coot. Now I know."

"I'm not so sure," said Abigail. "I'd just like to know what he was up to."

"He was cracked," Tick insisted. "He'd gone straight around the bend and thought he was Cesare Borgia."

"I wonder if he found a Lucrezia to help him," said Sarah. "I understand Professor Ufford preferred blondes."

"In my opinion, Versey preferred whatever he could get," snorted Melisande. "Shall I bring some more hot water, Mama?"

"Sit still, dear. I'll get it."

Max stopped her. "Before you go, Abigail, what's the status upstairs? Sarah's anxious to see her aunt."

"Of course she is, and so she shall. Bodie's fine, Sarah. Dr. Maude simply wanted to observe her reactions for a while, to make sure everything's in working order. Bodie was evidently drugged as well as being hit over the head. And I don't suppose being shut up all that time in the honey shed did her much good."

"Oh, the poor thing," said Sarah. "Why don't I run up now and see if she's fit to talk?"

"Why don't we all go?" said Tick Purbody. "The rest of us can stand outside and listen at the keyhole if Dr. Maude won't let us in the room."

Melisande's husband did have boundless energy, Sarah thought, watching Tick take the stairs three at a time. Then again, he might be in a tizzy over what Boadicea Kelling might have to say. Sarah was more than a little concerned herself.

It was Drusilla Gaheris who came out to meet them. "Good heavens, we weren't expecting a delegation," was her greeting. "I'm not sure how Dr. Maude will feel about six people at once."

"Then ask her, can't you?"

That was Tick, chafing at the bit again. Sarah got the distinct impression he didn't much care for his mother-in-law's old school chum, and wondered why. Had Mrs. Gaheris done something already to get his back up, or did he simply resent having a stranger around?

"It's all right, they can come in."

Dr. Maude was a short, stocky, cheerful woman with straight gray hair in a Dutch-boy cut, wearing a rust-colored suit with a tailored pink blouse. "Mrs. Kelling's doing better than I expected. Just try not to confuse her. I'd suggest her niece do the talking and the rest of you listen. I do have to leave now, Abigail, but you shouldn't have any problems. Mrs. Kelling understands she's to stay quiet until morning. I wish all my patients had her common sense, and took such good care of themselves. She's in amazing condition for a woman her age. If she weren't, things might have turned out rather differently."

"Do you know what the drug was?" Sarah asked.

"I'm guessing she may have got a lighter dose of the same tranquilizer that killed Rufus. There's a small puncture wound on her right shoulder. I've ordered lab tests, but the results may be inconclusive because of the time lapse. Whatever it was, she's fairly well rid of it now. Go ahead over to her, but please leave at once if she seems drowsy."

They filed in and stood around the bed. Boadicea Kelling

was propped up on several pillows, wearing a bright pink bed jacket with a great many lace-edged frills on it. Abigail's, no doubt. The effect was the reverse of sensible; it made her look like a sweet old lady trying to be brave. Sarah was rather taken aback.

"How are you feeling now, Aunt Bodie?"

"Tolerable, all things considered," was the brisk reply. "I expect you're here to find out what happened to me, so please don't interrupt with inane questions. Abigail, I'd like an eggnog at half-past nine if it's convenient, then I shall go straight to sleep. That leaves us just eight minutes to talk, which should be ample. Drusilla, you must be sick of hanging around here, would you like to say good night?"

"Oh no, Bodie, I don't want to leave you," Mrs. Gaheris protested.

"As you wish. I'd be bored stiff by now if the shoe were on the other foot. Sarah, if you're going to be spokeswoman for the party, sit down. It hurts my head to look up at you."

Sarah took the chair that had presumably been Dr. Maude's and refrained from asking inane questions. Boadicea took a sip from the glass on her nightstand and began.

"Having eaten what I deemed sufficient at the banquet and being for some reason inclined to take another helping of the frumenty, I determined to resist temptation by taking my usual four-mile walk while the rest continued their reveling. I set out from the pavilion via the path that led through the copse."

"A pertinent question, Aunt Bodie," Sarah broke in. "Did you see anybody there wearing a morris dancer's costume?"

"I did not. I saw nobody. I walked as far as the car shed, intending to rest awhile in one of the Rollses before continuing my stroll. Quite frankly, Abigail, your frumenty was sitting heavily on my stomach. I can't imagine what had possessed me to think I wanted more."

Abigail murmured something apologetic. Boadicea brushed her off.

"No matter, it was undoubtedly wholesome. In any event, got as far as the gate and found it locked."

"Was Rufus on guard?" asked Sarah.

"I've already told you I saw nobody. I was, I confess, somewhat indignant at being shut out." Boadicea shot a somewhat indignant glance at Bill, who opened his mouth to say something, then remembered he wasn't supposed to talk and didn't.

"Thinking there might be another entrance, I walked around toward the back of the shed. To my great astonishment, and I assure you I am not hallucinating however incredible this may sound, an entire section of the rear wall swung outward before my very eyes."

"You definitely weren't hallucinating, Aunt Bodie," Sarah assured her. "We know how it happened. Please go on."

"I stood rooted to the spot for some time. I can't tell you how long. The shock was great, and there was that frumenty to be considered. I was roused from my inaction by the sound of a car motor being revved up. I walked briskly toward the protruding section of the wall, a distance of perhaps twenty feet from where I'd halted when the wall swung out. I got there just in time to see the Silver Ghost emerge from the shed."

"Could you see who was driving?"

"Sarah, do stop interrupting. The car was moving faster than I'd anticipated. I narrowly escaped being run down. I uttered an ejaculation of some kind, I forget what, and the brakes were abruptly applied. After that I have only a confused memory of a clanking sound, a figure towering above me, and what felt like an explosion inside my head. Dr. Maude has explained that this was a normal reaction to a sharp blow on the cranium and is nothing to worry about."

Sarah ventured another interruption. "You say the figure towered over you. Do you mean it was a tall person?"

"I'm not short myself, and it loomed. That's all I can say."

"Have you any idea at all what it looked like? What color were the clothes?"

Boadicea Kelling shut her eyes. "I'm trying to visualize. I

think, and mind you this is only an impression, that the person was wearing one of the old dust coats and had something over his face. A driving veil would be a logical assumption but I'm well aware that assumptions aren't evidence."

"When Max and Bill found you, you mentioned a silly fellow in black who tied you up," Sarah prompted. "Do you remember that?"

"Vaguely. Dr. Maude assured me that confusion and possible hallucination would have been normal reactions to the combination of a blow on the head and an injection of a narcotic. Somehow, the black figure seemed to turn into Professor Ufford."

"It was Professor Ufford, Aunt Bodie."

"Then I was right in calling him a silly fellow. How reassuring. You must elucidate the matter when I'm in full possession of my faculties, Sarah. Right now, any infusion of narrative would only confuse me further. I believe I was under the impression we were participating in a rally together. That was a hallucination, surely?"

"It must have been."

"Excellent. We progress. Next question, please."

"Did you think you saw anybody else, Aunt Bodie?"

"No. The man you say was Professor Ufford pulled my hat down over my eyes. I remember that quite vividly. It seemed at the time an act of gratuitous rudeness, but I expect his actual motive was to prevent my recognizing him. I have an impression he was upset to find me alive. Somebody shrieked, I know that. I think I was struck again and that must have been when he tied me up because the next thing I remember is not being able to move my hands or feet and hearing a long, confused argument about who was going to kill me, and how and when. I kept wishing they'd make up their minds and be quiet so I could rest my head, which was aching quite badly. That was hardly a natural reaction on my part, so I suppose it was another hallucination."

Sarah doubted that very much. "Who did you imagine was arguing with him?"

"I thought it must be his wife. She was berating him quite shrewishly, calling him a coward and a fool because he hadn't done something or other about the cars. Perhaps that was how I got the notion we were at a rally, or else it was all part of the same fantasy. Professor Ufford isn't married, is he?"

"Not so far as we know."

"Hallucination, then. Now we're getting somewhere."

"Could you recognize the voice you thought was his wife's?"

"Sarah, you can hardly expect me to give a sensible answer about a figment of the subconscious imagination. It was all bits and pieces. There was a strange, mixed-up business about a coolie taking me for a ride in a rickshaw, which I now realize must have been Bill bringing me here in the electric cart. And voices, Drusilla's especially. I seemed to hear you wherever I went, Drusilla."

"But of course you would, Bodie dear." Mrs. Gaheris spoke gently, taking her old friend's hand. "I was with you, you know, when you recovered consciousness and I'd been talking to you for quite a while before that. Dr. Maude had said we should try to rouse you. And if you have any belief in telepathy, I have to say I'd been worried sick about you ever since you disappeared from the revel."

"Dear Drusilla." Boadicea Kelling clasped the other's hand for a moment, then let it go. "And now, since you've appointed yourself my guardian angel, perhaps you could assist me to the bathroom. Abigail, I shall be ready for my eggnog in three minutes. To the rest of you, good night."

21

"**C**an you believe that?" Even standing still, Tick was in motion, hands waving, foot tapping. "Bodie got there just in time to meet the Ghost coming out. Bill, I'm worried about that clanking noise she says she heard. You don't suppose the Ghost's got a rod loose?"

"I think we'll find the clanking noise was the missing *Totschläger*," said Max. "Didn't you say it had a hunk of iron attached to it by a short chain?"

"Yes, I did," said Nehemiah Billingsgate. "Good heavens, if Bodie was struck by that thing, it's only God's mercy that saved her from a fractured skull."

"I expect it was that God-awful old hat that saved her," said Melisande more prosaically. "So it looks as if whoever hit her dragged her into the Ghost, stuck her with the tranquilizer dart, then drove on into the honey shed thinking she was dead. The only person I can think of who'd be cool enough to do all that is Bodie herself."

"I don't know, Mel," her husband argued. "After what we've learned tonight about Versey Ufford, I wouldn't put anything past him."

"It can't have been Ufford," said Sarah. "He was sitting next to me during the whole first half of the banquet. Tom Tolbathy can testify to that. Tom and I were trying to talk and Ufford kept interrupting. I expect he was actually establishing an alibi."

"But if Versey didn't steal the Ghost, then who did?" Melisande demanded.

"If we knew that, we wouldn't be standing here talking about it," said Max. "Bill, you say the *Totschläger* still hasn't turned up. Did Grimpen's men search the house?"

"Why, I honestly don't know. They were messing around out by the pond for quite a while, as I don't have to tell you, then they went off with that wretched gun of Wouter's and were gone quite a while. When they came back, they searched for that syrup container, which they found, and then for that bicycle you phoned about, which they obviously didn't find. I hardly think they'd have had time to search the house. Did they, Abigail?"

"I don't believe so, dear. I was too preoccupied to think about it myself, what with having to cope with Rufus's funeral preparations and all that leftover food, and then Bodie."

"Then let's have a look now," said Tick.

"Great idea," Max agreed. "You and Melisande start in the cellar, why don't you? Bill, you and Abigail check around downstairs. Sarah and I will do this floor."

"Surely the house is the last place," Bill started to protest. "But then the honey shed was the last place, too, wasn't it. Come along, Abigail, if you're not too tired."

"No, no, I'd rather be doing something."

The four of them hurried downstairs. Sarah turned to Max. "I can't say I much relish the thought of prowling through everybody's bedroom."

"I doubt if we'll have to do much prowling," said Max. He led her away from Boadicea's room. "The one opposite is Mrs. Gaheris's, we can skip that. I was there earlier and it's bare as a baboon's backside."

He went on down the carpeted hall, opening doors and closing them again. Sarah followed him, tired and bewildered, wishing the next room could be her own. At the end, the hall broadened out to accommodate two spacious bedrooms side by side. One had to be the Billingsgates'. Through the open door, Sarah glimpsed massive Victorian furniture, crocheted dresser scarves, lovely old blue glass scent bottles, silver-backed brushes, crowds of photographs in little fancy frames. Max didn't even bother to look inside, but opened the other door.

"This has to be it. Okay, kid, go find the *Totschläger*."

"But this is Melly's room," Sarah protested.

"Précisément, ma chérie."

It was a lovely room, decorated years ago for a young girl. The furniture was pale green French provincial, picked out in cream. The wallpaper, the Aubusson carpet, the chintz draperies, even the flirty skirt on the vanity table teemed with pink roses. Mr. Hohnser would adore them, no doubt. The red satin costume Melisande had worn at the revel was tossed over the back of a slipper chair upholstered in tufted rose velvet. Tick's black leather dancing slippers looked huge and gross beside the rose velvet bedspread. Sarah shrugged her shoulders.

"If you say so, dear."

Eschewing more obvious hiding places, Sarah headed straight for the old-fashioned cast iron radiator that stood under the window, climbed upon it, and ran her hand over the top of the cornice box.

"I'm touching it, I think, but I can't quite reach. You try."

Being so much the taller, Max had no difficulty seeing over the top of the cornice. "My God, your aunt must have a skull like the Rock of Gibraltar."

"Take the thing down so I can see."

Instead he lifted her up. "We'd better leave it alone for the time being. Too bad Abigail's such a good housekeeper. Fingerprints in the dust would have helped, but there isn't any dust."

Sarah let him swing her down off the radiator. "It's dreadfully obvious, isn't it, darling? I did try to turn up an alibi for Tick, but all I got were holes."

"You had no luck with Lionel, either," Max reminded her.

"And I think I know why. I'll fix that right now. Is there a telephone on this floor?"

Max opened the drawer of Melisande's night table and

pulled out a pink princess phone, the kind that had been all the rage back in the fifties. "Try this."

"Oh, don't be so sickeningly omniscient. I suppose they've been putting the phones where they can't hear them on account of all those reporters calling." Sarah perched herself on the rose velvet bedspread and began to dial. The party at Bunny Whet's was winding down. Elizabeth sounded sorry she'd ever thought of it, but Lionel was still celebrating. He would be. Sarah wasted no time on the amenities.

"Lionel, I'm at the Billingsgates'. Get out here as fast as you can. Otherwise, Vare's going to get an earful about what you were really up to when you claimed to be taking part in that whale watch for Greenpeace."

Max could hear frenzied yowls. Sarah merely held the receiver away from her ear until Lionel simmered down, then went on twisting the screws.

"Lionel, don't try that nonsense on me. If you're not in this house within half an hour, I'll be on the telephone to Vare. Get started this minute, or you'll wish you had."

She tucked the phone back in the drawer and smiled sweetly up at Max. "There's only one way to handle Lionel."

"God, you're a vicious woman. What's his evil secret?"

"I haven't the faintest idea, but I knew he wasn't watching whales. Lionel's had a phobia about them ever since his father made him read *Moby Dick*. He's mortally ashamed of being afraid because whales are such an in thing these days, so he tells dreadful lies about going out among them in a little rubber boat to convince them we're all brothers under the blubber."

"I suppose I have to believe that," Max replied faintly. "And what do you think about Tick?"

"The same as you do, I expect. It's going to be horrid for the Billingsgates, but we know Bill suspected something like this from the start. Should we simply let them keep on hunting until Lionel gets here?"

"Why not? Maybe you'd like to go back and watch your aunt drink her eggnog."

"Yes, I believe I should. I'd hate for her to have a sudden relapse. What are you doing to do?"

"Stay here and phone the police station, for whatever that may be worth. Yell if you need me."

"I always need you."

Sarah gave her partner a highly unprofessional kiss and left the room. Max put in his call to the station, then took out his little black book and spent a mere twelve and a half minutes, thanks to the miracles of modern technology, getting through to the number he'd copied from Vercingetorix Ufford's telephone bill.

The woman who answered was kindly disposed, volubly distressed, and ultimately informative. Max made a number of careful notes, promised to drop by and say hello next time he was in Busto Arsizio, and stashed away the pink telephone again. As he was wondering whether to round up the searchers, Abigail came upstairs to tell him Sergeant Myre had arrived. Seconds later, Lionel panted across the drawbridge.

"Where's Sarah?" he bleated. "Tell her I'm here. Quick. It's a matter of life and death."

"Whatever is the matter with you, Lionel?" Abigail was demanding when Sarah heard the hullabaloo and came down.

"Lionel, quit blethering. You're under the wire. How on earth did you make it here so fast?"

"You said I had to."

"I didn't say to kill yourself speeding."

"It would have been the more merciful way out," he told her grimly. "All right, I'm here. What do you want?"

"I want you to come into the keep and sit down. Oh, Mrs. Gaheris." The houseguest had come down, too, carrying the needlepoint she'd evidently been working at to relieve the tedium of nursing. "Would you mind going down cellar and asking Tick and Melly to come up?" Sarah asked her. "Sergeant Myre, how nice to see you. Where's your dauntless leader?"

A smile of infinite beatitude illuminated the sergeant's plump and not unpleasing features. "He shot himself."

"Glad to hear it," said Max, who'd also joined the group by now. "How?"

"With the hippopotamus gun. When we got back to the station, Officer Swithin was on the desk. She's our token policewoman. So naturally ol' macho Grimpen starts handing her this big line about the dart gun. He'd got hold of a couple more tranquilizer darts over at the ballistics lab, small ones like you'd use for a mongoose or a coatimundi."

"Why a coatimundi?" Melisande wanted to know. "They can't be all that much of a problem in Massachusetts, can they?"

"You'd be surprised," said Myre. "People buy these so-called exotic pets, which are really wild animals straight out of the jungle. They grow up and turn ugly, so one day the owner kind of forgets and leaves their pen open. Next thing we know, they're killing the neighbor's Pekinese or taking a nip out of some kid who didn't have sense enough to keep away. So anyhow, Grimpen loads the gun to show Swithy how smart he is. He sticks it under his arm, leans over to see if he can get a gander down the front of her blouse, and accidentally hits the trigger. The dart hits him right in the jodhpurs and he's out like a stuck bandicoot. We carted him off in the wagon and told the hospital to put him in traction for a month or so. What's up, Mr. Bittersohn, or shouldn't I ask?"

"We've found the bicycle and the *Totschläger*."

"No kidding! Where?"

"The bike was under Rufus's bed in the gate house and the *Totschläger* on top of a cornice in one of the upstairs bedrooms."

"Which one?" demanded Tick Purbody.

"The one with your shoes and your wife's dress in it. I assume you didn't search either place, Myre?"

"No. I wanted to, but the chief told me not to be stupid."

"Chief Grimpen seems to be quite an authority on stupidity," said Nehemiah Billingsgate. "Max, may I ask whether you've been able to draw any viable inferences from these most recent discoveries?"

"Go ahead, Max," Tick grunted. "I know what you're going to say."

"Tick, how can you?" cried Melisande.

"It's fairly clear-cut, isn't it? I ride a bike. The car shed and the honey shed are my responsibilities more than anyone else's. I've worked with Versey Ufford a darn sight oftener than I'd have chosen to. I know all the radio stations and the people who work in them. I haven't always been in complete agreement with your parents' policies on either the stations or Apian Way, as you well know. Now Great-granddad's war club's turned up in the same place where I parked my dancing shoes, so that makes me the villain. Right, Max?"

"You left out the fact that you don't appear to have much of an alibi for the period during which Rufus was killed and the Silver Ghost moved," Max replied.

"How do you know when it was?"

"We know Rufus was alive shortly after the banquet started because Dorothy Dork saw him. We know he was dead when Boadicea got to the car shed, because she didn't see him. You heard her say so, and you knew Rufus. He had your father-in-law's strict orders to stay at his post. Would he have disobeyed if he'd been alive?"

"No. What else?"

"That's all I can think of offhand. How about that alibi? Can you give us any help?"

Tick Purbody shrugged. "How can I remember? I went to the bathroom after I left the dance floor, then to the pavilion. I've already told you that. I went back again a little while later to get a cushion for Ethelyn Frome's back. I've got to find a rental place that has more comfortable chairs next year, Bill. Providing I'm still around, that is."

"My boy, don't talk that way," Bill expostulated.

"Let's not get sidetracked," said Max. "Where did you take the cushion from, Tick?"

"The front parlor. It was nearest the door. Let's see, I met Lissy, our youngest daughter, as I went in. She was staggering out with a trayful of flagons. It was far too heavy for her, so I took the tray and let her carry the cushion. Then the bartender asked for more ice and the kids were all busy, so I ran back to the kitchen. Cook was meditating, so I ran down cellar and got some from the big freezer there. I think I went out the cellar door that time and ran around under the drawbridge."

"Not into the copse?"

"Of course not. I was carrying about fifty pounds of ice cubes, for God's sake! I just dumped the ice and—I don't know what I did next. I was all over the place. Trying to make the old people comfortable, watching the kids so they didn't begin sampling the mead, just doing what needed to be done. And I was hungry myself, you know. What I'd have preferred to do was just sit down and eat my dinner. But anyway, that's my unsatisfactory story. What are you going to do about it?"

"Ask some more dumb questions, I suppose." Max sounded tired. "Mrs. Gaheris, when you first told us about watching that morris dancer walk into the copse, you specifically mentioned the figure wasn't tall enough to be Tick. Would you care to amend that statement now?"

Mrs. Gaheris had taken up her needlepoint again. Now she let the canvas fall across the workbox she was holding in her lap. "How can I? You don't seem to realize, Mr. Bittersohn, that Abigail and I were at boarding school together."

"Mr. Bittersohn doesn't consider that touching fact germane to the issue at hand," said Tick Purbody. "I can't say I do, either. Go ahead, Drusilla, say what you think."

Mrs. Gaheris wet her lips. "I also mentioned, I believe, that it was difficult to judge heights correctly looking down from my window. I simply don't know. Can't we just let it go at that?"

22

"**D**on't let it bother you too much, Tick," said Sarah. "Lionel doesn't have an alibi, either."

"What are you talking about?" her cousin yelped. "Of course I do. I was with Mother."

"No you weren't. Your mother didn't sit down for ages, she was milling about chatting with everybody in sight. You never set foot inside the pavilion till at least half an hour after the rest of us did. Where were you all that time?"

"I—" confession didn't come easily to Lionel Kelling.

Sarah showed him no mercy. "Mrs. Gaheris, you must know Lionel was one of the morris dancers. Could he have been the man you saw?"

"My dear Mrs. Bittersohn, I've already told you I didn't know. I suppose I'd have to say he's as likely as anybody else."

"Thank you, Mrs. Gaheris. I might point out in passing that Lionel's taller than Tick. Now, Lionel, are you going to come clean? You and I both know where you were and what you were doing. It's what you always do when you get the chance, isn't it?"

Her cousin drew himself up and primmed his lips. "I'm sure I can't imagine what you think you're talking about, Sarah. Unless you're referring to my penchant for exercising my powers of observation to increase my store of knowledge. If so, I'm quite willing to agree with you."

"So you did go snooping."

"So rather than risk a bilious attack by consuming a heavy meal directly on top of a morning's strenuous exercise," Lionel had his mind ticking over nicely now, "I determined to satisfy a long-felt curiosity about certain architectural features of this intriguing old house. Since the estate had been thrown open to the revelers, of whom I was surely one, you can hardly be implying that I was guilty of an impropriety."

"Not at all," said Melisande with little conviction. "Did you have a good look around, Lionel?"

"I had a most interesting little session, thank you."

"And what did you find out?" said Sarah. "Spare us the architecture, whom did you meet?"

"I didn't meet anybody."

"Nobody at all? But servers were coming and going all the time, and Tick just said he was in and out."

"Yes, well, I confined my investigations to the upper regions. Not to be in anybody's way, you understand. I did hear voices and footsteps. And I heard you go thundering down the stairs, Tick. You said 'You shouldn't try to carry so much at one time, honey. You'll give yourself a hernia.'"

"I probably did," said Tick. "Why didn't you holler?"

"I was going to, but you went out. I heard the front door shut."

The door had been propped open, Sarah remembered, so that the wenches and potboys could pass through without hindrance. She let it pass. "Which of the bedrooms did you go into, Lionel?"

"I—er—was trying to determine the relative proportions."

"So you went into them all, and you still say you met nobody. Not at any time."

"Sarah, why do you keep harping on that? Why should I have met anybody? They were all out inside the pavilion."

"I wasn't." Mrs. Gaheris flipped open the lid of her workbox to select a different thread. "I came in to get my pills, as I told the others last evening. Too bad I missed you, Lionel. We could have explored together. I love houses."

"When did you come upstairs, Mrs. Gaheris?"

"Why, I can't say exactly. Early on, while some people were still clustered around the buffet. And I stayed in my room for—oh, three or four minutes, I suppose."

"You weren't there while I was there." Lionel forgot to be circumspect in his need to be right. "I spent a good ten minutes in your room. Checking the proportions." And other things, no doubt. "I didn't see you upstairs the whole time I was there. But I did see you going back to the pavilion. I didn't mention that before, Sarah, because I didn't think it counted."

"It counts," Sarah croaked, "Go ahead, Lionel. Where was she?"

"I was coming down the back stairway that leads into the corridor from the parking area to the front door. Mrs. Gaheris dashed in from the drive and went out to the pavilion ahead of me."

"She didn't see you because you ducked out of sight, I suppose."

"I didn't intercept her because she was obviously in a hurry," Lionel corrected. "She was making awfully good time for a woman her age, I must say."

Mrs. Gaheris failed to appreciate the compliment. "Lionel, don't be a fool. It's obvious to me and to everyone else that you're trying to cover yourself by making me the scapegoat. That must have been you I saw going into the copse. You no doubt caught sight of me watching you from my bedroom window and made up this taradiddle to save your own skin. Abigail, I hate to make a scene in your house, but I do think this has gone far enough. I must ask you to excuse me."

Nobody moved except Sergeant Myre. "I don't think you ought to leave just now, Mrs. Gaheris."

"You can't hold me! I have diplomatic immunity."

"I don't think so, Mrs. Gaheris," said Max. "That only applies when a diplomat's in a foreign country. Anyway, you weren't the diplomat. Your husband was, and he's dead, or so we've been given to understand."

"That was an unnecessarily cruel remark, Mr. Bittersohn.

f I was mistaken about diplomatic immunity, it's simply that
was accustomed to it for so long that I took it for granted."

"You take a lot of things for granted, Mrs. Gaheris, one
eing that we'd fail to make the connection between you and
ersey Ufford."

"What connection? I met him here in this house as a friend
f the Billingsgates."

"Whom you hadn't seen for thirty years or so?"

"That is correct."

"Then how do you explain all those overseas phone calls
Jfford made to you last month at the Albergo Verdi in Busto
Arsizio?"

"I don't explain them because they never happened."

"Oh yes they did. I'm sure you told Ufford to destroy the
phone bills, but he was a penny pincher. I expect he
ntended to take them off his income tax as business
expenses. Signora DiCristoforo asked me to let you know
he found that cassette tape you were so worried about. It
had fallen down behind the headboard. Her cousin Pietro's
going to play it so we can find out if it turns up in Ufford's
card file."

"I think you must be insane."

"The tape was in one of those padded envelopes with your
name and Ufford's return address on the customs slip."

There was dead silence. Then Nehemiah Billingsgate said
quietly, "I think you'd better explain, Drusilla."

She sat there quite a while, fiddling with the clasp of her
workbox. At last she spoke. "Very well, Bill, if I must. This is
painful for me. You see, my husband was not always faith-
ul. Years ago, in a stupid attempt to get even with him, I had
a brief fling with Versey Ufford, whom we'd met on a visit to
Rome. I soon wearied of the affair, but Versey didn't. He kept
n touch, and when my husband died, he tried to win me
back. He began a barrage of letters, phone calls, and small
gifts. I have to confess that I didn't discourage him at first. I
was lonely, and a woman my age can't help feeling a bit
grateful, I suppose, that any man cares enough to bother.
But Versey really was the most dreadful bore. He'd got

worse as he got older, and I soon realized I'd made a mistake letting him back into my life."

"Then why did you come here instead of to the Dorks'?" Melisande demanded. "You must have known he'd be infesting the place."

"I came here because I wanted to be with my old friend Abigail. It wasn't as if Versey actually lived in the house. I decided the nuisance of having him in the picture would be outweighed by the advantages of being in a social circle where I could really feel I belonged. Anyway, Versey was an unattached man and there are times when any escort is better than no escort, to put it as crudely as possible."

Mrs. Gaheris tried the effect of a wistful smile, but nobody smiled back. "Does that explain why Lionel saw you coming in from the drive?" said Sarah.

"Well, yes, as a matter of fact, it does. Versey'd insisted I meet him outside for a private interview. He was resenting the fact that I'd refused to acknowledge him to the Billingsgates as an old friend. I went because I didn't want him to make a scene in the pavilion, as I knew he was quite capable of doing."

"Was this before or after you went up to your room?"

"After. I did go to get my stomach pills. I knew I'd want them by the time I got through with Versey. Then I fiddled around the room postponing what I knew would be a distasteful experience, which it was. That was how I happened to be around to see your cousin going into the copse."

"Sorry, Mrs. Gaheris," said Sarah. "You didn't meet Professor Ufford outside. He glued himself to me the moment I entered the pavilion and stuck like a burr all during the banquet. Lionel didn't go anywhere except where he said he did. No morris dancer went into the copse. That was a flat lie, to distract attention from your having been out of the pavilion while Rufus was killed. We have all the morris dancers and all the costumes accounted for. I doubt whether the Billingsgates will care to go on sponsoring a guest who tried to frame their son-in-law for the murders she comnitted, and I'm sure Aunt Bodie's going to take umbrage in a big way when she finds out her old school chum hit her over the head with Bill's *Totschläger*. Grab that workbox, Max!"

Unfortunately Tick Purbody couldn't resist getting in on the action, and Tick was a little too far away. While he and Max were getting untangled, Drusilla Gaheris had time to open her workbox. It was Sarah who hurled the sofa cushions to deflect her aim and Melisande who wrenched the gun out of her hand. But Lionel Kelling was the real hero of the hour.

"I don't see what everyone's so wrought up about. Naturally I confiscated the bullets when I discovered the gun yesterday. You're old enough to know, Mrs. Gaheris, that one should never leave a loaded weapon lying around."

At least Sergeant Myre got to make the arrest.

23

Of course the dog work remained to be done. Not until Friday at teatime was there another gathering at the Billingsgates'. Abigail and Bill, looking careworn but relieved, were helping each other butter the crumpets. Sarah had met the flight from Busto Arsizio and brought Max out from Logan Airport. Acting Chief Reginald Myre represented the Fernwood Police. Lionel Kelling had been invited partly because Sarah felt a trifle ashamed of the way she'd bullied him on Monday and partly because her bullying had paid off so handsomely. Boadicea Kelling had driven from Wenham in her 1946 Daimler wearing her Queen Mary toque, which didn't look much worse than it had before.

Tom and Hester Tolbathy were there because everyone wanted it made clear that nobody was holding Wouter's doomful legacy against them. Mr. and Mrs. Purbody, however, had sent regrets. Tick was busy interviewing prospective assistant meaders in his new capacity as president of Apian Way Enterprises. Melisande was at a professional recording studio taping another hour of "Melly's Mellow Melodies."

Boadicea Kelling took an analytical sip from her teacup and nodded approval. "Just right, Abigail. I must say in retrospect that Drusilla always did have a duplicitous streak. She borrowed my best silk stockings once without asking and sneaked them back full of runs, thinking I wouldn't ıotice. And she was always smuggling in chocolates. She'd at them in bed after lights out so she wouldn't have to hare. I could hear the little papers rattling when she fished ıround for the caramels. Her cubicle was next to mine, you now. I never snitched on her before, but now that she's ried to murder me, I feel myself under no obligation to keep ilent."

"My loyalty went down the drain when I found out she'd ısed our hospitality to kill poor Rufe, swipe our cars, and try o put Bill out of business," Abigail agreed. "I still can't grasp ıow she managed it all, much less why. Were you able to dıg ıp any information in Italy, Max?"

"Plenty. For one thing, the late Gawain Gaheris was never a diplomat, though he often pretended to be."

"Whatever for? Was he a spy?"

"Now and then. Also a smuggler, a forger, and a few other things. He and Drusilla worked as a team. Their real forte ıppears to have been dirty tricks to order."

"Such as what?"

Max shrugged. "Spreading false rumors and planting evidence to back them up, staging entrapments, arranging quiet disposals."

"Do you mean murders?" Abigail asked bluntly.

"Sure. Nothing cheap or vulgar, you understand, they were always very careful and very clever. It did get to be noticed eventually that wherever the Gaherises went, accidents, suicides, shattered reputations, and depleted bank accounts tended to follow; but they never left a clue anybody could put a finger on. What's incredible is that they managed to keep it up for forty years or so, maybe even longer. They worked in Europe, North Africa, and places like Hong Kong; but they shied clear of the United States pretty much. She came back for a few brief visits, but he never did, as far as anybody knows. The inference is that he'd made the U.S. too hot for himself."

"Was he ever traced back here?" Sarah asked.

"Not successfully. He posed as an Englishman who'd been sent here as an orphaned child, which accounted for his

New York accent. He had the right papers, but a man of his talents naturally would. By the time anybody thought of checking him out, there didn't appear to be anybody left alive who could vouch for his identity."

"How old a man was he?" Bill asked.

"Seventy-two when he died, according to his passport—for whatever that's worth—but he was showing no sign of being ready to quit. It wasn't a heart attack that killed him, as his wife claimed, but a fall from an open cable car halfway up an Alp. The man from Interpol who'd been riding with him explained that Gaheris had stood up to get a better view of the scenery and lost his balance."

Lionel snorted. "Surely nobody believed that yarn?"

"I got the impression people had been lining up in rows to believe it," Max told him. "Anyway, the widow obviously decided to carry on the business. Just before Gaheris died, they'd been approached by what sounds to me like a neo-Nazi to lay the foundation for a propaganda network in this country. Gaheris would probably have turned him down, but for Drusilla alone this must have seemed like the ideal setup. She probably did want to come back to the States, as she claimed. She was clean with the authorities, she had a handy accomplice in Ufford, and she had the ideal cover: relatives who hadn't seen her in years and an old school friend living practically next door to her client."

"Lord save us!" Bill exclaimed. "Who was the client?"

"Hohnser the rose man. He met with the Gaherises at Busto Arsizio as representative for a neo-Fascist underground group so top-secret he refused even to tell them its name. He did write them a businesslike follow-up letter about this neighbor of his who owns a group of radio stations currently being used to disseminate dangerously subversive propaganda about racial equality, universal brotherhood, and other radical left-wing garbage."

"Did he actually say that in the letter?" Abigail demanded.

"That and a good deal more. He outlined in detail how he wanted them to infiltrate the stations with a dirty tricks campaign. Once they'd got the owner demoralized enough o quit, they were to buy him out with money obtained by capturing—Hohnser's word—and selling the neighbor's own collection of antique Rolls Royces. The stations would then be used to broadcast both overt and subliminal messages of what Hohnser described as 'the right sort.'"

"He must be crazy!" cried Hester Tolbathy.

"No doubt," Max agreed, "but he's an efficient organizer. He explained how he wanted the Gaherises to remove the cars by a series of clandestine operations utilizing a concealed door in the car shed which had been installed some time ago by a rival gang of subversive operators who were no doubt Russian spies. The owner had been absent at the time but Hohnser had naturally maintained close surveillance and discovered the mechanism that operates the door."

"Do you mean he's been spying on us all these years? And using Bob as a—" Words failed Bill.

Max shook his head. "Hohnser states that your gardener has remained obstinately loyal to you and should not be approached with bribes or other inducements, which have already been covertly tested and proven ineffectual."

"Why, that infernal scoundrel! He ought to be strung up by the boot heels. Forgive the intemperance of my language, but I find this revelation totally incredible. Hohnser's been a pillar of this community. He's served without emolument in town offices."

"Yeah," said Myre. "That's how come we got Grimpen for police chief. Hohnser ganged up with the chairman of the Board of Selectmen and they rammed the appointment through. I even heard it was Hohnser who took Grimpen's written exam for him."

Bill shook his head again. "I knew Hohnser was an enthusiastic supporter of Grimpen, but—good heavens! And to think we've lived right on the same road with the man all these years."

"And never heard a cordial word out of him the whole time," snapped Abigail. "You know what he said last Christmastime at the Fromes' about your little homilies, Bill. Your soft answer didn't turn away my wrath, I can tell you.

How did Versey get mixed up in it, Max? He wasn't really Drusilla's lover, was he?"

"Probably not, but he appears to have been on the Gaherises' payroll for a good many years. He did own a house in Venice, by the way. It was no palazzo, but it must have cost Ufford something to keep up. That may explain why he developed a sideline."

"But surely he wasn't sending out noxious propaganda over our stations all that time," Billingsgate protested.

"No, Bill. I'm sure this was a recent development. Otherwise Ufford wouldn't have been testing to find out whether his messages were going to work for the Hohnser project. There was no point to that 'eat the frumenty' stunt unless it was an experiment in mass persuasion to show Drusilla he was capable of handling the job. I expect he valued his long connection with you mainly because it gave him a legitimate excuse to be skipping back and forth on the Gaherises' errands. Like those so-called visiting lectureships he kept telling you about. Some of them may have been genuine, but I suspect a good many weren't."

"He seems to have got away with a great deal." Lionel Kelling spoke not in censure but in envy.

"He wouldn't have for much longer," Max assured him. "Ufford had been getting too arrogant and taking needless risks. The Italian police had been keeping an eye on him, I found out."

"Probably that was why Mrs. Gaheris decided to get rid of him," said Sarah. "The bicycle was definitely his, by the way. Brooks checked it out with the professor's landlady. They had a cup of tea and a cozy chat together. Brooks would, you know. The landlady says she saw Professor Ufford riding off on his bike about half-past one Monday morning, but thought nothing of it because he often did. He'd told her he liked to ride when the streets were empty of traffic, but she thought it more likely that he had some woman on the string whose husband worked the graveyard shift."

"Well, I'd say Versey booked himself for the graveyard shift when he got mixed up with our old school chum,

bby," Hester Tolbathy reached over to set down her empty
up on the tea wagon. "And to think Drusilla planned the
hole thing sitting right here with that everlasting needle-
oint."

"Wherever she planned it, she didn't do as good a job as
er husband would have, if you'll forgive the sexist observa-
on," said Max. "Gaheris would have known better than to
nderestimate the opposition."

Boadicea Kelling sniffed. "Drusilla always did think she
ould get away with anything. She was a positive menace at
eld hockey. She's kept herself in shape, though, you have to
and her that. Not many women her age could have got to
he car shed, killed Rufus and hidden his body in that bizarre
vay, driven the Silver Ghost to the honey shed, stopping to
ommit mayhem on my person and haul me aboard en
oute, hidden the car, then run the whole length of the
edgerow path, gone around through the house and been
ack inside the pavilion before anybody noticed she was
;one."

"You could have done it, Bodie," said Hester.

"I'm sure she could," said Sarah, "but I'll bet Drusilla
Gaheris didn't. My theory is that she told Rufe on Sunday
norning to drive the honeybug out to the honey shed and
eave it there. Melisande noticed after the revel, when she
nd I went for our ride, that the bug wasn't parked quite
vhere it ought to have been. She thought the kids must have
een fooling around with it, and said she was going to jump
n somebody's neck, but she probably forgot."

"Rufe wouldn't have taken an order from Drusilla," Tom
Tolbathy objected.

"He would if she claimed to be carrying the message from
Bill. She'd have known it was safe to lie to Rufe because he
wasn't going to be around long enough to—" Abigail choked
up.

Boadicea decided to be tactful.

"Having the electric cart left where she could quickly find
it and drive it back would certainly have been the practical
thing for Drusilla to do. My own feeling is that while she's in

excellent condition for her age, as I remarked earlier, Drusill
is by no means the athlete she used to be. She couldn't hav
put much of her old force behind that blow she dealt me wit
the *Totschläger,* or I shouldn't be here to criticize. Of cours
her arms may by then have been tired from pulling Rufus
body up into the tree," Bodie conceded as a gesture t
positive thinking. "I should have thought her ingeniou
arrangement of pulleys would have reduced the expenditu
of muscular force required, but perhaps I underestimate
the original degree of difficulty. What really puzzles me i
how Drusilla managed to install the hoisting apparatus s
expeditiously."

"That hoist must have been rigged in advance," Max tol
her. "Since Mrs. Gaheris used to be a mountain climber,
expect she could have got up the tree all right, but it's mor
likely the rigging was another of Versey's jobs. He probabl
biked out here Saturday night with the rope and pulleys
Getting them up in the tree wouldn't have been any big dea
for an ingenious guy like him."

"But why didn't anybody notice the rope on Sunda
morning?" Lionel demanded.

"Partly because of the thick foliage around it, partl
because everyone's mind was on other things, and partl
because the rope blended in so well with the tree trunk,'
Sarah told him. "It was the same dark brown as the one yo
use on your rock climbs."

"Ungh." Lionel didn't care much for that. "And woul
you kindly inform me as to when Mrs. Gaheris could hav
had time to throw the dart gun into the pond?"

"I don't suppose she did. She'd have tossed it in amon
the bushes or somewhere for Professor Ufford to find an
dispose of. That would explain what he was doing up on th
hill when I met him. I shouldn't be surprised if he had th
gun hidden under that full cloak he was wearing even whe
he claimed to be trying to date me up for the dance."

"Damn good thing you didn't accept," Lionel grunted.

"Men were deceivers ever." Tom Tolbathy was getting hi
spirits back. "But what about this business of the bicycle

Abigail? I was given to understand you and Drusilla spent the whole morning together in good works yesterday."

"We weren't always together. In fact, there was a space of time when I'd gone off to do a few errands and Drusilla stayed here. The idea was that she'd be helping Cook pack the rest of the food for us to take out to Milltown, but when I got back I found Cook meditating, which is a euphemism for taking a nap, and Drusilla nowhere near done with the packing. She made a little joke about having to work slowly so as not to disturb Cook's meditation, and I helped her finish up. It wasn't that much of a job, really, and I remember feeling just a trifle annoyed that Drusilla'd managed to drag it out so long. But you know how it is, working in someone else's kitchen. I thought perhaps she'd been unsure about what I wanted done, and blamed Cook for not staying awake to tell her. It just never entered my head that Drusilla Gaheris could be up to anything shady. How in the world did you get on to her, Sarah?"

"Max and I both wondered about her right from the beginning. You didn't actually know her, after all."

"We certainly didn't," Abigail replied bitterly.

"But of course you know and trust Tick Purbody implicitly, so when the evidence began piling up against him it seemed possible somebody else had marked him out for the scapegoat. Living here in the house, Mrs. Gaheris was in an excellent position to manage that. That story of hers about the wandering morris dancer made us wonder even more, especially when we found we couldn't identify the man she allegedly saw. But what clinched it for me was when you said the person who hit you was wearing a dust coat, Aunt Bodie. That costume Mrs. Gaheris had on was exactly the same color. I expect the veil you thought you saw was the wimple, pulled over her face."

"But Drusilla's not tall enough," her aunt protested.

"She'd be plenty tall enough standing up in the Ghost," Lionel broke in impatiently. "And at least you know now you weren't talking through your hat when you said you'd kept hearing Drusilla's voice while you were tied up in the car. How did you get on to Hohnser, Max?"

"Well, I'd thought it a bit strange, his insisting Bob work
for him both Sunday and Monday when he must have
known the Billingsgates would have plenty for Bob to do
here. Bob impresses me as being a bright, active guy; he
mightn't have been so easy to dispose of as Rufe was. But
thought maybe Hohnser had just done it to be ornery until
persuaded the Italian police to open a safety deposit box
Mrs. Gaheris had in a Busto Arsizio bank."

"Good heavens," Bill exploded, "do you mean she kept
Hohnser's letter? Why ever would she do a reckless thing
like that?"

"For insurance, I'd say offhand. The Gaherises may have
intended to finance a prosperous old age by blackmailing
their former correspondents. Only they didn't retire soon
enough. Getting back to Hohnser, once the preliminary
negotiations had been opened through Ufford, he came to
call on the Gaherises at the Albergo Verdi, posing as a tourist
named Brown."

"How original," Tom Tolbathy remarked. "Why Busto
Arsizio, Max? I know it's up near the Italian Alps, but I
thought it was a manufacturing town, not a tourist resort."

"It is, but it's also close to the Swiss border, you know, and
the Gaherises used to pop back and forth a lot, especially on
weekends. Signora DiCristoforo told me there always
seemed to be tourists passing through when the Gaherises
were there, and they always managed to strike up acquaintances. A nice elderly couple, possibly a bit lonesome and
bored, it seemed natural enough at first. After a while,
though, she began to get curious and had her nephew
Pietro, who's quite a talented fellow, run a few spot checks."

"How?" demanded Lionel.

"In Hohnser's case, by lifting his wallet. As soon as he
found out Mr. Brown wasn't Signore Bruno, Pietro took a
few snapshots and jotted down the real name and address
on the back."

"Sounds as if the DiCristoforos were taking out a little
insurance themselves," Lionel grunted.

"I expect it's a fairly profitable sideline." Max took out his wn wallet and extracted a small sheaf of plastic envelopes. These cost me fifty thousands lire apiece. There you are, ill. One of Ufford having an *aperitivo* with Drusilla on the rrace, one of Hohnser sitting at a table with the two aherises, a good, clear closeup of Hohnser himself, and ne of Mr. and Mrs. Gaheris watching him leave. It's okay, ou can pass them around. Just don't take them out of the nvelopes."

"So that was Drusilla's husband," said Abigail. "My oodness, he was a handsome rogue. No wonder she fell for im. He had a mean mouth, though. Don't you think so, odie?"

"Let me see." Boadicea Kelling put on her reading glasses nd took the photograph from her friend's hand. "Good eavens, that's Lance!"

"Your brother Lancelot? I thought he died years ago. odie, are you sure?"

"Of course I'm sure. Don't you think I know my own rother? So that's why Drusilla went to live in Europe. All nose years, sending me postcards and polite little notes, ever once letting me know Lance was alive and she was my ister-in-law. Drusilla always did have a mad crush on Lance, ven when she was captain of the lacrosse team. She roped im on the rebound, I suppose. Poor Lance, throwing his life way because of a heartless, scheming woman."

In mingled grief and righteous indignation, Boadicea hoved her reading glasses down to the tip of her nose and ressed a clean white handkerchief to her eyes. "I hope you ealize, Sarah Kelling Bittersohn, that if it hadn't been for our precious Aunt Caroline, all this would never have appened."

"If you say so, Aunt Bodie," said Sarah. "Actually, I never iked Aunt Caroline either. Abigail, if there's any more tea in he pot, I think Aunt Bodie and I could both use another up."

MORE MYSTERIOUS PLEASURES

HAROLD ADAMS
The Carl Wilcox mystery series

MURDER	#501	$3.95
PAINT THE TOWN RED	#601	$3.95
THE MISSING MOON	#602	$3.95
THE NAKED LIAR	#420	$3.95
THE FOURTH WIDOW	#502	$3.50
THE BARBED WIRE NOOSE	#603	$3.95
THE MAN WHO MET THE TRAIN	#801	$3.95

TED ALLBEURY

THE SEEDS OF TREASON	#604	$3.95
THE JUDAS FACTOR	#802	$4.50
THE STALKING ANGEL	#803	$3.95

ERIC AMBLER

HERE LIES: AN AUTOBIOGRAPHY	#701	$8.95

ROBERT BARNARD

A TALENT TO DECEIVE: AN APPRECIATION OF AGATHA CHRISTIE	#702	$8.95

EARL DERR BIGGERS
The Charlie Chan mystery series

THE HOUSE WITHOUT A KEY	#421	$3.95
THE CHINESE PARROT	#503	$3.95
BEHIND THAT CURTAIN	#504	$3.95
THE BLACK CAMEL	#505	$3.95
CHARLIE CHAN CARRIES ON	#506	$3.95
KEEPER OF THE KEYS	#605	$3.95

JAMES M. CAIN

THE ENCHANTED ISLE	#415	$3.95
CLOUD NINE	#507	$3.95

ED McBAIN

ANOTHER PART OF THE CITY	#524	$3.95
McBAIN'S LADIES: THE WOMEN OF THE 87TH PRECINCT	#815	$4.95

The Matthew Hope mystery series

SNOW WHITE AND ROSE RED	#414	$3.95
CINDERELLA	#525	$3.95
PUSS IN BOOTS	#629	$3.95
THE HOUSE THAT JACK BUILT	#816	$3.95

VINCENT McCONNOR

LIMBO	#630	$3.95

GREGORY MCDONALD, ED.

LAST LAUGHS: THE 1986 MYSTERY WRITERS OF AMERICA ANTHOLOGY	#711	$8.95

JAMES McLURE

IMAGO	#817	$4.50

CHARLOTTE MacLEOD

The Professor Peter Shandy mystery series

THE CORPSE IN OOZAK'S POND	#627	$3.95

The Sarah Kelling mystery series

THE RECYCLED CITIZEN	#818	$3.95
THE SILVER GHOST	#819	$4.50

WILLIAM MARSHALL

The Yellowthread Street mystery series

YELLOWTHREAD STREET	#619	$3.50
THE HATCHET MAN	#620	$3.50
GELIGNITE	#621	$3.50
THIN AIR	#622	$3.95
THE FAR AWAY MAN	#623	$3.50
ROADSHOW	#624	$3.95
HEAD FIRST	#625	$3.50
FROGMOUTH	#626	$3.50
WAR MACHINE	#820	$3.95
OUT OF NOWHERE	#821	$3.95

THOMAS MAXWELL

KISS ME ONCE	#523	$4.95
THE SABERDENE VARIATIONS	#628	$4.95
KISS ME TWICE	#822	$4.95

RIC MEYERS

MURDER ON THE AIR: TELEVISION'S GREAT MYSTERY SERIES	#725	$12.95

MARCIA MULLER
The Sharon McCone mystery series
EYE OF THE STORM   #823 $3.95

FREDERICK NEBEL
THE ADVENTURES OF CARDIGAN   #712 $9.95

WILLIAM F. NOLAN
THE BLACK MASK BOYS: MASTERS IN
  THE HARD-BOILED SCHOOL
  OF DETECTIVE FICTION   #713 $8.95

PETER O'DONNELL
The Modesty Blaise suspense series
DEAD MAN'S HANDLE   #526 $3.95

SUSAN OLEKSIW
A READER'S GUIDE TO THE CLASSIC
  BRITISH MYSTERY   #728 $19.95

ELIZABETH PETERS
The Amelia Peabody mystery series
CROCODILE ON THE SANDBANK   #209 $3.95
THE CURSE OF THE PHARAOHS   #210 $3.95
The Jacqueline Kirby mystery series
THE SEVENTH SINNER   #411 $3.95
THE MURDERS OF RICHARD III   #412 $3.95

ELLIS PETERS
The Brother Cadfael mystery series
THE HERMIT OF EYTON FOREST   #824 $3.95
THE CONFESSION OF BROTHER HALUIN   #808 $3.95

ANTHONY PRICE
The Doctor David Audley espionage series
THE LABYRINTH MAKERS   #404 $3.95
THE ALAMUT AMBUSH   #405 $3.95
COLONEL BUTLER'S WOLF   #527 $3.95
OCTOBER MEN   #529 $3.95
OTHER PATHS TO GLORY   #530 $3.95
OUR MAN IN CAMELOT   #631 $3.95
WAR GAME   #632 $3.95
THE '44 VINTAGE   #633 $3.95
TOMORROW'S GHOST   #634 $3.95
SOLDIER NO MORE   #825 $4.95
THE OLD *VENGEFUL*   #826 $4.95
GUNNER KELLY   #827 $4.95
SION CROSSING   #406 $3.95
HERE BE MONSTERS   #528 $3.95
FOR THE GOOD OF THE STATE   #635 $3.95
A NEW KIND OF WAR   #828 $4.95

AVAILABLE AT YOUR BOOKSTORE OR DIRECT FROM THE PUBLISHER

Mysterious Press Mail Order
129 West 56th Street
New York, NY 10019

Please send me the MYSTERIOUS PRESS titles I have circled below:

103 105 106 107 112 113 209 210 211 212 213 214 301 302
303 304 308 309 315 316 401 402 403 404 405 406 407 408
409 410 411 412 413 414 415 416 417 418 419 420 421 501
502 503 504 505 506 507 508 509 510 511 512 513 514 515
516 517 518 519 520 521 522 523 524 525 526 527 528 529
530 531 532 533 534 535 536 537 538 539 540 541 542 543
544 545 601 602 603 604 605 606 607 608 609 610 611 612
613 614 615 616 617 618 619 620 621 622 623 624 625 626
627 628 629 630 631 632 633 634 635 636 637 638 639 640
641 642 643 644 645 646 701 702 703 704 705 706 707 708
709 710 711 712 713 714 715 716 717 718 719 720 721 722
723 724 725 726 727 728 729 801 802 803 804 805 806 807
808 809 810 811 812 813 814 815 816 817 818 819 820 821
822 823 824 825 826 827 828 829 830 831 832 833 834 835
836 837 838 839 840 841 842 843

I am enclosing $_____ (please add $3.00 postage and handling for the first book, and 50¢ for each additional book). Send check or money order only—no cash or C.O.D.'s please. Allow at least 4 weeks for delivery.

NAME _____

ADDRESS _____

CITY _____ STATE _____ ZIP CODE _____
New York State residents please add appropriate sales tax.